Skrean Time

A Time Cycle Conundrum

Ace Skorig

M&B Global Solutions Inc.
Green Bay, Wisconsin (USA)

Skrean Time

A Time Cycle Conundrum

ISBN: 978-1-942731-55-9

Published by M&B Global Solutions Inc.
Green Bay, Wisconsin (USA)

Dedication

For my brother, Scott.

*One of the good guys
who deserved so much better!*

Contents

Contents

Introduction

"It's not going to be another *Star Wars* rip-off, is it?"

Those words, or something similar, conveyed the concern my high school English teacher had when I told him I had chosen science fiction as the genre I would use to fulfill my semester obligation. The poor fellow had likely encountered too many short stories that borrowed heavily from the George Lucas's movie of 1977.

No, I promised the soft-spoken instructor, no Han Solo, Princess Leia or Chewbacca for me. I had another idea. One that came to me on a carefree afternoon ripe with imagination.

Long before I had signed up for this class, the thought of creating an alternate reality fascinated. I produced comic books centered on a cast of robots. I penned a series of mysteries similar to those featuring Nancy Drew or the Hardy Boys. I even attempted to parody *Mad* magazine, getting no further than a fold-in and a front cover.

But this would be different. The fruits of my labor would be shared with my classmates, teenagers like me. Young adults who could devastate or uplift with a flippant remark or a brutally honest assessment.

So, pencil to paper – there were no personal computers then – I shaped my narrative. When I finished, my mother hammered out a typewritten copy that I turned in. I then awaited a grade.

As summer approached, we students, one by one, read our stories out loud to the class. We did so front and center, behind a lectern that provided little cover. It was a daunting task. Feedback would be immediate, honest, and broadcast to all. Hiding was impossible.

Was I anxious? Nonplussed? Confident?

I don't recall. What I do know is that the idea I hatched over forty-five years ago has stayed with me. So much so that I vowed to turn those ten single-sided sheets into something more. Making good on that promise proved more difficult than I could have foreseen. What you hold in your hands is the outgrowth of many false starts.

Nearly four decades went by before I hit upon the right approach, the right characters, the right relationships. Finally, I saw through to the end. Five-plus years of writing, polishing, and agonizing over what to include and what to exclude followed. Even now, my work complete, I'm still open to second-guessing.

I applaud anyone who can turn a blank slate into a novel.

In your hands you hold the outgrowth of a seed planted long ago. You, like the teens of yesteryear, will form an opinion as to what you encounter here. If your reaction matches that of a girl whose name I have long since forgotten, my effort shall not have been in vain.

Most of what transpired that day has been lost to history. What remains is a single comment, a single remark that let me know I had been heard.

That girl, a year older than me, gave me hope. She allayed my fear of not measuring up. She had me thinking that writing might be something I should pursue.

After I finished reciting the prose that had become part of me, she approached with a question. I continue to interpret her words as a compliment.

"What kind of drugs were you on when you wrote that?" she asked, laughing as she spoke.

What kind of drugs, indeed!

Ace Skorig

FYI: The original story referenced above is included at the back of this book.

We are each of us an endangered species.

When we die, our species disappears with us.

Nobody like us will ever exist again.

—Journalist Janet Malcolm, quoted in *Artforum.com*

Wednesday

Chapter One

"Have you found *your* governor, yet?"

Each morning, Hamelton Skrean emphasized the fourth word in his opening salvo. Each morning, when the answer came back negative, the old man's delivery turned more clipped, more derisive, more confrontational.

This unchanging reply, offered daily by Eugene Van Meyer, always came equipped with the coda that something was sure to turn up and soon. The hourly employee insisted he would leave no stone unturned in his search for the elusive politician.

The approach worked until it didn't.

"You don't find him, you're fired!" Hamelton boomed. "Understood?"

This noisome ritual – held over for a second week – had Eugene on edge before his first dose of caffeine. Didn't his boss have something better to do like pitch reverse mortgages? God knows he looked the part, dressed in a corduroy blazer with funky elbow patches.

The passage of time had not favored Hamelton, he being a dead ringer for the lesser half in Grant Wood's *American Gothic*. Sunken cheeks, tight skin, and a skull-like face, his looks scattered trick-ortreaters and Jehovah's Witnesses alike.

To combat his less-than-ideal appearance, Hamelton could have cultivated a pleasant demeanor. He could have embraced the qualities that foster long-lasting friendships.

No dice. That wouldn't have been Hameltonesque. The man who had hired Eugene deemphasized his own unpalatability only when it furthered his agenda. He came off as human only when seeking to influence others.

There was a reason for the 'm' and 'e' in the unorthodox spelling of his first name.

No, Hamelton Skrean could not have hawked mortgages – reverse or otherwise – any more than he could have windows or siding. He shilled but one product – himself. And if that meant selling his soul, so be it. In Grant Wood's iconic masterpiece, Hamelton would have been clutching the Devil's trident rather than a pitchfork.

But who was Eugene to judge? Middle-aged, balding, and with a paunch that sagged below his belt, the computer operator was no prize, either. Featuring a funny walk and halting talk, he compensated for his brand of unattractiveness with an authentic nature that was endearing.

Single and forty-five, he liked to think of himself as a work in progress.

"Fired, sacked, canned," Hamelton pledged anew with unbridled gusto. "Find your damned governor or find a new line of work!"

The broadside injected a new level of nastiness into this tiresome game of shriek and play dumb. It underscored the catch-22 that confronted Eugene. Should he locate said governor, his services would no longer be required. Should he fail in that regard, he would be shown the door. Either way, unemployment beckoned.

Eugene had no intention of surrendering his position. Not without a fight. Twenty years a church secretary in his previous employment, he had jettisoned the monotony of a liturgical year for the unpredictability of new frontiers. In leaving, he had thrown open a future in which he could make a difference.

Not that he didn't look back. Not that he didn't second-guess his decision. In stepping into the unknown, he operated without a compass or road map. In leaving the familiar, he risked getting lost.

What the hell had he been thinking?

Eugene had almost skipped the interview. Tummy roiling, breakfast in reverse, he turned down a side street to puke. And puke some more.

This was crazy. He was walking into a trap. He was setting himself up for failure. Why didn't he just admit that he drew comfort from the routine?

Hundreds would be competing for the same position as he. Every candidate more qualified. Every candidate more adept at small talk and building repertoire.

Better to turn tail and run. Better to save face. He could always slink back to the church, begging forgiveness.

But now, having prevailed, having outlasted all comers, having triumphed over his doubt-riddled psyche, Eugene would not abdicate. He would remain on Hamelton's payroll. And if that meant dragging his feet or breaking the eighth and ninth commandments, so be it.

Eugene The Meek would not disinherit what he had coming.

Five days a week – and sometimes on Saturday – Eugene operated courtside in the historic gymnasium at St. Anthony's. He and Verne – his co-worker and buddy – spent hours traveling to locations heretofore off-limits. The pair chose where and when to visit, and the length of their stay. They recorded each outing for posterity.

No two shifts were ever the same. Eugene called the shots. For the first time, he – and not someone else – drove the bus.

And so Eugene apologized to Hamelton for his lack of progress. He sucked up, promising to make amends. He turned one cheek while kissing two others. That the most beautiful woman this side of Eve worked in the same abandoned parochial school provided Eugene with further incentive to pacify his boss.

"I will find the governor," Eugene assured. "Signed, sealed, delivered."

That line, or some variation thereof, usually sent Hamelton scurrying off to climes unknown. Not this time. The white-haired geezer buzzed about like a fly, his bug eyes taking in Eugene's every move.

Why couldn't the overwrought pest make himself scarce? He had done it before.

For two decades, Hamelton had literally wandered in the wilderness. He had stayed out of sight, scurrying about the underbrush in the northernmost regions of the state. The Yeti got spotted more often than he.

But when Hamelton re-emerged – recharged and champing at the bit – he dropped the low-profile routine. Having been reborn, he strutted – chin high, face aglow, hair bathed white. He had been to the mountaintop. He had seen the light, and it was good. Very good.

Hamelton, you see, had made a discovery, one of such cataclysmic significance as to ensure he would walk alongside Newton, Darwin and Einstein in the pantheon of science. The technology he would bring to bear would revolutionize in a way that only the most game-changing of breakthroughs had throughout the ages.

How did Eugene know? Hamelton told him – repeatedly.

"Get ready for Skrean Time," the Inflated Ego gushed. "Must-see TV."

Fed a steady diet of Hamelton's self-aggrandizement, Eugene

sought to avoid the braggart. Evasion worked until the Old Goat began demanding these early-morning, in-person check-ins. With nowhere to hide in an office space measuring roughly 10,000 square feet, Eugene broke into a sweat anytime a door opened before the clock struck eight.

"I don't give a damn, Max," Hamelton shouted into his phone. "Noon tomorrow, or you and Sam don't get paid!"

Eugene was not privy to the reply, but Max must have poured kerosene onto the fire.

"Go for it. I dare you," Hamelton encouraged. "I'll take ten years off your life."

"Trouble?" Eugene couldn't resist after Hamelton finished spewing.

Android at half mast, Hamelton glared at his least favorite – and only – keyboard technician. He halved the distance between the two, inching closer until Eugene finally looked his way. Satisfied he held the upper hand, Hamelton ceased his visual assault and returned to fondling the handheld device that never left his side.

Eugene spritzed open a can of caffeine. It was the first of three or four he habitually would consume before nightfall.

The gymnasium at St. Anthony's could accommodate nearly a thousand fans in its heyday. Home to the Bulldogs, the court hosted the area's first televised high school basketball game. Athletes crisscrossed its hardwood floor for decades. Competition separated winners from losers.

Enrollment declined as migration to the suburbs intensified. Lack of funding forced the academic institution to close its doors. A homecoming of sorts was organized prior to the shuttering. Former students and staff returned en masse for one last walk down memory lane.

Abandoned, languishing, St. Anthony's stood ready to meet the wrecking ball. But the property gained reprieve when Hamelton and Darby Kyvelt purchased the land and buildings outright. For cash.

Talk about good fortune! Hamelton Skrean had a partner. One with deep pockets. One with whom he could co-exist. One willing to bankroll Hamelton's contribution to science regardless of cost.

How infuriating! How utterly unfair! The narcissistic self-promoter crosses paths with a walking, talking ATM and befriends him. Gets him to drop a dime whenever the mood strikes. A slate of blank checks earmarked for deposit into the Bank of Hameltonia.

And here sat Eugene, squeaking by, paycheck to paycheck, unable to pay off his credit cards and behind in his car payments. Mr. Anonymity, bedding down in a studio apartment where he dined on tuna with Theo, his cat.

Where was his lifeline? Where was his benefactor?

"My office at three tomorrow," Hamelton hissed, startling Eugene, who nearly sprayed soda out of both nostrils. "Everything you have on the governor. All of it. Understood?"

A nod, then another from Eugene. A conflict avoider, he would have agreed to a lobotomy if it meant hastening Hamelton's departure.

Eugene took a fresh drag from his soda and flipped the first of many switches that would actuate the massive computer Hamelton had named Verne. If no glitches occurred, the digital marvel would reach operational status in less than five minutes.

Verne, the elephant in the room, overspread more than half the basketball court. East to west, it stretched from one free throw line to the other. North to south, the standalone savant came within inches of the faint, but still visible, out-of-bounds lines.

An eight-foot high, steel-reinforced fence surrounded Hamelton's master work. Painted black, the enclosure had been erected at Darby's insistence. If Hamelton's second in command was going to pour millions into a computational colossus, he would protect it.

Hamelton, of course, had been dead set against the metallic moat. He wanted Verne's innards on display. He wanted the sleek metal and bright lights to dazzle. He wanted spotlights shining upon his crown jewel.

For days, the two men butted heads. Then, in what may have been a first, Hamelton backed down. He had little choice. No fence meant no additional funding from Darby.

And what lay inside the imposing barrier? Nothing but a self-contained binary ecosystem without rival, one that resembled the supercomputers of the 1960s, but on steroids.

Control for the elaborate data processor ran through an oversized console that abutted the south fence. The interface, as elaborate as any mixing board in a recording studio, had become home away from home for Eugene. He navigated its many controls better than anyone apart from Darby.

Separate from Verne, a silo – farm-like, only narrower – arose from the floor and exited through the ceiling. The cylindrical chute, offset from the console by a few feet, was unbroken save for a small door. Behind it, an intricate drone idled, ready to take flight.

"My office at three tomorrow," Hamelton reiterated, causing Eugene to again jump. "If you're not there, I'll come looking!"

Running his hands over the console, Eugene powered up the fifty-inch monitor that jutted out from the upper left of the console. At the same time, the jumbotron affixed to the rafters, brightened.

"Kill the Big Boy," Hamelton screamed. "How many times have I told you not to use it!"

Eugene cut the power. He had not synched the two units. Darby had. The self-made millionaire preferred his television larger than life.

The jumbotron, almost as wide as Verne, was not part of the original blueprints. Darby added it because he could and because it fit his personality. Why make a splash when a tsunami could sweep everyone off their feet?

Eugene faithfully avoided the big screen. The mammoth display with its millions of LEDs produced vibrant, high-impact visuals that could easily be seen from any seat in the bleachers. With it on, one could not work in secret. With it broadcasting, one could not explore places and times that otherwise were off limits.

"Yes, Brody, tomorrow is fine," Hamelton agreed, fielding yet another call. He signed off by agreeing with the party on the other end in an uncharacteristically pleasant voice: "Yes, we'll hit him with a blindside tackle. Yes, he'll never see it coming."

The hint of a smile crossed Hamelton's face. The slight creasing of his lips didn't go unnoticed by Eugene. Just what nefarious scheme was afoot?

"Three o'clock tomorrow," Hamelton sputtered yet again in Eugene's direction. "My office. Everything you have! Understood?"

Eugene nodded like a bobblehead. Anything to get rid of American Psychotic.

As Hamelton one-eightied, Eugene exhaled. Just as quickly, he sucked in air as a near collision ensued.

Cidally Short dodged left as Hamelton stumbled into the space she had occupied only a second earlier. Nimble as a lynx, she avoided the Geritol-swilling geriatric by the thinnest of margins.

"Good morning," she beamed. "I trust all is well here in the bowels of St. Anthony."

Cidally knew how to make an appearance. And she didn't have to wipe out Boss Man to do it. Eyes shifted when she entered a room. Conversations fell by the wayside. Whispering commenced.

No one could focus a group like Cidally Short.

Stylish in linen pants and a white blouse, Cidally looked as refreshed as if she had just emerged from the spa. Blue-eyed, tanned and athletic, she cast spells without a license to practice magic. She inspired double-takes, the popping of Altoids, and countless pickup lines.

And Hamelton thought he was all-powerful!

Eugene was smitten. He was in so deep that not even an intervention could shake his all-consuming infatuation. Rational thought disappeared when he was in her presence. Sentence formation deteriorated. The possibility of morphing into a babbling idiot became all too real.

Eugene so wanted to say and do right by Cidally that he risked paralysis. How could he possibly measure up?

Best to let her speak first.

"Darby wants to know what you think of this life-size cutout."

The custom cardboard, nearly six feet tall, likely had been created using a photo of the governor in campaign mode. The amiable politician had both arms extended as though shaking the hands of a constituent.

"What are you going to do with them?" Eugene asked, hoping his question didn't qualify as stupid.

"We'll use them at Yest Fest," Cidally explained. "We'll place them in the lobby and other common spaces. They will get people talking."

Yest Fest was to be Hamelton's coming-out party. It was there that Verne would demonstrate that he, and he alone, was the mother of all motherboards.

"What the hell . . . NO," Hamelton huffed. "I don't have time for this!"

"No" served as Hamelton's default. He spewed it more often than a toddler.

"*I* don't have time for this!" he roared, glancing over his shoulder as he walked backwards. "*You two* don't have time for this! Stop farting around and do your jobs. I'm not an effing babysitter!"

The tirade became more unintelligible as Hamelton grew more distant. It ended with the slamming of not one, but two doors.

Cidally winced.

"What a Grouchypuss! Who frosted his flakes?"

Cidally rarely swore, a quirk Eugene found endearing. Instead, odd expressions rolled off her tongue, a dialect he had dubbed Shortcusses.

Fit and trim, the former point guard wore her hair in a twisted fauxhawk and low pony, a carryover from her days on the basketball court. Her smooth, bronze skin glowed under the gym's uneven blend of natural and artificial light.

How could anyone with a pulse not be titillated?

"Darby ordered the cutouts, didn't he?" Eugene surmised.

"Just took delivery of them, "Cidally confirmed. "We have three different poses. Would you like to see the others?"

Eugene signaled affirmative. Anything for more time with Cidally.

"I'll snag a couple the next time I'm in the neighborhood," she promised.

Next time in the neighborhood? Was she wrapping up? Already? She had just arrived.

Eugene's brain shifted into overdrive. He had to entice Cidally to stay while making it appear he had no qualms about her leaving. Cool detachment. He had seen other guys do it. How difficult could it be?

Ten on a scale of one to ten. Eugene lacked the charisma and confidence to pull it off. He paddled in the waters of self-doubt. He bathed in the fountain of inadequacy.

Eugene's nature, rounded into shape during his formative years, continued to stymie as an adult.

"Darby needs half an hour at 11," Cidally informed. "That's 11 o'clock today."

Damn! That meant that Eugene had to give up Verne for thirty minutes. Far too long for him to be offline in his quest to find the governor.

Disruption aside, the request was not unreasonable. Darby asked for time alone with Verne at least once a week. Eugene always complied. To have refused would have been cruel.

"Darby understands your time is precious," Cidally acknowledged, "so he offers these suggestions."

The athlete-turned-program director pulled out a three-by-five notecard. She cleared her throat.

"No. 3, treat yourself to lunch – on your dime."

Excellent idea. Would Cidally join him? If only he could ask.

"No. 2, go for a walk."

Not as appealing, but doable. Again, would Cidally join him?

"And the No. 1 thing you could while you wait is..."

The hesitation that followed all but confirmed Cidally had not read the list ahead of time. She was blushing through her dimples.

"Well," Eugene probed. "What is it?"

Cidally passed the card over to Eugene. After deciphering the chicken scratching, the message came through loud and clear.

"Grow a pair!!"

Eugene would not – could not – look at Cidally. His manhood – thanks to Darby – had come under fire.

Flashback! Throughout his life, Eugene had been told he was too little of this or too much of that. From day one, he had had been informed he should be more of this and less of that. Everyone – strangers, even – believed they warranted a say in how the quiet guy should conduct himself.

And now Darby was throwing in his two cents.

Eugene grabbed the nearest pen. He would show Darby he could think on his feet. He would show Darby he had imagination.

If anyone deserved a comeback, it was Darby Kyvelt! Eugene inked his in all caps.

"I WILL NOT BE YOUR SURROGATE! YOU NEED A PAIR? VISIT BALLSFORHIRE.COM. GRASS FED AND FREE RANGE."

Eugene found release with each block letter. No longer was he a punching bag, the butt of jokes. He could hold his own in the court of jesting.

Satisfied and a tad cocky, Eugene paused. How could he possibly place this reply in the hands of Cidally?

"I should get going," she announced. "I believe you'll deliver that yourself?"

Absolutely. No need to drag her further into this juvenile imbecility.

Taking in her gaze once more, Eugene again wondered: Did Cidally ever think of him as more than a fellow employee? Did she ever – even in her loneliest loneness – think he might be the one?

Whoa! Cold shower. Mental health assessment. Eugene had gone delusional. He was conjuring up a scenario that couldn't possibly exist.

But he couldn't help himself. With Cidally, until he was told otherwise, he held out hope that fantasy could become reality.

"You haven't seen a set of keys floating around anywhere, have you?" Cidally asked, putting the brakes on her exit.

"No," Eugene replied. "But I'll keep my eyes open."

"The miniature basketball on the ring is a dead giveaway," Cidally informed.

Eugene made no promises. By not getting her hopes up, he would earn more points when he found them.

And find them he would. The governor could wait. He had been presumed dead for forty years.

Cidally was alive, vivacious – scrumptious, even. Eugene so wanted to win her over that he was game for just about anything.

Chapter Two

"Has your husband ever cheated on you?"

Hamelton released the hypothetical as effortlessly as a burp after a satisfying meal. As with expelled gas, he waited for a reaction.

With nothing forthcoming, he forged ahead.

"You have a husband, yes? Every beautiful woman has at least one."

If Hamelton's off-road musings offended Sasha Ankubar, she remained unmoved. The seasoned reporter had been subjected to worse.

Attired in a conservative two-piece suit and knee-length skirt, the Queen of the Query knew when to grant a subject some latitude. Hamelton's stream of consciousness – though mystifying at present – might yet elevate what had been a relatively unremarkable back and forth.

Eugene had the next three hours to himself with Hamelton and Cidally gone. He adjusted the small monitor attached to Verne's console. Despite being berated just minutes earlier, he had no interest in pursuing the governor. Truth be told, he had not delved into the case in more than a week. He would hold tight until he met with Hamelton.

Then, depending on how cantankerous the Officious Ogre might be, Eugene would offer up dribs and drabs of what he knew.

Rummaging through his front pocket, Eugene retrieved his Silver Bullet. The flash drive and its one-terabyte memory could always be found on his personage. Every piece of video he had gathered in his search for Governor William J. Allerspan resided within the drive's durable aluminum casing.

Eugene had much from which to choose. He had Allerspan as a child and as a young scholar in college. He had the attorney-to-be hanging his first shingle. He had the up-and-coming politician rising through the ranks.

Though the governor dominated the bullet of record, he had company. Clips of Hamelton, Darby and Cidally also resided there. The footage on each varied, with most confined to the walls of St. Anthony's.

Conspicuously absent from the portable storage unit: Eugene. He took pains to ensure his likeness never made it onto the thumb drive in the same way he kept the existence of his portable video collection a secret.

Simply put, Eugene did not like his picture taken. What developed was never good enough. He preferred to be seen from within rather than from without.

Photos had permanence. Goofy haircuts, ugly zits, or double chins lived on. There was always a chance those imperfections could resurface, lobbed as weapons of belittlement as in: "Hey, I might have it bad, but look at that poor sap!"

Once taken, who had control of the photos? How often would they be shared? Who could access them? To what end would they be put?

Eugene avoided those questions by steering clear of the lens. He safeguarded his appearance. He got to choose how he remembered himself because photographic evidence to the contrary was all but impossible to find.

Still stinging from Hamelton's early-morning rebuke, Eugene queued up Skrean v. Ankubar. Though he had watched it many times, he never tired of Hamelton getting schooled by the opposite sex – those unpredictable vessels of emotion the egotist deemed inferior!

Eugene slid the thumb drive into the USB slot on Verne's console. He uncorked another soda. He unwrapped a candy bar. Only theater-style popcorn could have made the occasion more complete.

Hamelton had contacted Sasha at the same time he hired Eugene. He asked that she profile him on her weekly public television show. She rebuffed him. Multiple times. Undeterred, Hamelton called in a favor. He met with the executive director of public media, who then orchestrated a meeting.

Miffed at Hamelton going behind her back, Sasha went from fair and balanced to prickly and wary. The veteran investigator treated Hamelton more as a hostile witness than a person of interest.

Despite their differences, the pair agreed to meet in the school's library. Both reclined in wingback accent chairs.

Nearby, card catalogues (the search engines of yesteryear) and bookshelves (warehouses for encyclopedias long out of date) lent a sense of gravitas to the proceedings. One half expected Alistair Cooke to saunter in and arbitrate the exchange.

His presence proved unnecessary. Even had the longtime host of *Masterpiece Theatre* been alive, he could not have matched the aplomb with which Sasha handled her Skrean test.

Hamelton pressed on with his infidelity setup. Whether Sasha had a husband or not was immaterial.

"So, if your significant other cheated, how would you know?" he asked. "Check his phone? Hire a private detective? Tail him?"

Hamelton pooh-poohed each.

"How quaint. How old school. Know what I would do?"

His lead-in complete, Hamelton allowed the question to hang. Counting three, the salesman pounced.

"What I have to offer will nail the cheater in the act. It will catch him with his pants down. It will expose him for the scoundrel he is," Hamelton strutted. "And – better yet – what I offer will stand up in a court of law."

Sasha's lips quivered ever so slightly. She had to admire – or, more likely, be amused by – Hamelton's chutzpah.

"You're talking time travel, aren't you?" she asked, certain of the answer.

Smugness radiated from Hamelton. Sasha had set him up beautifully. Botox and dermal fillers had not diminished her talent.

Eugene paused the video. How could anyone be so supremely confident?

On screen, the geezer's self-satisfied mug taunted. Eugene memorized every revolting fold and crease. All the better to contrast this holier-than-thou look with the sad-sack version soon to follow.

"Tell me about perpetual motion," she cooed, her probe striking a nerve.

Hamelton double clutched. Instead of expounding on the new and novel, he had to account for baggage thought lost and forgotten.

Oh, the indignity!

"That was long ago," Hamelton protested, his ship taking on water. "I'd rather talk . . ."

"Correct me if I'm wrong," Sasha overrode, "but isn't time travel all about looking back? Shall we then?"

Eugene again halted the video. Hamelton's mouth hung askew. The muscles in his neck tightened. Panic flecked his eyes.

Why, precisely, Sasha had chosen to goose Hamelton was anyone's guess. But she did, and that put her squarely in Eugene's camp.

Decades earlier, Sasha had hosted *In Her View*, a late-night offering in which she coaxed secrets from tight-lipped celebrities. As her star and telegenics faded, she adopted a more confrontational style. Getting an aging pseudo-scientist to revisit an epic fail played to her strength.

Yes, pseudo-scientist. Eugene had yet to be convinced of Hamelton's credentials. Sure, the discovery he claimed as his own worked. And yes, it promised to alter life in ways yet unknown.

But Hamelton was big picture. He didn't dabble in details. He was a BSer, one who'd rather blow smoke than expound on the particulates of which it was composed.

For all the flapping of his gums, Hamelton never once spoke about inspiration, the "aha moments" that led to his innovation. He displayed zero interest in discussing the theory behind his work. He provided no backstory as to its origin.

Eugene was no scientist. He couldn't distinguish argon from xenon. But, dollars to donuts, his boss couldn't either.

"That was eons ago," Hamelton complained anew. "I was young, impulsive, looking to make a name for myself."

Behind Hamelton, a portrait of St. Anthony kept watch. In it, the Christian monk clutched a scroll bearing the words: "I saw the snares that the enemy spreads out over the world, and I said groaning, 'What can get through from such snares?' "

Snares! Why, Sasha had hooked a big-mouth bass, one accustomed to playing by his own rules. How was he to break free?

Eugene knew the answer. Running the single-word solution through his mind, he relished the juxtaposition between saint and sinner: Anthony, the Father of all Monks, and Hamelton, the Father of all Nonks. Anthony embodied **humility**, the virtue that penetrates snares. Hamelton marinated in self-absorption, the kind that generates contemptuous stares.

The Nonk continued to blather: "My latest breakthrough has nothing to do with perpetual motion. What I have engineered – a mechanism to view the past – is unprecedented!"

Droplets of spittle punctuated Hamelton's assertion. Though out of range, Sasha involuntarily pulled back.

"Then as now, you make outlandish claims," she countered. "Why should anyone believe you?"

Hamelton swatted at a fruit fly.

"Yest Fest will shake up the world," he predicted.

"I see. Will this Yest Fest be another carnival road show to prove your invention works?"

Sasha had gone thermonuclear. She had teleported Hamelton back to a disgrace of his own making with a single question.

Hamelton had encountered resistance, disinterest – even hostility while hawking perpetual motion. To boost his claims, he shuttled an outsized power pack from town to town, dropping in on state fairs, rodeos, flea markets, any gathering of substance. He invited the young and old, the gullible and skeptical, to poke, prod and photograph his flimflammery. Occasionally, he'd get a scientist to attest to its legitimacy.

At every step, Hamelton boasted he had outwitted the laws of thermodynamics.

As the public shrugged its collective shoulders and Hamelton's fifteen minutes of fame waned, the do-it-himselfer promised more. His brainchild would light a city. His novelty would reverse the flow of a river. His lungs would supply an abundance of chicanery in the face of dwindling demand.

And then, the gaslighter simply dropped from the face of the earth.

Back in the library, Sasha had relented. She allowed Hamelton to pontificate about his latest project, a task he performed with less enthusiasm than intended.

Weeks later, *Man in Motion Driven to the Past* – aired with little fanfare. The piece bordered on a hatchet job: Hamelton a zany zealot out for personal gain.

Seething, Hamelton swore off interviews. He, and he alone, would control the narrative.

He took to the internet. He presented his case – on social media, in chatrooms, in podcasts and elsewhere – with a spin all his own. He clashed with cynics. He tangled with trolls. He lit up those who threw shade.

For all his effort, he scarcely moved the needle. Flat earth, yes! UFOs, sure! Big Foot, you betcha!

But tampering with time? That was too wacky even for the farthest fringes.

In the end, did it matter if anyone believed him? Yest Fest was coming. Sasha Ankubar would get an invite. So would a slew of other Doubting Thomases.

Once that curtain went up, they would believe. They would come around. Gobsmacked, every last one of them would be. Of this he was certain.

Chapter Three

"**Y**ou never told us he was a cop!"

Cidally's voice carried to the far corners of the gym. Legs pumping, arms swinging and friend in tow, she barreled straight for Eugene.

Her accomplice, nearly six-and-a-half feet tall, took in her surroundings as she drafted behind the straight-line speed of her friend. The newcomer covered the same distance, but with fewer steps, her long legs and gait reminiscent of a giraffe.

"I told everybody he was a cop!" Cidally's friend insisted.

Fight, flight or hang tight? Eugene considered all three as the out-of-breath duo wheeled his way. He settled on giving ground, enough to avoid getting swept up in the collision that ensued when Cidally hit the brakes without warning.

"This is Carrie Boll, the Banker," Cidally announced, raising and lowering her right hand as if revealing a showcase package on *The Price is Right*.

"And this is Eugene."

No flourish for Eugene. He got a backward thumb thrust in his direction.

"A pleasure to meet you," he said politely.

Then, in a stab at small talk, Eugene added: "Tell me, what is up with interest rates?"

"She doesn't work for a bank, you big nerd!" Cidally groaned. "She's our center. Bank shots. Money in the bank. Get it?"

A lioness bracelet dangled from Carrie's wrist. A leopard-print scarf spilled over her almond white shirt. Jeans and ankle-high boots completed the ensemble.

"He's a cop," Carrie proclaimed, her eyes twirling around the gym. "I wanted everyone to know."

"Bull cud," Cidally volleyed back, "and I'm going to prove it."

Cidally handed Eugene a slip of paper on which she had written a date, time and location. Eugene surmised that the destination – wherever it might be – would settle this cop/no-cop nonsense.

"The girls – Carrie and I, and a whole bunch of the team – had dinner the other night," Cidally began. "Had the Banker here told us her new boyfriend was a cop, I would not have gotten a speeding ticket a few days later."

"What do you want me to do?" Eugene asked, feigning ignorance.

"Don't sink stupid on me," Cidally shot back. "Take those coordinates and feed them to Verne. We have a restaurant to visit."

Eugene hesitated. Outwardly, he had to appear irritated that Cidally's request would take time away from the governor. Inwardly, he was all-in, eager to take a field trip with two women who otherwise would not have given him a second look.

So, he took the slip of paper and held it up to the light. He studied it. He turned it over. He admired the looping cursive.

Why did the hottest girls always have the sexiest handwriting?

"I should be ...," Eugene protested weakly.

"I get it," Cidally cut him off. "But Darby okayed this. Text him if you want!"

Eugene could have called her bluff, but that would have been bush league. Besides, chaperoning this trip promised to be the highlight of his day.

One problem: Carrie blocked access to the console. Mesmerized by blinking lights, whirring fans, and the size and scope of the operation, she had dropped anchor mere inches in front of command central.

Eugene cleared his throat. Securing Cidally's attention, he pantomimed picking up Carrie with his thumb and forefinger and moving her as if a chess piece.

"Really," Cidally mouthed back. She took her friend's hand and pulled her back a few feet to clear a path for Eugene.

"Did someone record us on their camera that night?" Carrie asked, pointing to the shimmering jumbotron hanging from the rafters.

"No," Cidally answered. "This is a time machine."

"Shut ... up," Carrie protested.

Her reaction was typical. When sold separately, time and machine flowed without prejudice. When linked together, the words met with opposition.

Blame Hollywood, where slipping between past, present and future was as easy as climbing into a DeLorean or relaxing in a hot tub. Movies that rearranged time as so many dominoes to be shuffled generated millions in ticket sales, often leading to a sequel or even an entire franchise.

Of course, theatergoers had to mute more than their phones for these films to work. They had to silence logic and reason as well, a tacit acknowledgment that time travel was pure hogwash.

Carrie's "shut ... up" surfaced because she could not suspend disbelief. Not in the real world. Discuss time travel with any degree of seriousness and pushback ensued. Index fingers traced circles near ears.

The concept of flitting between centuries was rejected so universally that even defenders of other forms of quackery – astrologers, crystal healers, moon landing deniers – soundly rejected it. Only the foolish – or the certifiably insane – dared rearrange timelines.

Enter Hamelton Skrean. The self-described agent of change promised a paradigm shift. Channeling Archimedes, he declared: "Give me a screen and an app and I will wow the world." For those partial to Willie Shakespeare, he also gloated: "As past is prologue, past shall be profitable."

Carrie, of course, had not considered any of this. She just wanted to make sense of the alternate reality into which she had stepped. She wanted to see over the fence – what lay beyond – so she raised herself on tip toe.

"You want to peek over the top?" Cidally asked. "Let me help."

A plastic chair slid to within a foot of Carrie. Rather than sit, the accidental tourist climbed atop.

"Whoa, it's like a public housing project in there! High-rise buildings one after another. Who pays your utility bill?"

"Sit, Big Dog, sit!" Cidally growled, thinking better of her chair proviso. "I don't need you breaking an ankle or worse."

Hands on hips, jaw jutted, Cidally waited for her guest to return to earth. If she had to go coach mode to get the Banker to comply, she would.

"This is Verne," Cidally began. "Don't be fooled by his size. He's a computer like any other except ..."

She trailed off and Eugene picked up the slack.

"He can revisit the past."

"This is a joke, right?" Carrie asked. "You're pranking me because the po-po did a number on your wallet."

"No joke," Cidally insisted. "Using GPS, Eugene will send Verne back to that night at the restaurant. We'll watch on the big screen."

Eugene opened the silo door.

"See the drone inside?" he asked, pointing to the unmanned vehicle. With its multiple propellers, the high-tech flying machine resembled a tandem rotor helicopter.

"That drone turns to pure energy before re-emerging in the time and place of our choosing."

"Right!" Carrie agreed without agreeing. "And I boinked the Easter Bunny!"

"Now I know why you laid an egg in that game against Aquinas. Goodbye, undefeated season!" Cidally razzed.

"At least I didn't foul out," Carrie returned.

"Wish you had," Cidally shot back.

Twisting an imaginary knife into Carrie's back, Cidally continued: "There are cameras on board the drone, and Eugene will choose the one that gives us the best view. Simple as that."

"Hey, let me look at that gizmo," Carrie said, leaning forward. "I bet that's how this trick works."

"No one messes with the drone," Eugene jumped in. "It's one of a kind, and we don't have the time or money to replace it.

"But you're right, Carrie," Cidally agreed. "This rocketman makes the show go. Now fasten your seat belt."

With that, Eugene took up his usual position. Rare were the instances in which he took charge. Nonexistent were those in which he had an audience.

As Eugene carried out the launch sequence, he envisioned Michael Collins, Buzz Aldrin and Neil Armstrong at his back. The Apollo 11 crew, the first to land on the moon, had been treated to a three-and-a-half-hour ticker-tape parade after they returned.

Eugene fancied himself the fourth musketeer of that group. Like those trailblazers, he guided a craft that mined history. He gathered knowledge that would benefit the planet. He reached deep into uncharted territory.

How could he not be revered for his role in unlocking the past? How could he not be lauded as humanity gained a better understanding of its roots?

Presidential Medal of Freedom, anyone?

Having confirmed his inputs, Eugene activated Verne. As he did, a Shepard tone issued forth from deep within the massive computer. This haunting sound – an auditory illusion – accompanied each lift-off.

Eugene had never heard of a Shepard tone until joining forces with Verne. Now he was eerily enchanted.

The tone – a superposition of sine waves separated by an octave – sounded as if it were rising or falling to meet a particular note. In reality, it was an endless loop that never reached its destination.

Eugene likened the tone to a balloon that continually fills with air yet never expands. Or maybe a mound of dirt that grows no smaller regardless of how much soil is removed.

The auditory experience – which had Carrie plugging her ears – continued until the drone, sufficiently amped, cleared the roof. Exiting at the speed of light – or so Eugene had been told – the little guy chewed backward through time as it traveled to the eatery Cidally had frequented with friends.

Images popped on the small screen to Eugene's left. Choosing one, Eugene dared splash it on the jumbotron above.

"Just so you know," he said, anticipating what he might be asked,

"I cannot stop the action, I cannot rewind, I cannot fast-forward, and I cannot reposition the camera. All I can do is zoom. Once the camera reaches its destination, it is fixed in place."

Senzotti's, Italian in name only, catered to those seeking scrumptious, low-calorie, farm-to-table cuisine. Chic in appearance and spacious in layout, the restaurant comfortably accommodated parties of all sizes. That included Carrie and Cidally's band of seven. They and five others from their high school basketball championship team clustered about two tables pushed together to make one.

At the far left, Carrie deposited a silver napkin ring into her handbag. At the far right, Cidally drained the last of a rosé. Settia, lithe and long-armed, high-fived fellow forward Leticia. Olivia, the off guard, sampled Carrie's linguini as the center considered what else she might pilfer. Tamika and Lauren, who rarely saw the court, reviewed the dessert menu.

As the Carrie on screen zipped her purse, the Carrie in the gymnasium unloaded: "There was no camera in that restaurant!"

"And there isn't one now," Eugene said. "The drone resides in its own space and time, a fraction of a second ahead of what we see on screen."

"Oh, my hair is atrocious," Carrie grimaced. "Why didn't you tell me?"

"Why didn't you tell me Rod Smith was a cop?" Cidally asked, throwing up her arms.

Oversized wine glasses – some aloft, some table-bound – sparkled amid refracted candlelight. Partially consumed appetizers and entrees ran the gamut, many having cooled to the touch.

At table's edge, far out of reach, the women's cell phones huddled together in a rattan basket. Eugene recognized Cidally's. Hers bore a juicy peach sticker that covered the Apple logo.

Once a year – sometimes more – these fast friends rejoined forces. Years of shared experiences and the pursuit of a common goal forged a oneness that the day-to-day routine of high school could not. Old stories resurfaced. Inside jokes returned. Past accomplishments were celebrated anew.

Only after fully exploring memory lane did the present become an avenue on which they traveled.

"I have news," announced the restaurant Carrie. "I had a blind date."

A fast break of questions erupted.

"What was his name?" "Where did you go?" "Who set you up?"

Eugene struggled to follow the cross talk. But even he clearly heard: "What does he do for a living?"

As always, Eugene concentrated on Cidally. She had tapped out seconds before the question of work was posed ducking under the table to retrieve a wayward fork on behalf of a nearby patron.

"He's a cop," Carrie buzzed, tilting her head while bending the wrist of her extended arm as if to accept a kiss.

Rapid-fire descended into chaos as the group dished on the budding romance. Questions and comments overlapped, a mish-mash that raised the specter of handcuffs, frisking and cavities – those not filled by a dentist.

Cidally, her body still below dining level, padded the floor with her hand. Glimpsing metal, she extended her foot in an effort to reach the shiny object.

"Have you seen his gun?" Leticia blurted out.

"Oh, he has great guns," Carrie admitted. "He's in the gym every day. He's also a hunter. Deer, bear, elk – you name it."

"Looks like Cupid is good with an arrow, too," Settia declared. "He's found his Bambi!"

Striking metal, Cidally bumped up against the tine of a fork. Wrapping her now-shoeless toes around the utensil, she came up for air and handed the missing silverware to the grandmother seated behind her.

The elderly woman's sincere thank you got lost as chants of "Bambi! Bambi! Bambi!" pinged off the walls.

Witnessing on the big screen what she had missed in person, Cidally owned up.

"I was wrong. Guess that's what I get for being a Good Samaritan. Had I known the Rod Smith that stopped me was your Rod Smith, I could have talked my way out of a ticket."

"Apology accepted," Carrie said.

"Is it okay to leave the restaurant?" Eugene asked as Cid and the Banker again carried on as if he weren't there.

A faint sound, not unlike that made by a descending elevator, signaled the drone was returning to its perch within the silo. The noise – almost imperceptible unless a person was clued-in to its presence – decreased until a thunk, like carbon steel on wood, announced the time traveler had touched down.

"Maybe I can help you out of that ticket yet," Carrie offered as she and Cidally headed for the exit. "I'm seeing Rod tonight."

"What is it about men in uniforms?" Cidally mused.

"I was once a Cub Scout," Eugene interjected, two fingers lodged above his brow. "I earned merit badges. Gobs of merit badges."

"Nice meeting you," Carrie said, not breaking stride on her way out.

Alone again, Eugene put the needle to Verne.

"You're quite the wizard, big fellah. You can take me back to any place at any time, and I respect that. But don't get cocky. As powerful as you are, you can't strip away twenty years. You can't make me young again.

"When you can, let me know. I'll be first in line."

Aw, hell! Even at twenty-five, Eugene had no chance with any of the seven girls at the table. They operated on a different playing field, engaging in a game for which he had no aptitude.

No, the best Eugene could hope for was that Cidally and Carrie might one day recall this virtual visit and ask: "Whatever happened to that guy who took us back to Senzotti's?"

Chapter Four

Darby Kyvelt arrived at eleven as Cidally had promised. Trim and fit, he sported an untucked midnight gingham shirt and jeans. He called the get-up – of which he wore a variation most days – business-as-usual casual.

Darby entered the gymnasium empty-handed save for a small pack of tissues, the kind distributed at funerals. He pulled them from his breast pocket and set them on the console. A quote printed on the outside wrapper hinted at where he was headed: "Sometimes memories sneak out of your eyes and roll down your cheeks."

"Spending time with Sabrina today?" Eugene asked.

"Yes, my talented little artist," Darby confirmed, pulling a well-worn photo from his wallet. The pony-tailed girl wearing a bright yellow smock had just turned five.

"Cute as ever," Eugene agreed with a cursory glance. "Say 'hi' to her for me."

Even before he finished speaking, Eugene had set his sights on the door. He had no intention of sticking around while Darby used Verne to revisit happier times.

Eugene had tagged along once, feeling more like a trespasser than guest. He listened as Darby read *Tacky the Penguin* to Sabrina. He watched as father tucked in daughter and kissed her good night. He offered condolences when informed of what lay ahead.

The trip broke Eugene's heart. He could not bear such sorrow. How could Darby? How could anyone?

At least once a week, Darby resurrected his only child. He basked in her wide-eyed eagerness, her willingness to embrace the new. He reveled in her unrelenting curiosity, her desire to comprehend. He cheered her every triumph, her perseverance in the face of setbacks.

Darby ached to again hold her hand, kiss her cheek, hug her close. But fate decreed otherwise. Life veered off course. Sabrina would not, could not, come home.

And so the ever-grieving parent turned to Verne. This idea of bridging the bygone – though imperfect – had swayed Darby to join forces with Hamelton.

Rebel, class clown, troublemaker, the younger Darbeau – so named for his maternal grandfather – had muddled through high school with middling grades. Apathy, not lack of intelligence, accounted for Darby's less-than-stellar performance.

Bored, restless, and no longer a teen, this son of a single parent audited classes at one Ivy League school, then another. He never enrolled, never received a grade, and never stayed beyond a semester.

Three years in, he declared himself graduated. To pass time, Darby drove taxi and sold timeshare properties. He turned a lens on photography and spun the potter's wheel.

The nonconformist didn't have to work thanks to a Powerball-like inheritance from his Uncle Floyd upon turning twenty-one. His mother's brother bequeathed the money to him with a simple request: "Do good."

Darby took to the air in his late twenties. A stint in accelerated flight school led to a career flying jets across the span of two decades. He met his wife while crossing the Rockies, proposed over Niagara Falls, and became a father while on the tarmac at Heathrow.

Darby's marriage was fraught with turbulence from the outset. He cheated, then she cheated. They reconciled. She strayed, then he strayed. They separated. She went to counseling. He strayed. She served divorce papers. He slept with his divorce coach. He lost his job.

Humbled but not chastened, Darby bought an RV. Unhurried, unworried, the vagabond crisscrossed the lower forty-eight states, documenting his trip in words and pictures.

Somewhere along the way from Cape Alava in Washington to West Quoddy Station in Maine, Darby bumped into Hamelton. A friendship blossomed. A partnership formed. Verne went from scale drawings to reality.

Darby would have traded every zig and zag of his unorthodox trajectory to have his daughter at his side. How could she be gone and not him? What kind of universe permitted such cruelty? To whom should he direct his anger?

Unable to create new memories with Sabrina, Darby fell back on what had been. He rejoiced in precious moments past. He took delight in every nuance and wrinkle that he missed in previous visits.

What else could he do? Verne could not reanimate the dead.

Having punched in the proper coordinates, Darby took a step back. The first glimpse of Sabrina always startled, a pinch-me jounce that confirmed that what filled the screen was real and not a dream.

There she was, crayon in hand, sprawled on the floor, open-mouthed and locked in to her coloring project. She applied generous helpings of blue to a monstrous sketch pad that was nearly as wide as she was tall.

Buster the cat napped on the loveseat, a well-directed beam of sunlight adding to his cozy. Half-dressed Barbies congregated on the carpet near the toy box. A six-foot teddy bear, purchased during a layover in Atlanta, reclined in a glider next to the grandfather clock.

Home sweet home. The Kyvelts had resided in the two-story colonial at the end of a cul-de-sac for ten years. Never had Darby remained in one place for so long.

Having finished with blue, Sabrina expanded her palette. Tongue burrowed in cheek, she test-fired red, then orange. Two more dropped by the wayside before scarlet made the cut.

"I'm making a birthday card for Mumma," Sabrina offered in a squeaky voice.

She directed her words to the Darby of the past who stood just outside camera range. He, like his counterpart in the present, was captivated by the tot who crafted with such singularity of purpose. Hyper-attuned to the sacredness of life, both men marveled at their miracle on a mission.

"Crap," the Darby of yesteryear gulped. He had forgotten his wife's birthday – again!

Not so the little girl spotted with freckles. She had been preparing for days.

So reminded, the Darby with fewer trips around the block saved face with roses and dinner that evening. But his gesture, while appreciated, could not compete with Sabrina's handiwork: art from the heart.

Armed with yellow, Sabrina fleshed out the radiant sun at the top of her drawing. Shifting to earth tones, she added volume to the hair on those assembled.

"Who are all these people?" Darby asked, moving behind his daughter and tucking in her shirt tag.

Scrunching up her shoulders until the gentle tickling on her neck subsided, Sabrina replied, "These are my friends."

"Wow! You are a popular person," Darby said, pointing to children of all shapes and sizes.

In the present, Darby reached for a tissue. He sniffled. He blew his nose. Tears emigrated to the surface.

On screen, Darby had a question. He had caught sight of the name printed on the side of Sabrina's Crayola.

"What color is that?" he asked.

"It's brown, Dad."

"Can you say burnt umber?"

Sabrina tried, each attempt dipped in cuteness. Taking the lead, Darby repeated the name – burnt umber – drawing out each syllable in a falsetto voice that had his daughter giggling. The tee-hees increased as his exaggerated high notes dropped to a baritone in which he clamped down hard on each word. So well-received was his low-range rendition that he reissued his basso profundo as an encore to conclude the exercise in pronunciation.

The laughter didn't last. This girl was not to be thrown off task.

"Who's the lady with the yellow hair?" Darby inquired.

"That's Mumma."

"And how about this fuzzy ragamuffin here?" Darby continued, awed by the detail in his daughter's work.

"That's Buster. He's taking a nap. He's always sleeping."

Enthralled, the two Darbys – on screen and in the gym – ceased to exist separate from the action playing out in front of them. Both had invested fully in the moment, one in real time and one in playback mode.

Sabrina tilted her head. She squinted and curled her nose. She smoothed a rumpled corner of the drawing.

How would the intervening years have shaped her? Would eagerness have given way to reticence? Would cynicism have replaced curiosity?

Would Darby's daughter – a living, breathing vessel imbued with potential and possibility – have subjugated her hopes, her dreams, her aspirations for another? Or, would she have remained true to herself?

Both Darbys trembled as they imagined walking her down the aisle on her wedding day.

"What, Dad?" Sabrina asked, sensing her father had drifted elsewhere. Her green eyes met his before falling back onto the page.

"I have a question." the as-yet-bereaved Darby asked. "I see your friends in your drawing. I see your Mumma. But how come I don't see me?"

The answer surprised then. It packed no less a wallop in subsequent recitations.

"You're not in the picture, Daddy. You're out playing with your friends."

Friends? Did she mean passengers? Crew? Other pilots?

Someday he would explain his absences to her. Someday he would find the time.

Someday never came.

Sabrina held up her masterpiece. She really could have been an artist.

"It's beautiful," remarked Darby of the past.

"You're beautiful," murmured Darby of the present.

His only child passed away a year later. His marriage dissolved that same year.

Darby sobbed openly as the girl on screen dashed off in search of the next mountain to climb. He would be back, he promised. Sooner rather than later.

For upwards of a minute, Darby remained frozen, moving only to dab his eyes or grab more tissues. His collection of discards expanded as unabated grief battered at high tide.

"I'm back," Eugene whispered. He had been ordered to return after an unexpected run-in with Hamelton outside the principal's office.

"Life," Darby shouted to the callous that was the cosmos. "Life, my friend, is blatantly unfair! Totally, utterly, blatantly unfair!"

Only Darby didn't say "blatantly."

Chapter Five

"**I**f you could go back in time and change one thing about your-self," Hamelton asked, "what would that be?"

Aside from the perfunctory "Can we get you something to drink?" the question was the first posed to Eugene when he interviewed for the position of computer operator. Aimed to unsettle, the off-speed curve ball sped by the plate with enough topspin to compel even the best batter to swing and miss.

Fortunately, Eugene had toyed with this idea before. He had more than one answer in his arsenal.

Should he go humorous or go profound?

For Hamelton, his ploy served to bolster the illusion that he was a deep thinker, a philosopher seeking to understand the human condition. In actuality, the exercise was a gotcha, an opportunity for him to inveigh his perceived superiority. The Swelled Head took pleasure in picking apart responses he found wanting or those he just flat out didn't like.

Even Darby had been subjected to the pitch. But the wallet of the operations effectively removed Hamelton from the mound by stating he would withhold further funding if such drivel continued.

Darby could afford to crack wise. Eugene could not.

Sitting cross-legged on the floor of the gymnasium, Eugene tied his shoelaces. Taking a swig from soda number three amid a mid-morning break, he allowed his memory of that first encounter to play out.

If glossophobia – the fear of public speaking – ranked number one among social anxiety disorders, interviewing for a job had to be a close second. Such inquisitions always seemed to trip a breaker – often more than one – in Eugene's delicate circuitry.

Hamelton had kept Eugene waiting for more than an hour before Darby opened the main entrance to St. Anthony's. During that time, Eugene had fallen asleep. Head resting against hot brick, he slumbered below the sign whose message – *"Celebrate endings for they precede new beginnings"* – hadn't changed since the school had closed its doors for good.

Once inside the building, Eugene was directed to an armless guest chair in what had been the attendance office. The student-abused one-seater offered little support and creaked with the slightest movement.

Hamelton and Darby, outfitted with clipboards, operated from behind a U-shaped reception desk. To the left of the walnut structure, a stackable letter tray, dented and in need of paint, remained empty save for a dried-up wad of chewing gum. To the right, where the desk bumped up against the wall, a perpetual block calendar displayed the date as May with no date, two of its wooden cubes having gone missing.

As Eugene sized up his surroundings, the question came again: "If you could go back in time and change one thing about yourself, what would that be?"

Pen to paper, Eugene's potential boss awaited a response to the puzzler he so loved.

"I have to be honest." Eugene confessed, slowing his pace to convey introspection. "I do have regrets. My life is not perfect."

Heart thumping, adrenaline flowing, Eugene repositioned himself. Creak!

"I prefer to work on the future," he continued. "That's where I can engender change."

Eugene prayed his words – even the high-falutin use of "engender" – came off as unrehearsed. His answer always sounded good in his head, where the mellifluous James Earl Jones did the reciting.

Of course, the classically trained actor – his pipes deep, resonant, and no nonsense – possessed the power to transform bromides into bona fides. Eugene had no such gift. His delivery came off as stilted, hollow and spurious.

And just like that, Eugene wanted to go back and change another thing about himself.

"You can't change the past," Hamelton scolded, another sucker having fallen into his version of quicksand. "What's done is done. But thanks to me, you can view the past. And if I hire you, you'll be spending long hours in the long ago."

Then, as if addressing the village idiot, Hamelton reiterated: "View the past, yes! Change the past, no! Simple, don't you agree?"

Holy cow! Hamelton carried on as if he had just revealed a hot scoop out of *Time Travel for Dummies*. Eugene deep-sixed a snicker. One titter and he was done.

Having zapped another with his standard zinger, Hamelton yielded the floor to Darby, who adopted a more conventional line of inquiry.

"Why are you looking to leave the church?"

"My work, and by extension, my life has become repetitive," Eugene replied. "I'm looking for new challenges."

Too formal? Too professorial? Eugene couldn't decide.

"Care to elaborate?" Darby invited.

Sure, but how to do so without sounding like a disgruntled whiner? Like an ungrateful malcontent?

Oh, dear Jesus!

Repetitive only scratched the surface when describing Eugene's duties at the church. The office manager could cycle through a liturgical year as if an auctioneer.

"Who'll bid Advent?
I've got Advent, now Christmas.

Who wants Christmas?
Lots of presents. Lots of cheer.

Next up Epiphany.
How about Epiphany?
Do I hear gold? Frankincense? Myrrh?

Now Lent. Six weeks of fasting. Forty days of repentance.
No takers? No surprise!

Let's move on. Easter. What am I bid for Easter?
A cross? Death? Resurrection?
Thirty pieces? Is that right? Thirty pieces of silver?

Thirty going once.
Thirty going twice.
Sold!
Sold out by a guy named Judas!

The constant recurrence, seemingly arriving faster with each no-vus annus, moldered in monotony. The spin cycle of the sacred had Eugene repeatedly breaking the Eleventh commandment: thou shall not capitulate to boredom.

His routine remained unchanged: Unlock the building; turn on the lights; power up the computer; check emails; slide open the window at the business end of the office.

"Hello, Mr. Hamster! Hello, Mr. Wheel! How 'bout another lap?"

Each week, a sermon and a bulletin. Each month, a newsletter and a staff meeting. Each year, an annual report and an appeal for more money. Always more money.

And in between: copious amounts of ordinary time – boredinary time – snoredinary time. Enough to turn saints into sinners. Enough to drive atheists to pray for relief.

"No two days are alike here," Darby pledged after listening to Eugene's more diplomatic description of why he sought change. "We'll keep you on your toes."

As Eugene and Darby conversed, Hamelton scrolled through his phone as if it were a Rolodex.

"What's your greatest weakness?" he demanded, face firmly plant-ed in his handheld.

There it was! The dreaded question! The colonoscopy of the ego administered to ferret out deficiencies, inadequacies and incompe-tencies. A nail gun to one's pride that forced a candidate to cry out: "Hey, everybody, I'm no good, but hire me anyway!"

A baited trap, Eugene always fell hard. He lacked the skill to tiptoe around it and the ingenuity to neutralize it.

The creepy smile on Hamelton's puss only added to the pressure.

"I have been told," Eugene brightened, having hit upon the perfect comeback, "that I spend too much time in the past."

"How so?" Hamelton probed.

Eugene arched his back. "I love history. I enjoy collecting coins, comic books. I visit antique malls. I feel at home surrounded by the past."

"That's not history," Hamelton corrected. "That's nostalgia. History is messy. Complicated. Misunderstood. It's more than lava lamps and Pokémon cards!"

With Hamelton pontificating, Eugene redirected.

"I majored in history," he noted. "The United States in particular. GPA of 3.8."

Nothing but the facts. That ought to lower the thermostat.

"Who was the only president to win a Purple Heart?" Hamelton challenged, unloading an ear-high fast ball.

Eugene swung for the fences: "John Fitzgerald Kennedy. The injury he sustained after a Japanese destroyer collided with his patrol boat brought chronic pain. He wore a back brace for most of his life."

Hamelton scowled. "Nobody likes a showoff!"

"Well, I guess that should do it," Darby concluded, squaring up the papers he held.

"Hold up," Hamelton interjected. "Tell me what you know about Hamelton Skrean. What's the word on the street?"

His butt compressed and tingling, Eugene aborted his effort to stand and plunked back down. Creak! Was that hard plastic or aching bone?

What to say? That he had read an article entitled *Skrean's Bogus Energy Machine*? That Hamelton's attempt at a patent had been roundly rejected? That testing of his device, after he had fled for parts unknown, conclusively proved it did not export more energy than it consumed?

Better to play ignorant. Better to kill with kindness.

"With all due respect," Eugene thrummed. "I know nothing about either of you. But I look forward to getting to know you in the weeks and months ahead."

Three days after the interview, Eugene got the job. Only later, with the help of Verne, did he learn why.

"He's as boring as a houseplant," Hamelton spit up as he and Darby reviewed their list of potentials. "As charismatic as a wet sock."

"Honest and intelligent, if you ask me," Darby defended.

"He's a blender! Plain and simple," Hamelton grumbled.

Blenders disappear into the background. Blenders get overlooked.

Eugene stood out because he did not stand out. He would follow orders. He would do as he was told.

And those qualities – more than any others – were of utmost importance in a blockbuster production that could allow for but one name – Hamelton Skrean – above the opening credits.

Chapter Six

Middle age formally introduced itself to Eugene in, of all places, a vintage vinyl flea market.

Meandering through a maze of tables, Eugene hitched himself to one specializing in releases from a half century ago. The old records – he had a collection as a teen – had him thumbing through box after box of familiar artists.

While Seals and Crofts' *We May Never Pass This Way (Again)* played overhead, Eugene pivoted to a surface piled high with forty-fives. He brought one closer to better read the frayed title: *Old Days* by Chicago. A favorite.

That's when the realization hit. The number of RPMs stamped on the label matched exactly the number of revolutions he had made around the sun. He had logged more post-college than pre-college miles. He was freefalling on the downward slope.

What a cruel joke. Drum riff, anyone?

Weeks later, the what-have-you-done-with-your-life questions took hold. The unexpected reckoning in a race half over left him inside out and upside down. One mental health day, then another turned into a week.

So what if he had refused to get out of bed? Permanently? Would anyone have cared? Or would he have wasted away unnoticed, a blip on the radar only when the coroner came to dispose of yet another John Doe?

What, exactly, had Eugene accomplished? Where was his passion? How had he advanced the common good?

That Eugene skewed inward didn't help. He had no presence on social media. He clung to a land line and owned no cell phone. Telemarketers and robocalls were the only voices that reached out and touched him.

And what was up with all this phone phoolishness anyway? What buffoon had decided that everyone needed a face magnet? And why had so many consumers answered that call, one that had everyone jumping on a line while extending a rude busy signal to those engaging with them face to face?

This baffled Eugene, as did other trends. Eugene didn't follow the crowd. He didn't stay current in so many ways, the most noticeable being his out-of-style clothing: cargo shorts and a polo shirt, differing only in color depending on the day.

Maybe Hamelton and Gov. Allerspan had been right in taking a sabbatical from the breakneck speed at which the world turned. Maybe taking a step back and disappearing into the ether was the way to cope.

Twenty years adrift had Hamelton coming back stronger, refreshed, and armed with new ideas. He was poised to stamp his ticket to everlasting fame. He would be no John Doe.

And Allerspan? The governor's story had yet to be told. But the mystery surrounding his disappearance would get solved, his name passed down through generations as being central to demonstrating that time visitation worked.

What, exactly, had Eugene accomplished?

To his credit, he had been gainfully employed. He had no run-ins with the law. He had voted in most elections. He hadn't gotten anyone pregnant.

To his detriment, he had not saved a life. He had not fostered a child. He had not cured a disease. He had not earned mention in the tome of history.

Title his autobiography *He Had Not*, with each chapter a discourse on a particular shortcoming.

Eugene attributed his penchant for inaction to his reflective nature. He fancied himself a philosopher or at least a contemplationalist. He tended to ruminate, not ambulate.

Most of Eugene's mental machinations began and ended with "why." Why was he put on this earth? Why here, why now? Why so many unknowns?

Why? That yearning to understand, to make sense, was such that sometimes even those directly involved were at a loss to explain. Why did Bob kill his neighbor? Why didn't Hannah help the underserved? Why didn't Otto remember Ava's birthday?

Mother Nature, especially, factored in to the inexplicable. Why did one sibling contract leukemia and not the other? Why did one species go extinct while others thrived? Why did a plague have to wipe out tens of millions of lives?

Of course, Eugene's Pilates of the mind didn't stop at why. But the hows often gave up their secrets, and any reporter worthy of his standing could supply the who, what, where and when.

So, the whys dominated. All whys. Which led to another: Why was Eugene vexed with this need to know?

At first, believing in a supreme being helped. There was comfort in having a powerful ally. Don't worry; be faithful.

But as he matured, Eugene came to understand that humans manufactured their gods, not the other way around. The divine had been assembled in India, the Middle East, Saudi Arabia or elsewhere, with each location imbuing its creator with different attributes. One size did not fit all.

Two questions – both of the why variety – led Eugene to conclude that god's creation was less than divine.

First, why would an all-knowing, all-seeing, all-present being have a need, a desire, a want to create? Was it lonely? Bored? Unemployed? Out on a lark?

Remember, this is the Big Kahuna, not a slob like one of us. This entity lacks nothing. It is existence itself.

So, why? Why create?

Second, why would this totality, this sum of everything, settle on the human race, a species so vastly inferior? Did the Ultimate Life Giver run out of options? Lose a bet? Go on a bender?

Humans – really? What satisfaction could a god derive from animals so far down the cerebral spectrum? Fragile souls who, when spooked, murmur: "God has a plan."

Eugene didn't banter with bacteria. He didn't party with protozoans. He didn't date single cells.

No, a god bent on giving rise to other life forms would have created equals. What could possibly be gained from manufacturing a complex of inferiority?

Was this not common sense? Had Eugene been a god, he would have formed Cidally. He would have sacrificed a rib, his sense of humor, ten years of his life to shape clay into his version of beauty personified. He would have aimed higher, not lower. Lower was easy, lazy, a human contrivance.

Eugene wondered if he skewed autistic. Social difficulties, fixation on an idea, a preference for routine, a dislike of change – those traits manifested themselves early and only intensified. He shunned the spotlight as an adult, yielding the floor and often operating in a silo of his own making.

That wasn't to say that Eugene lacked for ideas or opinions. He knew where he stood on most issues.

But he tread reticent because others talked over him. They elbowed him to the margins. They percolated confidence while he dripped hesitancy and trepidation.

"There are two important days in your life," a marine biologist once noted. "The day you were born and the day you find out why."

Eugene, now in his fifth decade, waited on that second day. He insisted he would have a hell of a lot more to say once he found his calling.

But time was not on his side. The neck of the hourglass widened. More and more, the sand above refused to defy gravity.

Eugene understood almost from Day One that life was fleeting. As a kid, he had chiseled a date into the trunk of a tree: a month and year so far in advance that he told friends they might never see the day.

How foolish! In five years, the tree and calendar aligned. In another five, Eugene finished college. In another five, he attempted to strike the carving from his memory as what lay ahead shrank in comparison to what had come before.

"I can't wait," disappeared from Eugene's vocabulary. He embraced retro. He longed for the unchecked, unhurried days of yore that promised a reassuring familiarity. He knew his place, what to expect, how it played out. The script did not deviate.

"You're stuck in the past!" he was told more than once.

"So are you," he'd reply to those who labeled his compulsion a disability. "So are you."

Walk outside, he'd say. Every home, street, tree and shrub you see was there yesterday. And the day before. The eye takes in the present, but the brain processes the past.

"Show me a man who dreams solely of the future," Eugene's grandfather liked to say, "and I'll show you a man with no foundation."

No one sheds the past, the elderly man continued. It piggybacks with every step, attaching itself like burrs to the subconscious.

So why not celebrate yesterday? Historians did. Filmmakers did. Authors did.

Much of Eugene's youth *was* worth revisiting: sleepovers in the tree house, badminton tournaments behind the garage, rock climbing in the quarry. He relished those moments then. He cherished all he could recall now.

And in the end, what did it matter if others took exception to his outlook on life? It was his bus to drive. What harm could possibly come from an occasional glance into the rearview mirror?

Chapter Seven

"We have a skeptic in our midst!" Darby broadcast with a volume that carried to the cheap seats.

"Devoid of imagination!" Hamelton tacked on, his diagnosis more reserved. "Incurable in all but the mildest cases."

Back straight, rigid as a Marine at attention, Eugene straddled a dull grey metal shop stool. Eyes dancing, senses on overload, he sized up the metallic monument that was Verne.

At a width of fifty-four feet and a depth of thirty, Hamelton's baby boasted more square footage than some condos. If this was a computer, it had been weaned on Miracle Grow.

The eight-foot-high fence that surrounded Verne's internal organs was impervious to anything short of armor-piercing weaponry. The video scoreboard was a smaller version of the one found at AT&T Stadium, home of the Dallas Cowboys. The console, which Eugene was expected to master, was as complex as the flight deck of a 747 airliner.

Those were the facts as embellished by Hamelton Skrean. He wanted to stress that Eugene had not left the miraculous behind in leaving the church.

The new hire was not about to argue. Being the chosen one from a slew of applicants had Eugene believing in the "I'm possible."

All the talk of time travel during the interviewing process had led here. And that's what it had been: talk.

Like overprotective parents, Hamelton and Darby had not allowed any potential hires into the gymnasium. Only staff members had access to the basketball arena that would feature a different kind of traveling.

Now in the fold, they had to let Eugene in on the secret. He had to be convinced that what the pair was selling was real.

"This man has no faith in the power of Verne," Darby continued as he and Hamelton circled like vultures.

"He needs to be shown the truth," Hamelton declared.

Eugene removed his glasses. He was about to dab at the never-ending smudges that grimed his lenses when Hamelton grabbed his arm.

"Do you believe?" the bad actor inquired.

Encroached upon, Eugene felt obligated to respond.

"I guess," he shrugged, not wanting to appear contrarian so early in the morning.

"I knew it," Darby smirked, slapping his thighs with gusto. "This boy lacks conviction. A non-believer through and through."

The large screen blazed to life. "Skrean Time Productions" stretched from left to right. The accompanying logo – the evolution of man chart reversed; that is, upright man descending to hunched-over ape – only reinforced the notion that Eugene was no longer in Kansas.

"I need a moment from your life," Darby prodded. "Something big, something memorable, something you'll never forget.

"Your first car, your first love, your first kiss, your first ...!"

"Down, boy," Hamelton cautioned.

"Yes," agreed the seeker of indelible moments. "We'd better keep it clean or the old fart will keel over from a heart attack."

In amassing big-ticket experiences, Eugene lagged most of his contemporaries. He had not gone to prom, gotten sloppy drunk, or served in the military. He had not found his soulmate, gone skydiving, or run a marathon.

The "E" that began his first name did not stand for excitement.

"How about your high school graduation?" Darby suggested as Hamelton clicked and unclicked his ballpoint pen.

Deep six that! The ceremony that rewarded years of study had been a disaster. Eugene had been given the wrong diploma. His last name had been butchered. His left foot had snagged carpet, sending him – arms and legs akimbo – sprawling nose-first into the stage.

The pratfall rocked the auditorium. Laughter and finger pointing broke out as the prone figure's face reddened. In hastening to return upright, Eugene's Oxford cap and parchment went flying, sending the audience into a second round of convulsions.

No way Eugene was going to revisit that farce.

No, he needed an alternative. Something that wouldn't make him cringe with embarrassment.

"Come on, man!" Hamelton carped. "We're not asking you to pass the bar exam!"

"Old Pop Top," Eugene sputtered as if coming up for air after an extended stint under water. "I'd like to see Pop Top."

Eugene's frantic, high-speed search of his memory banks zeroed in on a homeless man who used to pick through trash left curbside. Unkempt and unshaven, the nomad crisscrossed the city in search of aluminum.

"Date, time and location," Darby ordered. "The more precise, the better."

Like flies to roadkill, Pop Top and garbage day arrived in tandem. Every Friday, the vagrant pedaled his Schwinn tricycle along the sidewalks in Eugene's neighborhood. His cargo basket at capacity, the resourceful scavenger tied plastic bags to his handlebars, which increased the poundage and clankage of his excursions.

On lazy days, Eugene and his pals would surveil the mysterious stranger as he moseyed from can to can. They watched from behind bushes, trees – anything that provided cover – squirming and giggling until the tinging of metal and squeaking of wheels warned them to fall silent.

One encounter stood out.

"My tenth birthday," Eugene said, rattling off the date and his street address. "Nine a.m."

During the week leading to becoming a double-digit preteen, Eugene had collected aluminum as if it were gold. He visited stores, restaurants, and bowling alleys in pursuit of the precious metal. He asked friends and family for donations. He downed an entire case of soda to further the cause.

Something inside had motivated him to help the solitary figure that most in town ridiculed.

On Thursday night, Eugene stuffed everything he had into white plastic bags. The next morning, he set those apart from the rest of the family's refuse. He attached a note to the fruits of his labor.

A Shepard tone rousted Eugene from his thoughts. Startled by the repetitivity spiraling throughout the gym, Eugene glanced at Darby.

"I've shifted our vehicle into reverse!" Darby announced.

Eugene gasped as the front yard of his childhood residence bounded into view. Maples flanked the two-tone split level that abutted Prescott Street. Banana-seat bikes lay abandoned behind the beige Ford Sierra in the driveway. A train wailed in the distance.

Squirrels zigzagged across the dandelion-dusted lawn. A robin poked the earth in search of worms. Old lady Miller walked her pug, the dog watering more than one lawn.

"Lame-oh," Hamelton grumbled. "I don't have time for this!"

The sourpuss rocked back and forth. As he did, a head poked out from behind the bushes. Then another. Before Hamelton could get to his feet, four boys – Ben, Rich, Tom and Eugene – stared out from behind the shrubs.

"How many teeth you think Pop Top has?" Tom asked.

"Same as his IQ, about six," Rich guessed.

With the pressing of a few buttons, the shifting of a lever, and the flip of a switch, the scene had teleported back thirty-five years. The faces of Eugene's youth – those best buds with whom he had cultivated adventure – shined brightly as if yesterday was dawning for the first time.

But this was no re-creation. The young lads rustling leaves were not actors. The whiffleball, plastic bats and other toys left out overnight were not props. The homes, the black-topped street, the power lines did not exist as part of a soundstage.

This was Eugene's old stomping grounds, the turf he roamed as a kid. Had any detail been out of place, he would have noticed. This was Eugene reconnecting with his childhood in a new and intriguing way.

Metal struck metal. Plastic scrunched plastic.

From the left, a tire, handlebars, and then Pop Top himself ambled into frame. Clad in a sleeveless shirt and shorts, the wizened man applied the brakes and dismounted. He approached the white bags.

In the gym, Eugene held his breath. So, too, did the youngster he had once been.

A smile parsed Pop Top's lips. In a quavering voice, he read Eugene's message.

"These are all the cans I could find. I'll get more next week."

The stooped figure waved the note as if it were a flag. Taking a last look, he folded the paper and tucked it neatly into his back pocket.

Was that a tear in his eye?

One by one, Pop Top tied down the unexpected bags of loot. So great was this additional stash that he would have to convert what he had into cash before setting sail again.

Finished, Pop Top returned to the saddle. He spoke directly to the shrubbery.

"You are most kind! You made my day."

Years later, Eugene's friends had insisted Pop Top did not speak that morning. He was a mute. His vocal cords had been severed in an industrial accident.

Everybody knew that. Eugene was hearing things.

Damn right he was. The drone's built-in microphones had no trouble picking up Pop Top's expression of gratitude. The words came through loud and clear. Eugene had made a difference, and society's cast-off was grateful.

The encounter was the last between Eugene and Pop Top. After that morning, the odd fellow ceased to make his rounds. He faded from view, no one the wiser.

"Well, that will cure my insomnia!" Hamelton groused. "Xanax through and through!"

The return to the present jarred Eugene. So fully invested in yesterday, he balked as the screen darkened and his preteen self retreated. For an instant, Pop Top – not Darby – worked Verne's controls. Ben, Rich and Tom tugged at his peripheral vision, not Hamelton.

The images hung on until Eugene's mind and body reconciled, and the stool beneath him again became solid.

"Is that the way you remember it?" Darby asked.

Eugene picked a piece of lint from his shirt. "Pop Top didn't look as old as I remember."

Darby slapped Eugene on the back: "You've put on a few years since you last saw him. Welcome to the team."

Tom, Ben and Rich had grown older as well. Tom, always one to check the coin returns on vending machines, had settled in as executive vice president at one of the region's largest banks. Ben, who sold cookies adjacent to other children's lemonade stands, had flourished in business. Even Rich, who battled brain cancer before dying in his early forties, had made a name for himself as a singer/songwriter based in Nashville.

And Eugene? He was the odd man out. Whatever he achieved never measured up. He always trailed the pack when tallying up accomplishments.

But now, for the first time, Eugene might catch up. With Verne as his guide, he could make up lost ground.

Seeing his friends as they appeared back in the day reminded Eugene of the home movies he had taken. Whenever moved, he would pull out the old 16mm Bell and Howell given to him by his grandfather, and point and shoot. He recorded sporting events, vacations, birthday parties – essentially life as it happened.

Eugene documented the happenings of his inner circle much like pioneer filmmakers did with players on the world stage. Enoch Rector captured Robert Fitzsimmons dethroning "Gentleman Jim" Corbett in a heavyweight boxing match on St. Patrick's Day 1897. Jack Lieb, too old to be drafted, landed on Utah Beach and filmed the invasion of Normandy, a decisive victory for the Allies in World War II.

Most impressive: Thomas Craven. Craven stood his ground when the Hindenburg exploded in flames in Lakehurst, New Jersey, in the spring of 1937. The out-of-work photographer reloaded his camera multiple times and shot more than 800 feet of film. Despite being a mere 200 feet from the fire by his estimate, Craven kept his lens trained on the German-made air ship – one that relied on highly flammable hydrogen for liftoff – as it crashed and burned.

With his trip back home still unspooling in his head, Eugene realized he could be the next Rector, Lieb or Craven. Hell, he could be all three rolled into one.

Verne and his trusty drone could go where no man (or woman) had gone before. Position the camera correctly, and Eugene could record every sweaty pore of Fitzsimmons and Corbett. He could document and relay to relatives the final words of men dying in combat. He could capture the horror on the face of Captain Max Pruss after that fateful spark ignited the dirigible.

All the emotion and drama that unfolded years ago could be funneled to the present in high definition cinéma vérité. Eugene would mine the past as never before. He'd shed light, glean details, and fill in gaps. His efforts would force a re-evaluation – perhaps even a re-writing – of history. His contribution to the human experience would be immeasurable.

Church secretary no longer, Eugene sat ready to roll back the odometer. All he needed was someone to show him how.

Chapter Eight

In the beginning, Darby piloted Verne and Eugene took notes. The navigator par excellence expertly manipulated the knobs, buttons and switches that cajoled the electronic marvel into doing his bidding.

Darby and his pupil began with the basics – the layout of the machine, the location of the drone, how to power both on and off – before graduating to the more advanced. At every turn, Eugene scribbled as if a stenographer without mechanical assistance.

The configuration of the console presented the greatest challenge. Eugene had to commit to memory the name of each control and its function. He had to recite which worked in conjunction with others and which operated as sole proprietors. He had to understand sequencing and how to abort.

Darby sprinted through the lessons. He addressed launching the drone as if fast-rolling the closing credits of a movie. He covered the Global Positioning System as if economy of words mattered. He talked of entering coordinates in more than one way: from month, year, time of day to mathematical expressions involving members of the Nominal family.

Eugene's pen bobbed left and right – like a boxer training for a fight – as he fought to keep up. His right hand calloused and tingled as he scribbled. Mentally run down, little registered in his brain.

At noon, Darby suggested they stand and stretch. Setting his notebook down, Eugene shook his cramping legs as he made his way to the far corner of the gym. Placing his hands against the brick to the left of the drinking fountain, he ripped off a dozen wall pushups. The physicality of the workout provided a welcome change of pace from the brain-bending backflips he had been performing.

When he returned to his seat, Eugene's notebook had gone missing.

"Kid, you have the world's largest, most expensive note taker in front of you. Stop with the novel writing," Darby ordered.

"But, I ...," Eugene protested.

Darby crossed his arms. "Don't you get it? You can YouTube everything we've done this morning."

"Explain, please," Eugene begged. "And slowly!"

"I know you have questions. That's natural. But all you need to do is send Verne back to when we covered a particular topic and you can watch what we did again and again until it makes sense. Simple, right?

"I tell you what. Before we head home, I'll send the drone back to eight this morning and have Verne record everything we did. First thing tomorrow, we'll recall the drone and – voila – there will be a file on the C drive containing everything we did today. We'll do that every day we train. Then, you can watch and rewatch as needed. How 'bout that?"

Eugene could have said no, but to do so would only set them back further. Darby was not about to be dissuaded from his preferred method of instruction.

The tutor uncrossed his arms.

"Relax. Observe. Ask questions. I'll drive and then you will. You'll get there."

Eugene's first solo flight took place on Day Five. Darby, running errands that morning, left two sets of coordinates on Verne's console. Eugene was to input those, head back in time, and provide summaries of what he had seen.

Furthermore, Darby had ordered his student to splash everything onto the big screen.

Hazy sunlight streamed through dirt-spattered windows as Eugene entered the gym. With each step, Verne grew larger. With each step, the rookie operator felt smaller.

"Morning, buddy," Eugene called out to his inanimate co-worker. "You're looking chipper."

In learning to bike, Eugene had ended up in a flower bed, flat on his back. In learning to drive, he had taken out a mailbox and a lawn gnome.

Only Pinkerton knew where this inaugural safari in cyberspace might lead.

"We're going for a little spin," Eugene began. "Nothing crazy. Point A to Point B."

Cracking open a soda, Eugene welcomed the first slugs of caffeine. He reached for the two sticky notes Darby had left. More Mandarin Chinese than Latin script, the handwriting would require some deciphering. Maybe that was part of the test. Rattle the newbie.

That could easily happen. The omission of a single digit or the transposing of others could knock Verne hundreds of years or hundreds of miles off course. And in this case, Eugene would be none the wiser as Darby had refused to divulge where he intended to send his pupil.

"Sink or swim. We'll sort it out when I return," Darby had reassured before leaving.

Eugene rocked on the heels of his feet. He interlaced his fingers, cracking his knuckles, and clenched his jaw.

Time to rip off the Band-Aid.

Taking a deep breath, Eugene hit go. The Shepard tone commenced, sine waves twisting and intertwining as the pitch moved up and down. Inside the silo, the drone supercharged, protons and electrons reconfiguring. Incoming static suggested a transmission was imminent.

In a gymnasium in which the eyeballs of thousands of fans took to the court, Eugene's headed skyward. He did not seek live action, only reruns of what had come before.

On screen, a slender, athletic women emerged from a white Land Rover. Coffee in hand, briefcase in the other, she drove her hip into the driver's side door to close it.

Eugene scrambled for a nonexistent pause button.

"You can't stop time any more than you can stop aging," Darby lectured, this time inside Eugene's head.

Okay! How about a screen shot, then?

Mouth agape, pupils dilated, Eugene progressed from impolite staring to felony leering. Though he could have spent the morning admiring the woman's backside, he prayed she would turn and face him. If anterior matched posterior, slap a sticker on his driver's license and call him an organ donor. He had just given away his heart!

Outfitted in a stretch tie-neck top and dark blue jeans, the perfectly proportioned blonde had her hair up in a crown braid. When she began to walk away, Eugene shouted "Wait up!" as if she could hear him.

What a moron! She transacted in the past. He operated in the present.

Why had Darby chosen such a stupid setup? He, better than anyone, knew the camera could not be repositioned once in the past. Unless the drone were recalled and sent back with different coordinates – an impossibility given his limited knowledge – Eugene was locked in to this position.

Why not come at her from a different angle?

This was all Darby. He knew exactly what he was doing. Tantalize with a once-in-a-generation head turner and laugh at helpless Eugene as she zoomed off to parts unknown.

Zoom. Eugene could zoom. By god, he would push that focal length until he could push no more.

At the far end of the parking lot – Holy crap; this was outside St. Anthony's! – six middle schoolers lined up for a free throw. All were roughly the same height except for the one closest to the basket on the left. He was a head shorter than the others.

The player who had been fouled rhythmically bounced the ball at the charity stripe. Staring straight ahead, he gathered the orange sphere, held it above his head and let fly.

Immediately sensing he had misfired, the shooter jumped into the lane. The other five followed suit as the ball caromed off the backboard.

Despite a solid jump, Short Stuff came away clawing at air. An opponent had sneaked past him and collected the miss.

"Hey, guys!" the Cover Girl to their left interrupted. "Got a minute?"

Heads spun as the tweeners halted play. Their annoyance evaporated as the reason for the stoppage strolled onto court and kicked off her shoes.

"My name is Cidally. May I have the ball?"

Turned to stone, the rebounder remained unmoved until twice

nudged by teammates. The entire group then did a double take after Cidally accepted a chest pass, squared up and rainbowed a twenty-footer.

"Pretty good for a girl, right?" she teased.

Damn! Who was this woman?

As the ball rolled onto the grass, a new sport took hold: rugby. Body parts intermingled as the slippery prize squirted from one determined youngster to the next. Each wanted the honor of returning it to the sharpshooter with the long lashes. The oldest prevailed, grinning as he made the presentation.

"Line up for a free throw," Cidally ordered. "Everyone in the same place as last time."

The turf-stained youth hustled to comply. Cidally's looks had arrested their attention. Her talent added to the intrigue. She didn't have to win them over with a motivational speech. Like lemmings, they would have followed her off a cliff, Eugene leading the way.

"What's your name?" Cidally asked Short Stuff.

"Clarence," he stammered, a couple of low-level "ooohs" adding to his embarassment.

"Well, Clarence, I'm going to take your place."

"He rebounds like a girl, anyway!" offered a member of the peanut gallery.

"Let's hope so," Cidally said. "Cleaning the boards is woman's work, right?"

Coaching basketball, letting the air out of gender stereotypes – Cidally Short was stacking Ws before her day had officially begun.

"Shooter, I want you to miss again and miss left," Cidally directed. "Can you do that?"

After receiving a grunt in the affirmative, Cidally sized up her competition. All were roughly her height. One or two weighed more than she did.

"Shooter, when you're ready."

Cidally bent her knees, turning slightly toward her left. She spread her arms wide, her right limb perilously close to the body next to her. Rather than back down, the young male leaned in. Whatever she could do, he could do better.

A high lob, deliberately off kilter, arced through the morning air. At liftoff, Cidally pivoted to face the rim. With the leaner a step behind, she thrust her tush outward. Wherever he moved, she moved, cutting him off and keeping him at bay.

After colliding a second time with Cidally's caboose, the gung-ho athlete broke off his charge. Red-faced, he pulled up as the only girl in the paint pulled down the intentional miss.

"It's all good," Cidally said, sensing the young man's discomfort. "Basketball is a contact sport.

"Box out. Take up your position. Use your body to wall off the bad guys. Size doesn't matter as much if you keep the big dudes away."

Seven heads nodded in unison with Eugene's jouncing as if a spring-loaded nodder.

"Remember," Cidally advised while placing the ball on her finger and spinning it. "Practice makes perfect."

"Show us how to do that," a chorus of voices pleaded.

"Another time, guys," Cidally said, tossing up a second net-rippling shot. "I have to go."

As one who had never driven the lane for a layup, Eugene had to reconsider his dislike for the sport. How could he have been so blind to the beauty of the game?

Years ago, when he still held out hope of finding Ms. Right, Eugene believed the girl of his dreams awakened each morning under the same sun as did he. She might live halfway around the world, but she was real and could be his if he persevered in his search.

As cynicism replaced idealism, Eugene wrote off finding someone, his perfect mate alive only in his mind. Though he could talk endlessly about attributes, he could not visualize what his heroine of the heart might look like.

Now, he knew.

"Encantada de conocerte *(nice to meet you)*, Cidally Short," Eugene playacted. "Puedo tener tu mano en matrimonio? *(Can I have your hand in marriage?)*"

Over in the corner, the water fountain's refrigeration unit kicked in. Eugene gulped down more of his syrupy drink. Though he wanted the imprint of what he had just witnessed to remain forever, he had another assignment. Eugene entered the target coordinates. Perhaps Darby had taken pity and this second look back might involve another show stopper as well.

Wishful thinking. As the screen brightened, an annoying zizzing sound pierced the gymnasium. A yellowjacket, trapped inside a rest room, banged from light to light.

Three stalls – the middle enclosure occupied – commanded center stage. Water – was that water? – burbled. Squeaking – that had better be squeaking! – emanated from behind a closed door.

Toilet paper circled round. Weight shifted. Wiping commenced.

In the name of decency, whomever lurked upon the throne should have been afforded privacy!

Eugene waved his hands over the console like a spasmodic mime. Fingers flitted from control to control – swooping close, then pulling away – as if touching molten lava.

Lunging for his notebook, Eugene flipped it open so violently that the wire-bound pages smacked into a slider bar. The collision only served to drive up the volume.

A volcanic flush thundered. Gushing water – as if a dam had broken – rushed in to replenish the bowl for the next customer seeking relief.

Hinges squealed. Metal creaked. A door opened.

Hamelton, his load lighter, headed for the sink. Instead of washing his hands, he ran tongue over teeth. He flicked at the moistened crumbs, some sticking to the mirror.

Yanking free a paper towel, Hamelton voided his nose. Coughing up phlegm, he hocked a loogie into the lime-stained porcelain.

Eugene doubled over, his gag reflex having kicked in. Dry-heaving, he chugged what remained of his soda to quell the insurrection.

Peals of laughter cascaded from the rafters. A firehose of gotcha glee flooded the premises.

Up in the bleachers, Darby convulsed turbulently. He nearly peed his pants.

Eugene had been set up. An unsuspecting sap, he had fallen face first into the trap.

The Jolly Jester hadn't gone out of town. He had been lying in wait.

"You bastard!" Eugene screamed, his words swallowed up by gut-busting guffaws.

Darby pounded the wooden seats.

"You ... you should have seen your face," he croaked. "Greatest reaction video ever!"

His face crimson, nerve endings frazzled, Eugene stomped his feet. He flipped the bird. No reputable HR department would have signed off on this training exercise.

"Now you know," Darby said, breathing in gulps as he descended from on high, "Now you know Ham Sandwich is a sitter!"

Reaching floor level, the prankster placed a hand on each of Eugene's shoulders to steady himself. Tears rolled down his face, plinking onto the hardwood court.

"Not only is he anal retentive," Darby began afresh. "He's ... he's urinal abstentive."

The remark sparked a new outburst. Eugene shook, so robust was Darby's rollicking. He dared not pull away for fear the man might collapse without his support.

"I have to give you credit," Darby said, struggling to complete a sentence, "you picked the right journey to abort."

"How did you know I wouldn't barge in on Hamelton first?" Eugene questioned.

"You follow directions. I knew you wouldn't swap Trip No. 1 for Trip No. 2."

Darby flopped onto the stool in front of Verne. Disheveled, flush in the face, he ran his fingers through his hair.

"I'll introduce you to Cidally tomorrow," he promised. "Even more awe-inspiring in person. Just remember to keep it tucked in your pants."

There it was! The escalation from casual to sexual. Why did so many guys do that?

Eugene chewed on a hangnail: "You had to see everything I saw before I saw it, right?"

"Damn straight," Darby confirmed. "And I watched that first trip more than once!"

"Then why don't I see a record of your visits in the log here?"

"All gone buh-bye. I deleted them." Darby confessed.

"You're not supposed to do that."

"And I shouldn't be spying on a crochety old man in the bathroom, either," Darby self-reprimanded with more than a hint of sarcasm. "But what Hamelton doesn't know won't hurt him. Remind me, and I'll show you how to delete a file."

Eugene had endured detenticn once in high school. Darby must have had his own desk.

"We're Peeping Toms," Eugene blurted out.

"Guilty!" Darby agreed.

"And that doesn't bother you?" Eugene questioned.

"Let me ask you this. Why does everyone have their nose planted in those face magnets we all carry around? Because we're interested in everyone's business but our own.

"So, we're going to elevate people watching to a new level. 'Don't fall behind. Rewind.' 'Smile, you're on can/did camera!' "

Eugene blanched: "That your sales pitch?"

"None needed. People will flock to this like seagulls to bread crumbs."

Darby adjusted his collar: "Won't be long before I have people deciding how to market this technology. Won't be long before I have people brainstorming slogans. This will be a game changer!"

"For the record," Darby interjected, "Hamelton likes the slogan 'Screening history through the lens of time.' I prefer 'Time Visitation: TV for the ages.' What do you think?"

"What about burnout?" Eugene asked. "Have we not reached screen saturation?"

"You tell me," Darby dug in. "Cameras in phones, pens, doorbells, at every street corner and intersection. Screens in the bathroom, bedroom and boardroom. Get your fill in the checkout aisle, in the waiting room, while pumping gas or folding laundry. Hell, your doctor doesn't flinch while touring your colon with a camera."

"If I have learned one thing on this journey," Darby concluded. "That apple in the Garden of Eden – it was an iPhone! The public will eat this up, like Adam and every other soul that craves forbidden fruit."

Chapter Nine

"**R**emember the Alamo!" Darby shouted, hands cupping his mouth.

"Where were you when Kennedy was shot?" Hamelton returned fire.

The high-volume tug of war played out in the hallway, ten paces from the school's trophy display. Neither combatant exhibited a desire to bolster his case with a cogent line of reasoning. Instead, both men resorted to repeating their calls to arm like petulant children.

Eugene, who passed by the brightly lit shelves and shiny hardware en route to the gymnasium, stopped short of turning the corner. Better to listen out of sight and avoid becoming collateral damage in the dust-up.

Scowling, hands on hips, Darby and Hamelton dug in. Theirs was an on-again, off-again battle of wills that would not end until one cried "uncle."

"Everyone remembers exactly what they were doing the day John F. Kennedy was killed," Hamelton averred, "Crockett was long gone. No one cares!"

"Everyone, old timer?" Darby goaded. "Really? Everyone?"

"Damned right," Hamelton doubled down. "A flashbulb memory! An event so tragic, so remarkable, it gets seared into the public's consciousness!"

"Hey, Eugene!" Darby called out to the hidden eavesdropper. "Where were you when Kennedy was assassinated?"

How had Darby sensed Eugene's presence? Sonar? Radar? Thermal imaging?

So much for remaining under cover. Darby had blown Eugene's to pieces. No use in pretending he wasn't there.

"Ah, here's what we call an ordinary man," Darby announced as Eugene approached. "Tell me, sir. What were you doing when President Kennedy met his fate in Dallas?"

Regardless of how he answered, Eugene would inflame one of his bosses. Best to err on the side of truth.

"I wasn't born, yet," he monotoned.

"My point exactly," Darby pounced. "Those alive when Kennedy passed are a shrinking minority. Everyone knows Davy Crockett. Immortalized on screen and in song. Coonskin cap. Rifle. His story has endured for centuries."

"Crockett died at the Alamo. It's a clear-cut fact!" Hamelton sputtered, his index finger in Darby's face. "But who killed Kennedy? That simple question spawned a cottage industry that rages today."

"Oh, my God," Darby exploded. "Here we go again. Grassy knoll this and grassy knoll that. What a gassy knoll of crap!"

Eugene backpedaled. He'd find a more circuitous route. Anything to circumvent this corridor kerfuffle.

Unfortunately, fleeing proved impossible. Like a cop bearing down on a suspect, Darby ordered Eugene to freeze. With one difference. Instead of informing the detainee of his right to remain silent, Darby expected Eugene to weigh in on the heated exchange.

"I don't give a damn what this kid has to say!" Hamelton objected. "His take is meaningless!"

"Well, I want to get another perspective," Darby insisted. "Can we at least agree to that?"

Hamelton backed off. The prospect of tearing apart what Eugene had to offer was incentive enough to hold his tongue. At least for the moment.

"Here's our problem," Darby began. "How do we show the world we can visit the past? How do we show them we can do what we say we can do? If we fail at that, we might as well dismantle Verne and sell him for parts."

Convincing one individual was straightforward. Circle back to a personal moment and a devotee is born. For Eugene, that meant Pop Top and his early-morning aluminum prospecting. For others, that might entail a poignant visit with a departed relative or friend. Something from a person's past that could not be faked. Or as Darby framed it: something real to seal the deal.

Convincing a mass audience would be more problematic. Revisiting an event – no matter how iconic – likely would not lead to a unanimous verdict or even a majority ruling. Not in this age of disinformation and AI, where skeptics trip over themselves to point out flaws and inconsistencies. Too many would grouse that what they saw was a re-creation. Too many would accuse Verne and his handlers of perpetrating a scam.

"So, I suggested we trek to the Alamo," Darby continued, waving off Hamelton, who squirmed as if a defendant under a gag order. "We celebrate the fighting spirit of those men. We make real the struggle to liberate Texas."

"Why not dial up Custer's Last Stand or the sinking of the Titanic?" Hamelton needled.

"Get this," Darby plowed ahead. "My mentally deficient colleague insists we revisit the Kennedy assassination. That's a no-freaking-win situation. Whatever Verne finds will be nullified by conspiracists who won't accept any outcome regardless. We'll be labeled frauds, dead in the water before we get started."

Hamelton growled like a cornered animal. Darby snarled back, morning breath offending from behind clenched teeth.

"Which one? Dallas or San Antonio?" he asked.

"You want me to decide?" Eugene asked incredulously, as if inches from the third rail. "Me?"

"Dallas," Darby clipped the name, "Or Saaaan Antooooonio!"

Eugene couldn't recall the last time anyone had waited on his opinion. Certainly not with this much riding on how he ruled.

"I like both," Eugene declared, emulating Switzerland. Just weeks into his employ, he could ill afford to tick off either man.

"Useless," Hamelton retorted. "Totally useless! He's a waste of time!"

The verbal right cross landed hard. Eugene spun 180. Tired of doubling as a punching bag, he put a dog in the fight, one with teeth.

"I have a third option," he said. "We clear up a mystery, one that could only be solved by visiting the past."

"I don't have time for this," Hamelton protested, shaking his phone like a maraca.

"Then leave," Darby called the old man's bluff. "I'm willing to listen to reason."

"Kennedy or Crockett is not your problem," Eugene advised. "High definition is."

"Wrong!" Hamelton jumped. "Everything you see is high def. We cleared that hurdle long ago. This is why I don't pay you to think!"

Sidestepping the insult, Eugene continued: "Think about it. We've all seen footage of sporting events from way back. They're either black and white or, if in color, they're faded or washed out. They LOOK old.

"So when you come in with crystal clear images of Crockett or Kennedy, you'll put an audience on alert. You'll be up against a roomful of disbelievers before you can even begin to make your case."

Hamelton lowered his phone.

"Twenty-five years ago, John Wayne sold Coors beer. Fred Astaire danced with a Dirt Devil. Those watching knew what they saw had been doctored, but they played along.

"Not so today. Anything even the least bit suspicious will be flagged, written off as fake or AI. Kennedy or Crockett in 4K will make you video magicians, not time travelers. The more you insist you're on the level, the more your viewers will demand to be let in on the trick.

"Whomever you profile should be a means to an end, not the end itself. Your choice should force the past to give up a secret, one that could only be ascertained if Verne truly is the real deal."

Accomplish that, Eugene promised, and Hamelton and Darby would have an army of allies.

"And your recommendation?" Darby asked.

"Governor William J. Allerspan," Eugene submitted unceremoniously.

"That two-bit hack?" Hamelton recoiled. "The only unknown is how he survived his time in office!"

"He went missing when I was in grade school," Darby recalled. "Former governor, exploring a comeback. Stymied at every turn by a legislature that didn't want a black man to succeed. He had ideas. Good ideas."

Hamelton adjusted his waistband. "Why not flag down Amelia Earhart?"

"That would work," Eugene agreed, "IF the drone could stow away on the journey from New Guinea to Howland Island. But it can't. It can't move about in the past.

"So, where do we send it?" Gardner Island? Howland Island? Somewhere in between? At what altitude? For how long? Essentially, we'd be flying blind."

"Don't be a wise guy!" Hamelton sneered.

"How is Allerspan any different?" Darby wanted to know.

"He disappeared somewhere within the state," Eugene explained. "We'd have a lot less ground to cover."

"Allerspan!" Hamelton scoffed. "Put John Kennedy's motorcade on screen, his wife Jackie in that pink pillbox hat, and we have a show."

Hamelton held up his phone. He had pulled up one of the hundreds of videos that focused on the tragedy in Dallas in 1963.

Eugene gave a passing look. "This event you are always talking about—what's it called? Yest Fest?"

Darby nodded.

"Picture Yest Fest a crime scene cordoned off by yellow tape. The night a whodunnit with a big reveal."

"Not bad." Darby said. "Tell me more."

Bingo! Eugene had the ear of the partner who controlled the purse strings. Maybe having a financial backing could knock some sense into Hamelton, a lifelong practitioner of selective hearing.

"Why not Jimmy Hoffa?" Hamelton proposed. "The former Teamsters union boss is the godfather of missing persons. Everyone knows Hoffa."

Hamelton had a point. When compiling lists of the world's most famous disappearances, Hoffa was sure to make the cut.

Darby chimed in before Eugene could.

"Hoffa was likely shot in the head and incinerated. Ever hear of Central Sanitation? We're not going to find his body."

"And we might not find Allerspan's either," Eugene appended. "But ..."

"But if we do," Darby took up the baton, "the curious, the kooks – anyone with a shovel – will come out. We tell them where and they'll dig. They will recover the body."

"And you," Eugene concluded, "both of you will have your picture on the cover of *Discover* magazine!"

"Mr. DeMille, I'm ready for my close-up," Darby Gloria Swansoned.

"Wrong, wrong, wrong!" Hamelton protested. "I have no intention of being the next Geraldo Rivera. I will not be the butt of a pathetic joke!"

"What?" Eugene asked, unfamiliar with the reference.

"You're too young to remember," Darby said. "Geraldo Rivera hosted a two-hour television event called *The Mystery of Al Capone's Vaults*. The former network correspondent had everyone buzzing as to what treasures might lurk within."

"The door was opened and nothing!" Hamelton spewed. "Nothing but dirt, debris and a few empty bottles. What an embarrassment! What a load of crap!"

"No worries," Eugene came back. "If Allerspan doesn't pan out, we find someone who will. More than half a million people go missing every year in the United States. We won't go into Yest Fest empty-handed."

"Damn right," Hamelton roiled. "We're going with Kennedy, not some long-forgotten colored fool in over his head. Understood?!"

As usual, Hamelton got his way. In the days that followed, Darby positioned the drone on Elm Street as Kennedy's motorcade wound its way down that street. He had wanted to park it at the location where Abraham Zapruder, using a high-end 8mm Bell & Howell Zoomatic camera, had recorded the assassination. But of course, Darby could not pan the camera as the clothing manufacturer could. He had to let the President come to him.

Hamelton uploaded the resulting video to YouTube. He included this disclaimer: "What you see is real. It is not a re-enactment. It is not computer-generated. We obtained this footage by sending a camera into the past. In that, you are watching history in the making on two fronts."

Hamelton solicited feedback from viewers. He got plenty.

"Amazing CGI," marveled one.

"Deep fake in the Deep South," posted a second.

"Artificial embellishment ... or superficial intelligence ... you make the call," remarked a third.

Hamelton's *60 Seconds in Dallas* drew enough attention to elicit a tongue-in-cheek reply. In it, a cartoon Kennedy returned fire, hitting Lee Harvey Oswald, who fell to his death from the sixth floor of the School Book Depository.

Alerted to that animation fabrication, Hamelton relented. The hunt for Governor William J. Allerspan commenced the next day.

Chapter Ten

"There's no use arguing. You've been given a Ham job!"

Bits of sub sandwich flew from Eugene's mouth. Masticated particles strafed the table, the floor and his companion, the one who provoked the mouth-emptying spit take.

"Correction: we've all been given Ham jobs," Darby continued, expanding on the line that had Eugene spewing like a Roman candle. He dabbed at the debris that had spattered his clothing like excreta from a passing bird.

Seated at a bench table in the cafeteria, Darby and Eugene had been riffing on nicknames for Hamelton Skrean. They had touched on the obvious: Ham Sandwich, Ham Fisted and Ham Hock; the arcane: Eventual Motion; and the uninspired: Dumb Ass.

Leave it to Darby to hit it out of the park.

As both toweled off with napkins, Eugene kicked himself. He knew better. One should never stuff his face while eating with the Wicked Witticist.

Three months. Three months had passed since Eugene joined the Skrean team. Three months spent wandering the halls of an institution he believed he had left behind for good.

But here he was, horsing around with a colleague that – had the years aligned better – could have been a classmate back in the day. Goof-offs both, their inner child none the worse for wear.

Yes, here he was, back in high school – albeit not the one he had attended as a teen. The return had him revisiting his formative years. Would he fit in? Would he earn the respect of others? Would the female population acknowledge his existence?

Five years short of a half century, Eugene had re-enrolled. He had reawakened a roll-call of memories, some best left buried. In the band room, he and Toby Demmings puffed cheeks in yet another face-off for first-chair clarinet. On a landing between floors, Kelle Satinski again declined a birthday invitation, unmoved by the intricate hand-crafted card she had been given. In the science wing, an F-bearing midterm awaited, one that took on added weight as red ink mixed with tears.

An edifice turned time capsule, St. Anthony's persisted in the past. Stickers – some profane – clung to lockers that housed no belongings. Teachers' names – some legible – adhered to mailboxes empty on the inside. Desks – some still aligned – congregated as they had when summer drained the last flesh and blood from campus.

Out in front, the sign under which he had fallen asleep remained unchanged: "Celebrate endings – for they precede new beginnings."

Unlike Eugene, his co-workers appeared unburdened by their surroundings. Cidally took up residence in a science lab equipped with a generous supply of windows that overlooked the front entrance. Darby planted his flag in the guidance counselor's offices, doling out unsolicited advice as if paid by the word. Hamelton set up shop in the principal's office because, well, he was the head honcho.

"How do you like working for Sir Hamelot?" Darby asked, a tuft of lettuce drooping from his lower lip.

"He reminds me of Pastor Paul," Eugene said.

"An old boss?" Darby guessed.

"First one and one I'd just as soon forget," Eugene replied. "That wasn't his real name. I called him that because he would rob Peter to pay Paul. Couldn't be trusted around money."

"That pesky Eighth Commandment," Darby lamented. "Always getting in the way, right?"

"He dipped into the parson's purse – money earmarked for the less fortunate – as if it were his own slush fund," Eugene continued. "He'd drain it and ask for more. There was no oversight.

"I caught on after opening a few bank statements. The timing of too many withdrawals lined up perfectly with the satellite radio, big-ticket items and vacations that he bragged about."

"What did you do?" Darby asked, downing the last of his flavored water.

"Kept my mouth shut. This shyster would buy things for the church – Christmas decorations, flowers for the altar, meals for the youth – and have the treasurer reimburse him."

"Sounds reasonable," Darby said, brushing away crumbs.

"The SOB would then turn around and claim those items as donations on his taxes. He bragged to me – more than once – that he had been audited for being too generous. Too generous. What a crock!"

"You know what the Bible says about the love of money," Darby volunteered.

"And don't get me started on his housing allowance," Eugene added, "one that continued long after he had paid off his home."

"No one held him accountable?"

"Who would have taken the word of a church secretary over that of an esteemed pastor with a direct line to God? I would have lost my job and any chance of getting hired elsewhere. He would have ended me and danced at my funeral."

"What would Jesus have done?" Darby reflected.

"He would have stood up to Paul. Told him to his face what a fraud he was. Stealing from others. Pathetic! A worthless pastor and even less of a man. Unforgivable!"

"Whoa. Slow down, Hoss," Darby said. "Didn't mean to rile you."

"Gotta give Ham credit," Eugene conceded. "He pretty much leaves me alone."

"So, why *did* you take this job? Why abandon saints to hang with sinners?"

"I wanted change. I wanted something different?" Eugene explained. "Here, I might make history."

"If you do, don't expect to get any credit," Darby cautioned, wiping the last of salami and rye from his face. "In case you haven't heard, this is Skrean time."

Eugene stacked his potato chips until they toppled. Undeterred, he placed one atop the other, aiming to go higher.

"Gotta wonder why he's so ornery, though," Eugene mused.

"Simple. He had his head handed to him on a platter," Darby summed up. "For a guy who can admit no wrong, that ate him alive."

"Perpetual motion?" Eugene guessed.

"Throw Hamelton's name into yorenewspaper.com sometime." Darby suggested as he launched his brown bag in the direction of the garbage. "See what comes up."

Darby helped himself to another soda from the fridge.

"You say you want to make history. Any idea of how many books have been written about Abraham Lincoln?"

"Not even going to guess," Eugene deferred, removing the wrapper from a sticky bun.

"Roughly fifteen thousand," Darby stated. "More has been written about him than anybody other than your pal, Jesus Christ."

A hiccup punctuated the fun fact.

"But," Darby cautioned. "How well do we really know that old rail splitter? All those tomes, all that verbiage. Did they get it right?

"Riddle me this: Did Honest Abe sing in the shower? Did he tip the wait staff? Did he pay for the car behind him in the drive-thru lane?"

Eugene set down his dessert. Darby was looking to brew more than coffee.

"Suppose instead of one drone, we have thousands," he continued. "And we send a fleet of them to record Lincoln as he ambles from borning cry to death rattle.

"Further, our immobility problem no longer exists. We can manipulate those drones – regardless of location – in real time in the present. Even better, all those worker bees come equipped with facial rec. They attach themselves to Lincoln like magnets on metal and shadow his every move! They track him without us having to lift a finger.

"Want more? Instead of having to wait fifty-six years – the lifespan of Lincoln – we speed up the process and have the drones back in hours, not years. We could – theoretically, at least – document an entire life in less time than it takes a woman to give birth."

Darby spoke with animated fury, as if he had shotgunned a flight of energy drinks.

Eugene took a gulp of his own. "Not to rain on your party, but who is going to sort through years and years of video?"

"We'll index it through a computer," Darby explained. "Cue up a date such as his first inauguration and – boom – you're there."

What Darby proposed represented a massive upgrade. An automation of the clunky process Eugene dealt with every day.

"What if someone wants access to all of Lincoln's encounters with Stephen Douglas, but has no idea of when those meetings occurred?" Eugene questioned.

Darby beamed as if a halo sat atop his head.

"We will document Douglas's life as we did Lincoln's. We'll do the same for Lincoln's wife and children. All the major players. We'll feed everything into a computer, which will note when various lives inter-sected.

"Once finished, you can query Lincoln-Douglas, and you'll get ev-ery instance of the two men interacting. Knowledge at the touch of a button."

Impressive. But how much of Darby's spiel was pure hype? How much was wishful thinking?

Eugene didn't know. Until recently, he had thought time travel to be a pipedream.

Of course, that changed as Verne escorted Eugene to places he had never thought possible. His electronic co-worker regularly exhumed the long gone and forgotten.

So maybe Darby's video library of the historically significant might someday come to fruition. Perhaps science could be injected into what sounded like pure fiction.

Still, Eugene had his doubts. For all the ballyhoo spouted by Hamelton and Darby, their prized baby crawled – not sprinted – along the long-stretching timeline of existence.

Further, these two self-professed stable geniuses had but one drone, not an endless supply. And when it fussed, flub-ups followed. Video came back raw and unsorted. Images blurred or disappeared. Cameras malfunctioned. Missions ended prematurely.

With the simple as yet unperfected, what chance did Darby's am-bitious agenda have of succeeding? Cost alone would be prohibitive.

The visionary did not seem fazed.

"People will pay," Darby said confidently. "Audiences will down-load or stream or binge watch, powerless to look away. They will clamor for more.

"Books will become obsolete. Gutenberg's invention – a mainstay for centuries – tossed aside like so much wastepaper."

Darby's lunch, apparently, had been topped with hallucinogens.

"Still not sold?" he said, sensing the younger man's skepticism. "How about celebrities? Think tabloids with moving pictures. You skipper the cruise as you hop from scandal to scandal and all ports in between. Nothing left to the imagination. All the tawdry details!"

Then, Darby unloaded his trump card.

"Still wavering, my friend?" his voice a whisper. "How much would you pay to have an all-access pass to Cidally Short?"

Alarm bells jangled. Trumpets sounded.

Had Eugene tipped his hand? Did Darby know he was sweet on Cidally? Did she? Had he been that obvious? Had his puppy dog eyes – boy, how he tried to avoid them – given him away?

Worse – far worse – had Darby discovered that Eugene had used Verne to record Cidally? Had he come across a stray file, one that should have been erased?

Eugene had been so careful. He checked and double checked the hard drive many times a day. He never left the gym until he was sure he had covered his tracks.

For the record, he justified his clandestine excursions as opportunities to get to know Cidally better. He excused his behavior because he steered clear of compromising situations. His portfolio contained only G-rated material.

Mostly, he defended his check-ins because of role reversal. Had Cidally been the one guiding Verne, Eugene would have been thrilled to find out she had been spying on him. Her displaying any interest at all – especially when no one was looking – would have had him jumping into the surf to frolic among the endorphins.

"Whoo boy! She has you good, doesn't she," Darby chuckled. "Just remember: She chooses her man, not the other way around."

"Let's change the subject," Eugene pleaded, loathe to incriminate himself further in matters involving Cidally.

"Fine," Darby agreed, basking in his companion's discomfort. "How close are you to finding the governor?"

Well, well! There it was. The real reason Darby had asked Eugene to lunch this Wednesday. With Yest Fest approaching, his superiors wanted a progress report.

No doubt, Hamelton had orchestrated the whole affair.

"Feed the kid. Put him at ease. Poke fun at my expense, if necessary," he had likely ordered. "But find out where he stands with the governor. Happy salmon him in the face if you have any reason to think he's been stalling!"

That thought, and the territory into which the conversation had drifted, added to a growing queasiness in Eugene's stomach. He took that as a signal to excuse himself, hashtag men's room.

Chapter Eleven

The claim, if true, would shake up the scientific world.

Hamelton Joseph Skrean, self-educated engineer, says he has invented a machine that produces more energy than it consumes.

"This creation," Skrean boasts, "will absolutely end our dependence on utility companies and fossil fuel. This breakthrough is revolutionary!"

Those lines, the opening to a human-interest piece decades old, filled Verne's small screen. The article was one of dozens that appeared when Eugene conducted a search at yorenewspaper.com using Hamelton's name.

Spurred by Darby's comment at lunch, Eugene intended to spend the afternoon learning as much as he could about his boss through the online newspaper archive. Information was power, and the more Eugene could glean the better.

The governor could wait.

To avoid getting caught, Eugene looped footage of his search for Allerspan on Verne's large screen. Anyone entering the gym would encounter the display and assume he was engaged on that front.

The trick served Eugene well. He spent considerable time coloring outside the lines without incident.

Funny. While repelled by Hamelton in the flesh, Eugene gravitated toward him in the past. What made the old man tick? Why had he withdrawn from civilization? How had he hit upon time visitation?

At what age did ulcerative colitis set in?

Most important: Why did Hamelton face no competition in bringing his technology to bear? Charles Darwin and Alfred Russel Wallace hit upon the idea of evolution by natural selection at roughly the same time. Sir Isaac Newton and Gottfried Wilhelm Leibniz introduced calculus within years of each other.

Why, then, did Hamelton have no rival in his pursuit? Why did it seem the powerful energy companies were not threatened? The more Eugene read about the man's devotion to perpetual motion, it couldn't be because of his intelligence.

Is Skrean the second coming of Thomas Edison – or is he the very reincarnation of P.T. Barnum? Time will tell.

Eugene clicked on another story, one that ran months later. After weeks and weeks of bold talk, Hamelton finally ponied up and built a prototype. The resulting test case – "a homemade concrete mixer mounted atop a wafer cone of pressed wood, cross-hatched slats and metallic trim" – overran his garage and weighed more than five tons. A patent was pending.

"Everyone who's been out here – physicists, engineers, other scientists – they all come away absolutely amazed," Hamelton enthused. "This machine puts out more energy than it takes in. Do you have any idea what that means?"

When the flow of onlookers to his residence slowed to a trickle, Hamelton took to the road. If the masses declined to come to his monstrosity, he would bring his monstrosity to the masses.

Loading his ugly stepchild onto the back of a flatbed, Hamelton carted it to carnivals, county fairs, festivals – any gathering with warm bodies. He gushed how he, in his infinite wisdom, "would light up the world for a song."

A circus-like atmosphere greeted Hamelton at every stop. In exhibiting his ware, he attracted the fringe, the gullible, the low IQ segments of the population he deemed unworthy of his standing. But, like any good showman, he held his nose and preached with the passion of a televangelist.

His act landed him front and center in more than one prominent tabloid.

Hamilton Skrean has made good on his vow.

The self-proclaimed Jack of All Trades hammered that point home as the flatbed truck carrying his shiny, 9,500-pound energy machine backed into the arena at the county fairgrounds. Microphone in hand, Skrean urged the crowd to "strap on their seatbelts," as they were about to fast track to the future.

Skrean ordered his assistants to start a countdown from ten. This they did as the oversize unit – described by one spectator as "a large tub from which one might make bootleg liquor" – coughed to life.

After the demonstration, Skrean lobbed a parting shot.

"The proof of the pudding is in the eatin'," he stated. "Y'all got your fill today."

Representatives from the local university assured those gathered that the machine had produced more energy than it had taken in. An impossibility, they conceded, but one that came loaded with promise.

Eager to stay in the public's eye, Hamelton sold T-shirts emblazoned with an expression that placed "e=mc²" atop the symbol for infinity. He promised cash to anyone who could prove his invention was fake. He offered to power any business or city willing to tap into his never-ending stockpile.

Determined to obtain exclusive rights to his creation, Hamelton turned to the US Government. His application fell flat. The Office Action authored on his behalf detailed the reasons for his rejection.

"You cannot patent fairy dust!" chirped one sage.

Hamelton appealed the decision and was denied. He protested what he insisted was shabby treatment as vociferously as he had promoted his work. He claimed the establishment was conspiring to shut him down. Free energy meant an end to the grid, to government control. If they could come for him – whoever *they* might be – who would be next?

In the end, Hamelton simply ran out of money.

On a hunch, Eugene entered Hamelton's name into his browser. Did video exist of the clown prince at the height of his infamy? One piece surfaced, its once-vibrant color having degraded to a faint pink. A local outlet had conducted the roughly minute-long interview.

The clip offered no new insight, but did provide further evidence as to how far divorced from reality Hamelton had become. When asked how he should be remembered, the self-proclaimed genius asserted, "Alphabetically, between Roentgen and Tesla."

The quip hit without a hint of irony. Eugene shook his head. This guy could sell manure to a cattle farmer.

Eager to continue his deep dive, Eugene mouthed an "Aw, man" after glancing at the scoreboard at the south end of the gym. Most of the afternoon had expired. Time enough for one last search. Had anything been written about Hamelton during his years of self-imposed exile? Anything at all?

Eugene got one hit and it knocked him sideways. He had to reread the headline more than once: "Local Resident Found Dead."

Clicking on it, he got more than he bargained for. Not from the story, but from within the gym itself. Two feet landed with a thud. Darby had been watching from the bleachers.

"Did you find any dirt on our boy?" the stealth ninja asked.

Eugene stammered, brain and mouth out of sync. How the hell did Darby slip in unnoticed? Cursing himself for having gotten caught, Eugene's fingers tripped over one another in a clumsy attempt to hide his fishing expedition.

"Leave it on," Darby instructed, removing a flash drive from his pocket. He waved Eugene away from the console and inserted the device into the nearest port.

So much for Eugene covering his tracks.

"I come into the gym. I see the governor kissing his wife. I see him drive away. I see him turn left. I see him turn right. I see him kissing his wife," Darby explained as he moved about the controls. "Next time, might I suggest a longer loop?"

Ouch! So much for his little ruse. Perhaps Eugene should retain a hotshot lawyer from the firm Beg, Supplicate and Grovel, and throw himself on the mercy of the court.

Screw that! Darby had all but dared him to check into Hamelton's past. He was following orders.

"You're downloading Verne's history into that thumb drive, aren't you?" Eugene guessed.

"Afraid of what I might find?" Darby asked.

Afraid, no. Terrified, yes!

What sane person wanted his online history made public? What reasonable individual welcomed a spotlight exposing what should remain hidden?

Eugene had yet to clear his browsing registry, something he usually did every hour or so. He had been so wrapped up in tracking

Hamelton he had overlooked this simple routine.

"You haven't been erasing anything?" Darby asked, pulling free the flash drive.

"No, sir. Scout's honor," came Eugene's truthful reply.

"Hamelton wants everything you have on Allerspan. For your sake, I hope there's enough here to satisfy him. You don't want to piss off the old goat."

Roger that. But something shady lurked in Hamelton's past, and that transgression – whatever it might be – needed to see the light of day. Eugene would tread lightly. He needed time – already in short supply – to keep digging.

"I suggest any skeletons you go in search of are the type to have held public office," Darby offered as he finished transferring data.

Would the files Darby had collected be enough? Eugene always ensured Verne had enough Allerspan-related material to satisfy the curious. The good stuff – that which carried real meaning – never left the plastic stick buried deep within his front pocket.

Of course, Ham would want more. He always did. Old Grouchy-puss – thank you, Cidally – had descended from the snake in the Garden of Eden. And he had Eugene square in his sights.

Who would prevail? The slippery, slimy slitherer or the caretaker who sought answers from the Tree of Knowledge?

"Why did Hamelton give up on perpetual motion?" Eugene probed, brushing aside Darby's warning. "I mean, aside from the fact that it's pure fantasy."

"He feared for his life," Darby replied, opening the silo door. "He picked the wrong crowd to finance his scheme. The group shared with him – in graphic detail – how they planned to kill him if they were not repaid with interest. That got his attention."

"So, Ham high-tailed his way out of Dodge?" Eugene asked.

"Stayed hidden until the last thug died."

"Completely off road?"

"Yep. Out in the boonies with nothing but time to think and sulk. I would have thought that would have driven him bonkers. Instead, inspiration struck.

"And, as luck would have it," Darby continued pointing to himself, "he gained a partner who only occasionally dreams of killing him. Figuratively of course, not literally."

When it came to whether Hamelton should live or die, someone ought to poll the hired help, Eugene chuckled to himself.

"Everything looks in order," Darby noted, rapping his knuckles alongside Verne's exterior. "Listen, I have to cut out early tonight, so you'll have to leave, too."

"What about Cidally?" Eugene protested.

"As you well know, she comes and goes as she pleases," Darby reminded. "But you, my friend, are not allowed in unless Hamelton or I are present."

Damn that Ham! He had refused to supply Eugene with a pass code. Something about a snot-nosed kid requiring babysitting.

Protestation was useless. He would never be given free rein.

So, Eugene ceased his squawking. He could peruse yorenewspaper.com at home where, without interruption, he could learn more about a dead body in a remote cabin.

"Those who foresee the future and recognize it as tragic are often seized by a madness which forces them to commit the very acts which make it certain that what they dread shall happen."

—Novelist John le Carre, quoted in *ArtJournal.com*

Thursday

Chapter Twelve

"**H**ave you found *your* governor, yet?"

The voice, deep and husky, cut through the morning air like a shudder-inducing arctic blast. The speaker – mimicking Hamelton at his irascible best – made sure to stress the fourth word as if having caught a knee to the groin.

Startled initially, Eugene regained his footing. A trace of whimsy accompanied the feigned gruffness, a slip-up that revealed the interruption to be a tactic meant to sow panic.

How true! When Eugene turned to confront the mischief-maker, Cidally shook with laughter. Backing up a step or two, she held up a hand to buy time.

"You think you're pretty damned funny, don't you!" Eugene said, a smile building from within.

"You must be part kangaroo!" Cidally exclaimed, agiggle in goofiness. "Did you see how high you jumped?"

"I coulda been a rebounder," Eugene proclaimed, summoning his best Marlon Brando.

"Got your attention, didn't I?" Cidally boasted, dabbing her eyes.

Since Day One. Unwavering and undivided.

That Cidally had taken time to prank him increased Eugene's desire for the woman twenty years his junior. For her to engage on this level, she must see something in him, right? Otherwise, why go to the trouble? Why make such an entrance?

Oh, how he hoped. When it came to women, Mark Twain had served as Eugene's wingman: better to appear foolish by not speaking than to open pie hole and remove all doubt. His voicebox inoperative, Eugene would smile, half-wave, or inspect the laces of his shoes when in their company. To start a conversation meant having to maintain a conversation. And in that, his every word would be evaluated: by her ("Boring!") by him ("God, that was lame!") or by others ("Is this schmuck for real?")

So Eugene scratched himself as a competitor. He admired the fairer sex from a distance. He encased himself in bubble wrap, a hangdog, hands-off affectation that effectively kept him out of the market.

That is until Cidally hit below the belt. Eyes alive, handshake firm, she approached him – not the other way around – at their first meeting. Intoxicatingly close, she did not waver or lose interest as Darby made introductions. Her warmth, her genuine delight in being there, had Eugene craving more. And her parting shot: "Don't be a stranger!" buckled his knees.

What was wrong with her?

Growing up, no girl had chased Eugene on the playground. No girl had volunteered to be his partner in science class. No girl clamored to sit near him on the bus and certainly not in the cafeteria.

Not that women found him ugly or repulsive or disturbing. They just looked past him knowing something better was right around the corner.

Eugene offered little in terms of his build or the way he carried himself. He came off as quiet, reserved, tentative. He leeched gray in interactions that cried out for color.

But that wasn't entirely fair. The real Eugene – fun-loving, upbeat, engaging – appeared once he warmed to others. But that required time, effort and perseverance. Why invest in him when so many socially gifted males splashed about in a pool in which he dogpaddled to stay afloat? What woman had the patience to wait him out?

Maybe one who interacted with him daily. Maybe a co-worker with whom he conducted business outside the realm of dating. Maybe someone who did not expect Eugene to soar to impossibly high heights to get noticed.

Forced proximity. It had Eugene's blessing. He never would have met, much less engaged with, someone like Cidally of his own volition.

"Ever think of finding your governor as a metaphor?" Cidally asked.

"You mean like finding a governess, the woman of your dreams?" Eugene ventured, hoping to ascertain her level of interest in him.

"No, you dope," she scolded. "Something that gets you going every day. Something that drives you."

"Men!" she muttered. "Always a woman. Since Day One, always a woman."

Yeah, and what's wrong with that? Eugene wanted to say. Not my fault you're so damned irresistible.

"Give me an example," he said instead.

"I'll give you three: preteen chess master, pianist in diapers, tennis champ who cannot vote."

Ah! Child prodigies. Those who peaked early. So talented. So soon. So little room for improvement.

So not Eugene. He had exited the womb sporting a sash that had "simpleton" written on it. He had no inkling of where or how he should fit in. Or what gifts he might possess. Or how to best use them.

All the reflection in the world did little to clarify his calling. Where others had taken the stage or claimed a seat in the overarching Amphitheater of Always, Eugene trudged aimlessly through the aisles.

"Maybe a governor is something that holds you back," Eugene suggested. "An insecurity, a fear, a roadblock."

"Way to go negative," Cidally congratulated. "But, your Danny Downer act provides a nice segue into why I'm here."

Cidally, a vision in blue jeans, dark turtleneck and leather boots, doubled back to the stands. She returned with an object – roughly six feet in height – covered with a sheet.

"I bring you motivation," she declared, placing the wooden base on the ground.

"I have my caffeine," Eugene noted, reaching for a can amid his ever-present supply.

"That's an addiction," she corrected. "This is inspiration."

Cidally removed the oversized linen with the flourish of a magician. The cotton covering collected in bunches at the feet of a Hamelton replica cast in cardboard.

Mouth agape, teeth flashing, and hands on his hips, the life-size replica harkened back to a Hamelton of an earlier age. Thick, dark hair swirled atop a head devoid of age spots and sebaceous cysts.

"He stays with you until you find the governor, Darby's orders." Cidally stated.

"You're kidding, right?"

"If only I were. Darby was going to deliver this himself, but I thought I'd have a little fun with it."

"So, what do I do when Hamelton shows up?" Eugene stammered. "The guy's not blind."

"Cover him. Put him in a corner," Cidally replied, launching the sheet at him. "Remember, Darby expects to see this cardboard cutout every time he visits."

With Darby's penchant for showing up unannounced, that could be anytime.

"Tell me," Eugene began after moving the faux Hamelton out of sight, "what do you know about Hamelton Skrean?"

"Lifetime bachelor. Socially awkward. Borderline creepy," Cidally summed up.

"Anti-social?" Eugene offered.

"I wouldn't go that far," Cidally cautioned. "Deep down, I think he desires closeness. But he holds everyone to impossibly high standards.

"So, when he finds someone who checks all the boxes – and I'm assuming that would be a woman ..." Cidally began.

"He dreams up additional requirements that can't possibly be met. He'd rather dump the woman than risk intimacy," Eugene finished, patting himself on the back for his insightfulness.

"I was going to say," Cidally restarted, "I think Hamelton rejects her because he figures something must be wrong with her. In his heart of hearts, he believes he is unlovable. He's a guy who would never join a club that would have him as a member."

"Psychology major?" Eugene guessed.

"Enough to be dangerous." Cidally warned.

Hold the fort! If Cidally could encapsulate Hamelton so easily, what was her assessment of him? She could probably hammer out a ten-page paper as to why he wasn't Mr. Right faster than she could click-clack a breakup text.

Eugene loathed being the subject of study. Fortunately, as a wallflower, he tended to stay out of the crosshairs.

Time to redirect.

"What I meant was, what do you know about Hamelton's past?"

"Simple. He's plagued by an acute case of PMS."

The diagnosis – stark and succinct – puzzled. The cryptic reference circled round Eugene's head as if on a rotisserie.

"Perpetual motion syndrome," Cidally explained. "It haunts him. It fuels him."

Eugene had to agree. Hamelton's failure in that regard had driven him to produce something – anything – that would endure after he passed.

Time was no ally. Nearly eighty years old, Hamelton had little margin for error. To ensure his legacy, he had to act, consequences be damned.

And Methuselah was succeeding. He lived rent-free in Eugene's mind. To the point of distraction.

Prime example: here was Eugene, the longest of long shots, chatting one-on-one with Cidally and delighting in her company. But instead of talking about her, he was diagnosing and assessing an old fart.

Someone ought to take away his man card!

"I have something else," Cidally announced, pulling a half sheet of cardstock from her back pocket.

On one side was a reprint of the front page of a newspaper. The headline "Former Governor Gone Missing" stood out above the text.

On the other side, five paragraphs set the mood:

Forty years ago, William Allerspan disappeared. He vanished during a weekend in which he mulled a return to politics.

Declared dead a decade later, Allerspan remains an enigma. Did he meet with foul play? Did he kill himself? Did he change identities?

Tonight, we pull back the curtain. We retrace Allerspan's final steps. We reveal the unknowable.

To do so, we return to the past. No longer will yesteryear remain hidden. No longer will bygones remain bygones.

Nothing can elude the lens of time. Every move, every deed, every action shall be uncovered for all to see. Past becomes present, and its presence shapes the future.

"Melodramatic and over-hyped. Pure Darby!" Eugene concluded upon a second look.

"Not a fan of my work?" Cidally remarked. "I am deeply offended."

Eugene cringed. Cidally had written that? How to remove foot from mouth?

"I like it," Eugene scrambled to save face. "May I keep this?"

"Oh, I can't lie to you," Cidally confessed. "Darby wrote it. One of these will get tucked into each invitation to Yest Fest. They go out next week."

So soon?!

And with that, ladies and gentlemen, the pretext for Cidally's stop became apparent. Darby had put her up to this. Send the pretty girl in with a gentle reminder to get to work. Eugene will fall in line. He'll do anything she says!

What a weasel! Using Cidally as a pawn.

Still, she was too smart not to have seen through Darby's ploy. She had to know what he was up to.

So, the fact that she agreed to serve as messenger meant what? That she wanted to see him? That she wanted to spare him a visit from Darby? That she viewed this as just another task in getting Yest Fest up and running?

Eugene didn't know. He just wanted to return to the promising vibe that had kicked off their morning together. Something to rekindle the easy back-and-forth that had distracted from the work at hand.

"I have something for you as well," Eugene announced, dashing to his jacket near the scorer's table. There, loose change, breath mints and a comb clattered to the floor as he rummaged through the pockets.

Cidally, bemused, debated whether or not to offer assistance.

"Are these yours?" Eugene asked, holding aloft a set of keys. He scurried back, trying to tone down his labored breathing, a byproduct of having forsaken cardio exercise.

"How did you find them?" she asked, turning them over in her hands.

"I looked in the last place you left them," he beamed.

"Did you get help from Verne?"

"Oh, no, no," Eugene protested. "I, I, — well, maybe a little."

"Thank you," Cidally said, reaching out and gently squeezing Eugene's forearm. That he had tracked down her keys – that he had even remembered she had lost them – affected her more than she expected.

That brief contact – affection in Eugene's mind – stayed with him. Her touch lingered long after she left. He vowed to keep that skin-on-skin connection alive for as long as he could.

He replayed the encounter often throughout the day, careful not to attach too much significance to it. And, really, what had happened, exactly? Cidally, delighted to have gotten her keys back, had reached out in an uncharacteristic display of emotion.

She was probably not even aware of what she had done. And even if she were, she had long since moved past the gesture that continually injected itself into Eugene's consciousness.

Give him credit, though. In making found what had been lost, Eugene had gone from nice guy to thoughtful nice guy. That had to count for something. Yes? No way thoughtful nice guys finished last. Or did they?

Chapter Thirteen

A ninety-year-old man was found dead in a cabin Tuesday night. Authorities identified the decedent as Clancy Wigwort, a self-described hermit who had lived in the area for decades.

Wigwort's body was discovered by Hamelton Skrean, a neighbor. Skrean said he regularly checked in on the elderly man.

Deputy county coroner Douglas Kolatch pronounced the man dead at the scene at 9:30 p.m. Kolatch said it appeared the man died sometime during the day from natural causes. It is believed the deceased had no living relatives.

Hamelton Skrean, a neighbor? So much for property values.

Sent home by Darby the night before, Eugene worked his laptop at home. Disappointed that the "Dead Body Found in Cabin" article contained only three paragraphs, he fed Wigwort and Kolatch's names into yorenewspapers.com and scored a few hits.

One proved helpful. Six months after Wigwort's death, a fire reduced the last remnants of the poor man's life to ashes. Arson could not be ruled out. Further, the story revealed the location of Wigwort's dwelling: Twigs Gathering.

Eugene dispatched Verne to learn more. As the drone sent back images, the human half of the team clapped his hands. His choice of coordinates had scored a hit.

Tucked away from civilization, Twigs Gathering came postcard ready. Birch and maple trees arrayed side by side, their branches gently swaying in the wind. Leaves shimmered in the sunlight, a vibrant mix of red, green and yellow. Fawns nibbled on vegetation. Squirrels and other pocket-sized mammals scampered along the forest floor.

In the distance, Eugene spotted a building. Could it be Wigwort's cabin?

"Time out!" boomed a voice from behind Eugene, who jumped as if a car had backfired.

"Hey, Grasshopper, why so jumpy?" Darby laughed.

His startle reflex activated yet again, Eugene forced a deep breath.

"You remember Sam and Max, don't you?" Darby asked, nudging the two men forward. "They are going to grab some additional footage. Shouldn't take long."

Great. Just great. Tweedledee and Tweedledum. Weren't they scheduled for noon?

"You're putting me in Hamelton's doghouse," Eugene griped. "How am I supposed to do my job?"

"Gotta prepare for the unexpected," Darby admonished. "Have to get on base even when life throws you a curve."

"So right," Eugene agreed. "How about a head-high, line drive screamer back to the pitcher?!"

Darby raised his arm as if to snag the imaginary ball. Then, fist above head, he signaled Eugene out.

Specialists par excellence, Sam and Max had been commissioned to produce a series of four videos for Yest Fest. The final video hinged upon Eugene finding the governor.

"We're going to concentrate on the console this morning," Sam said. "Give everyone a taste of its complexity."

"Stick around," Darby told Eugene. "They may need help."

With their wardrobe, yes. With their craftmanship, not so much. Hawaiian shirts open at the belly, socks tucked into sandals, the wardrobe saboteurs had taken home multiple Viddy awards. The mismatched pair generated buzz (and views) with their unique approach to product promotion with videos that ranged from funny narrative to product demos to customer testimonials. Hamelton had come across an early entry of theirs late one night.

Tired of your name surfacing in searches on the web? Want to erase your digital footprint? Get e-spungement: Whiteout for the World Wide Web.

Amused, Hamelton investigated further. He was fascinated with how effectively the duo showcased even the most mundane merchandise and locked up their services. Verne would be presented in the most flattering light.

Eugene dropped bottom in the bleachers. He would cite Sam and Max as yet another reason why he had not found the governor.

A camera cover clattered to the floor. Max scurried after it. As he bent to retrieve it, his butt crack made a hairy cameo.

Aha! One more reminder that Eugene was getting further behind in his work.

Freelancing to the extent Eugene had been doing was already fraught with risk. And now this delay! Yest Fest – long an amorphous concept in the distance – now loomed on the horizon. With invitations going out, the countdown had begun. Sandbagging to extend one's employment would require additional finesse.

Eugene had been told little about the event. Hamelton had barred him from attending any of the weekly planning sessions.

No surprise there. Being excluded was a long-running theme in Eugene's life.

As a college freshman, Eugene gave Greek life a try by spending five days at Beta Theta Pi. He ate, slept and partied there. As Frosh Week neared its end, Eugene strolled campus, head up, alive with possibility. He whistled – out loud – as he purchased books, supplies and the requisite allotment of alcohol. No dorm was going to hold him, he boasted. He would be hanging with his band of brothers.

Wishful thinking. The Friday before classes were to begin, two seniors took Eugene aside: "We don't see you as fraternity material. We'll help you get housing through the university."

They did, and Eugene selected a single room, far from the site of his expulsion. Outed as unworthy, he became an avoider. Never again did he set foot in that section of Fraternity Row.

Then, rejection spawned dejection. Now, rejection would spark in-jection.

Despite not being invited, Eugene attended every one of Hamelton's organizational meetings. He did so by going back in time and view-ing the proceedings on the small screen after the fact. He came away knowing as much about Yest Fest as any of the Big Three.

Newsflash! With Verne on duty, neither Eugene nor anyone else would ever again be excluded.

Yest Fest would commence at one in the afternoon at the Excalibur Performing Arts Center. Five hundred invitees would gather in the lobby, bumping up against cardboard cutouts of the governor. Actors would mingle with the crowd as music from the 1980s played, asking if anyone had seen the missing politician.

Darby, of course, would serve as master of ceremonies. He would inform the 500 that they, like John F. Kennedy, Davy Crockett and a host of others, were history makers. They had been selected person-ally to serve as witnesses to the ultimate shakeup: the reversal of time itself.

Roll *Gone Gov*, Sam and Max's first video of the afternoon. Using archival footage, home movies, television clips, and interviews with family and friends, the biopic would recount Allerspan's rise to power and, ultimately, his vanishment. By the end of the thirty-minute documentary, audience members would have come to know and care about the barrier-breaking politician.

Cue Cidally. After a break, she would address time travel and its role in pop culture. She would hit the highlights in literature – from Johan Hermann Wessel's *Anno 7603* to Isaac Asimov's *The Dead Past* – and the movies – from *Back to the Future* to *The Butterfly Effect*.

Hers would be the only segment with no video. Her looks and sparkling personality would more than compensate for the lack of moving pictures.

With Cidally having stepped aside – likely to a standing ovation – Max and Sam would roll *Ham on Why (and How)*, their second video. Through interviews and casual conversation, Hamelton Skrean would expound on his theory, its genesis and development. He would address the transformation he underwent in the wilderness. He would outline how Verne had come into existence. He would prime the audience for a virtual meet-and-greet with his pride and joy.

Then, drum roll, the Big Dog would enter – in the flesh. Hamelton would segue into the third feature, *Verne-Acular: Language from the Past*. The virtual tour – that which had Sam and Max busy at the moment – would touch upon every facet of Verne. From power source, to memory banks, to all that lay beyond the fence, the excursion into the inner workings of the Portal to the Past would create a buzz ahead of dinner. The shining sentinel was sure to be the topic of conversation as attendees partook of grilled salmon and wild mushrooms.

Before sending his audience to supper, however, Hamelton would disclose the mistake behind Verne's name. He'd blame it on Darby, a once avid reader who believed Jules Verne had authored *The Time Machine*. Knowing better but refusing to set the record straight, Hamelton – with a mea culpa to H.G. Wells – let Darby's ignorance carry the day. That way, the latter would be reminded of his slip up every time Verne's name was invoked.

Hamelton had all the charm of halicephalobus mephisto, the Devil's worm.

A shout went up from the gym floor. Max had walked into Sam's shot.

"If I wanted someone to show off this machine, I would have asked for that Silly chick, not some spindly legged, balding goofball! Get out of my way!"

"You mean SidSilly," Max corrected.

"Wrong!" Eugene shouted from his seat. "It's Suh-Dilly! Get it right."

"Whatever!" the Tweedles replied in unison.

"Don't make me come down there and e-spunge you two," Eugene wanted to say. Instead, he sat back down. He could ill afford to pick a fight. Not if he wanted to expedite a return to Twigs Gathering.

Damn! Darby had returned. He huddled with Sam and Max. The three went back and forth as if game officials deciding on a call.

As the confab went into overtime, Eugene sat back down. If this much rigamarole went into completing a piece on a machine that lacked legs, how long would it take the pair to piece together the grand finale?

That video, *Gone Gov*, would bring Yest Fest to a close. Darby would sum up and review as folks filed back into the auditorium following dinner. He would stress that William J. Allerspan had been missing for forty years. No one – not psychics, nor amateur sleuths, nor law enforcement – knew his whereabouts. Only by turning back time could the mystery be solved.

Gone Gov would rely totally on footage gathered by Eugene. It would highlight the final week of Allerspan's life. It would retrace his final steps. It would reveal the location of the politician's body.

"And now you know," Darby would intone in his best attempt at Paul Harvey as the stage went dark, "the rest of the story."

The real fun would begin in the days following. Folks from all walks of life would set out to recover Allerspan's remains. The first one there would get bragging rights. The first one there would confirm Verne could visit the past.

Investors, Silicon Valley, venture capitalists, entrepreneurs – anyone with ideas and money – would clamor for a piece of Hamelton's Time Traveling Wilbury. The ways in which Verne could be utilized would be limited only by the imagination of those who secured rights to him.

Hamelton's achievement would dominate the news. The genius who threw open the doors to antiquity would become a media sensation. Man and machine would be immortalized. The Bloviating Boor would make money Ham over fist.

One Verne would become two. Then four. Then eight. In time, Verne would become as ubiquitous as the smart phone, more prevalent than the automobile. Verne would shape the human condition based upon the needs, desires and whims of his users.

Or his abusers. Eugene feared he might not recognize subsequent generations of his favorite CPU.

Laughter intruded upon Eugene's thoughts. Poised at the console, Max and Sam pretended to have sent the machine deep into the Old Testament.

"Look at Noah," Max howled, pointing at the blank screen. "He had two of every animal on board – except for the three-way involving your mother."

Sam cuffed his colleague upside the head.

"Yeah, well, your Mama was so ugly, Noah logged her as the second baboon on his passenger manifest."

Eugene unkinked his legs. Time to send the clowns packing.

"You guys should do open mic," he suggested, easing his way to floor level. "You'd make one helluva an animal act."

Cases clicked shut. A backpack landed on a shoulder. Pants got hiked. Max and Sam – so animated seconds earlier – filed out in silence.

"One more thing," Eugene shouted as Heckle and Jeckle made tracks. "Verne doesn't do fairy tales."

The mid-morning sun shimmered through the vented glass block windows to the east. Refracted rays bathed Verne in a dingy, smoky gray. He looked downcast, almost forlorn.

"Forgot those morons," Eugene encouraged. "They're idiots!"

"I don't care how often they clone you," he continued. "There'll never be another like you."

Chapter Fourteen

Auguste Rodin's *The Thinker* had nothing on Clancy Wigwort. True, the sculpture loomed larger and more imposing than the genial Wigwort. And, yes, the bronze figure boasted more muscle and definition than the roly-poly man born with a surname.

But, despite being something of an unknown, Wigwort generated far more brain power than the nude inanimate. And old Clancy did so without resorting to the classic head in hand, crouched in sober meditation position.

Wigwort had a calling. He would improve the human condition. He would let rational thinking guide him in achieving that goal.

Problem: As he contemplated how to make a difference, Wigwort's mind wandered. Standing, sitting or lying in bed, his train of thought invariably derailed, sidetracked by the trivial or the random.

Wigwort did not allow himself to get bogged down for long. He would eliminate distraction. He would cure what had befuddled every individual who set out in pursuit of a goal.

"Say hello to senseless goggles," boasted one publication available at yorenewspaper.com:

Staying on task has never been easy. One is constantly bombarded by stimuli that interfere even in the most remote of locations.

A rain-spattered window, the howling of a coyote, the pungent plumes of a wood fire – sights, sounds and smells nip at the senses. Once detected, they worm their way in, gathering strength with each effort to suppress. They whisper. They cajole. They collude. "Pay attention!" they demand.

Soon, even the most disciplined is off task, having fallen prey to the hobgoblins of hindrance. What's a person to do?

Eugene had to laugh. Was Wigwort for real?

To don the senseless goggles was to invite ridicule. The extra-wide rims and temples hugged the skin, forming an air-tight seal. Like blinders on a horse, the eye pieces bugged out and cut off peripheral vision. The lenses – mere slits – allowed one to home in on the task directly ahead.

The crazy setup came equipped with various offshoots. Ear plugs blocked all but the loudest of noises. Electrodes, when affixed to one's forehead, stimulated the prefrontal cortex, thus improving concentration. Nose filters pumped in oxygen to regulate improved breathing and ward off sleepiness.

The length and level of detail within the article astonished. Wigwort included intricate diagrams and explanations. He provided reasons for every design decision. He even modeled how to use the goggles in a series of photos that detracted more than helped his cause.

Earnest to a fault, Wigwort opened the floodgates to derision and scorn. He could not fathom why his solution – functional and effective – failed to gain traction. He had identified a human weakness and provided a remedy. Why the putdowns and scant praise?

Eugene chanced upon a particularly caustic letter to the editor.

Dear Sirs:

Wondering where I can purchase one those goofball goggles. Looking to add them to my backlog of moronic miscellanea that includes the rectal toothpick – "come at the problem from the other end" – and the sensory-deprivation casket – "dead or alive, you'll rest in peace."

Had Wigwort been privy to this disrespect? Did the vitriol prompt him to pack and head for the hills? If true, then Wigwort's decision to isolate himself from the public he sought to help came laden with irony.

Irony had nothing to do with Wigwort and Skrean crossing paths. How and where the two met remained a mystery. Perhaps a shared sense of failure drew the two together. Or maybe a mutual determination to prove they were no jack-a-lents.

At day's end, how the men met was of no importance. Knowing how they parted had a greater chance of shedding more light on the relationship between the two oddballs.

With Sam and Max having moved on, Eugene programmed Verne to take him back to Wigwort's final hours at his cabin in the woods. Douglas Kolatch had said the loner died of natural causes, which seemed plausible given Wigwort's age. But Kolatch didn't have Verne at his disposal. Eugene did. And Verne, even without a medical degree, might turn out to be a better coroner than Kolatch.

Towering, knotty pines interlaced to form a cathedral-like ceiling over the cabin, a hand-hewn structure consisting of two stories. Wisps of smoke curled from a crumbling brick chimney. A battered air conditioner protruded from an upper-floor window. Wooden steps, sans railing, provided less-than-safe passage to a boarded-up front door.

A Dodge Dart rusted nearby, coated in a veneer of sap, pollen, and insect carcasses. With its single headlamps and padded bucket seats, it could have passed for the one owned by Eugene's grandfather.

"That's got to be Wigwort's place," Eugene declared. "How about picking the lock and getting me inside, Verne old boy?"

Eugene let out a "huzzah" as his first try landed him inside the living room. A massive fireplace stretched to the ceiling, the stone structure cold and foreboding. The mantel shelf, which rested on a pair of log corbels, was barren save for a tintype of an unsmiling woman.

Within the four walls, clutter co-mingled with disarray. Asymmetrical stacks of books, magazines and newspapers elevated the printed word to new heights. Binders, notepads, file folders, and more scattered about every surface.

The never-ending paper trail had long ago encroached upon the floor. Confetti tossed into an industrial fan had more organizational integrity than Wigwort's filing system.

So where was the architect of these unsightly messes?

Wigwort's bald pate poked out from the back of a long sofa, one that faced the fireplace and not Eugene. Was he sleeping? Reading? Dead?

With only an inch of head visible, Eugene could only guess. He needed a view from the opposite side of the davenport.

Eugene had become skilled at repositioning the drone. Another fifteen feet and he could get a decent shot of Wigwort from the front.

Even so, every recall, recalculation and relaunch took time, a waiting game that could not be rushed. And if the new coordinates did not yield a decent view, a second round commenced.

Not this time. As luck would have it, Eugene's adjustments put the camera right where he wanted it.

Wigwort, as peaceful as the setting sun, sat slumped at sofa's end. In his left hand, his reading specs. In his right hand, well, that paw rested atop a large book as if being sworn in to provide testimony.

Decked out in a red and black flannel shirt, Wigwort resembled a pudgy lumberjack. Make that a wet, pudgy lumberjack. Perhaps a hole had opened in the roof, or a rain cloud had followed him that day. Either way, the old man's clothing had been the intended target as areas nearby appeared dry.

In the distance, Wigwort's kitchen displayed all the signs of the dereliction found elsewhere. Bacon grease coagulated at the base of a frying pan. Half-eaten muffins and fruit took up positions along table and countertops alike. A trash can had been upturned, eggshells and pork rinds thrown clear.

The coffee maker noted the time: 6:30.

A large ant zigged and zagged across Wigwort's chin. Slowing down, the insect got cheeky, then scooted out of sight.

Had it sensed the terrain cooling beneath its spindly legs?

Eugene closed his eyes. A moment of silence for the deceased.

A soft, sliding sound intruded upon Eugene's thoughts. Barely audible, it returned a second time. Then a third.

Eugene scanned the bleachers. He eyed them row by row. No Darby.

A fanning of paper came next. Then a slight clunk. Then more sliding, more fanning, and a vigorous shaking.

The thud and expletive that followed left no doubt; these sounds originated with Verne. Someone or something was moving about in Wigwort's home.

Eugene groaned. He would again have to recall the drone and send it back. But where? The waiting game he had to endure when working with Verne now had the potential to become an extended play album he could ill afford to play.

Why did negotiating the past have to be so problematic?

Eugene landed in Wigwort's bathroom on his first attempt. His second placed him in a broom closet. And his third put him nose to nose with a stuffed bear.

Damn, damn and damn! This guessing game had him all over the map!

When he finally touched down in the master bedroom, Eugene couldn't have been any less surprised. There Hamelton Skrean pulled books – one by one – from the shelves that lined three of the four walls.

The misanthropic meddler glanced at each tome. Some he turned over. Others he shook with gusto, sending bookmarks or tucked-away tidbits to the ground. Occasionally he'd fling a binder off the wall, always in concert with a choice word or two.

Hamelton slogged through each shelf, working left to right. Reaching the end of one level, he dropped down to the next.

On the bed, pillows, blankets, pajamas and underwear lounged atop bed linens that had yellowed with age and neglect. Every so often, the interloper kicked at the dirty clothes nipping at his feet.

Wigworth's mental acuity: top shelf. His upkeep and deportment: bottom of the barrel.

Kicking aside a pair of pants, Hamelton made his way to another wall of literature. Like a typewriter, he moved left to right, carriage return, left to right, carriage return until he finished the bookcase.

What was he after?

Having thumbed through Wigwort's library, Hamelton set upon the bureau. Thrusting open every chamber, he rototilled through the contents. Clothing, medications, playing cards, scissors, a tape measure and more headed skyward as he powered through what had to be a junk drawer.

Then, sucking air as if he had been jumping rope, Hamelton dropped to his hands and knees. He rotated his head like a miner's light, sweeping every darkened inch under the bed. Encountering nothing but dust bunnies, he clambered back to his feet. The infantile intruder tramped from the room stomping and screaming to the heavens.

Great! Just great!

Eugene pulled the drone back into the present. Where was Hamelton headed?

Odds-on favorite: the great room. Sure enough, Eugene came face to face with the rabid ransacker rifling through a mélange of materials at a table within spitting distance of Wigwort. In his flurry of hurry, Hamelton drove a stapled stack of papers and its neighbors over the edge.

With speed that surprised, Hamelton dived for the fallen. Bypassing the extraneous, he homed in on what had first caught his eye. He latched onto the assembled pages, scanned the cover page, and let out guttural cry. Placing the document to his lips, he kissed it and held it aloft.

"I got it," he whistled. "I freakin' got it.

Exhilaration carried Hamelton to the sofa. He plopped down at one end, Wigwort rising at the other as if the two were on a teeter-totter.

"Thank you, my friend," Hamelton said, nodding in the direction of his former friend. "You did not die in vain."

Hamelton skimmed through his hard-won discovery. He cycled through pages, paused, then started again. Exuberance flowed unchecked, but what escaped his windpipe sounded more like a moose in heat than elation.

If this was Hamelton at his most excited, pity the woman who could take him there.

Satisfied he had the real deal, Hamelton set his prized possession on the arm of the sofa. He positioned it in a way that prevented Eugene from reading the cover page.

"I know you're tired, Verne," Eugene consoled. "But we have to come at this from a different angle!"

After a few adjustments, Eugene returned the drone to the exact moment the document left Hamelton's hand. With the camera higher up and facing downward, Eugene expected every word to jump off the page. What he didn't anticipate was the item in question to be missing. Not only the item, but Hamelton as well. The entire right side of Wigwort's couch was empty.

Cussing, the kind that erupts in the wake of repeated failure, reverberated throughout the gymnasium. A second, more profane outpouring, exploded on the heels of the first.

Eugene slammed his right fist into his open left palm. Verne, the drone – the works – everything needed recalibrating.

Chapter Fifteen

John Hasmire's classroom had long been a haven for the misfit and the marginalized. Shaded by a pair of towering oak trees, the third-floor outpost was the farthest one could get from the main office at St. Anthony's yet remain within the building proper.

Hazz's Hangout, a sanctuary for students lingering past three o'clock, remained open long after classes dismissed. At its busiest, the oasis resembled a flea market with kids playing board games, thespians running lines, and achievers – over and under – mindfully or mindlessly thumbing through textbooks.

Hasmire, math teacher, and Jerome Zeppner, metal shop instructor, encouraged the youth, lending an ear, offering advice and factoring the most daunting of polynomials. While other staff dashed for their Buicks or BMWs, Hazz and Zep slow-walked the next generation toward the future.

Eugene, who attended school nearby, happened upon this scene just once. His mother had ordered him to drop off a package with the son of one of her friends.

Waiting for the boy to emerge, Eugene gaped at the ant hill inside. Two girls sketched a third, who gabbed more than modeled. A card-carrying geek badgered an unsuspecting mark to pick from a rigged deck. A hot head flipped a chess board, then the bird when asked to take his tantrum elsewhere.

Overcome by the hustle and bustle, Eugene clung to the door. His superpower – invisibility – helped keep him out of harm's way.

"You looking for me?" demanded a teen rife with indignation and armed with an oversized Adam's apple. Eugene recognized him as the intended recipient of his delivery.

Lip quivering, Eugene thrust forward the cardboard box. The malcontent, not extending a thank you or an invitation to join the party, took charge of the package before returning to friends. There, he slaked their curiosity with the words "some dorky loser."

Well, that dorky loser now had Hazz's Hangout all to his own. Eugene came and went as he pleased, usually to avoid Hamelton or, as in this case, because of Verne's faulty calibration.

As always, Eugene locked the door. His hideout secure, he placed his backpack on the rectangular table where chess matches had incited Tarrasch talking. He powered up his laptop at Hasmire's desk and dimmed the lights as was custom on test-taking days.

Dust and cobwebs aside, little had changed in the land of logic where talk of denominators had once been common. A faded calendar, set to June, hung by pins nearly sapped of push. A poster tacked to the bulletin board – the ten commandments of math – warned students to avoid such sins as dividing by zero and failing to honor the correct order of operations.

Above the chalkboard, a number line stretched from one wall to the other. Arrows at both ends signified the two-dimensional construct carried on to infinity in either direction.

With Verne under the weather, Eugene cued up a favorite video from his flash drive. Labeled, "Lunch Date," the file's title was not entirely accurate. Though eating had taken place, the meeting had not been prearranged. For the noshing to have been planned, Eugene would have had to have visited the great and powerful Oz. Only then could the Cowardly Lion have summoned the courage to ask Cidally to sup.

"Happenstance" or "Happenchance" better summed up the encounter. Eugene's decision to nuke his pizza rather than come at it cold precipitated his noonday delight. Whether in his mind or on his laptop, he relived it often.

Four weeks in, having been harangued yet again by Hamelton, Eugene headed for the only working microwave in the building. Throwing open the door to the faculty lounge, he abruptly stopped – one foot dangling in midair – as if he had collided with a hot stove.

Eugene could have bolted. He could have shifted into reverse. He could have closed his eyes.

Instead, he seized up, every muscle and connective tissue on lockdown. Neuromuscular paralysis set in as if he had been envenomed by a poisonous snake.

Cidally, her back to Eugene, had just removed the last pin holding her hair in place. In slow motion, her liberated locks unraveled, spiraling downward in a Rapunzel-like bun drop that left him slackjawed. Wave upon wave slipped free, a glowing auburn avalanche that gained speed as it twirled past her shoulders, back, hips and buttocks. Hitting bottom, it billowed outward like curtains blown open by a summer breeze.

Cidally she couldn't have been more arresting had she been nude. She raised and lowered the massive tumble, hands extending outward from her neck. As she kneaded her scalp, reddish-brown poofiness undulated with the back and forth of her fingertips.

Warm pizza. Hah! Eugene could have flash-burned an entire pie with his bare hands!

"Don't mind me," Cidally said, dipping and adjusting until every strand found its place. "I'll be just a moment."

No rush, Eugene thought, his motor skills yet unresponsive. Like the Tin Woodsman, he might require a few shots of oil to become ambulatory.

At least his tongue had stayed put. He could take pride in that.

In the distance, the microwave beeped. The intrusion reminded Eugene that unrequited gawking could be construed as sexual harassment. If he didn't cease and desist, this meal might be his last as a free man.

Cidally popped open the microwave. She pulled out a steaming bowl of rice pilaf that sent an enticing scent of onions, garlic and sweet broth wafting upward.

"All yours," Cidally announced, running a spoon through the vegetable delight. Her stirring of ingredients only intensified the aromatic infestation abounding in the teacher's lounge.

Head down, eyes to the floor, Eugene felt about inside his tattered brown bag. As inconspicuously as he could, he slammed what had been a midnight snack into the electronic warming device. Hitting go, he watched the combo of pepperoni, bacon, sausage and hardened cheese go 'round. With each revolution, he second-guessed his choice. Day-old greasy carbs didn't belong in the same room as the Garden of Perfection.

"Ah, a meat lover," Cidally observed as she passed behind him.

Best not to offer her a bite. Supermodels don't fall prey to empty calories as do schlubs who refuse to cook.

Taking a seat, Cidally placed her food, protein shake and silverware atop an oversized napkin.

"You're welcome to stay," she offered.

His vocal cords still on the fritz, Eugene loitered near the refrigerator. He read through the list of ingredients found on the side of his soda. Just how much sodium benzoate and erythorbic acid had he guzzled in his lifetime?

"Sit," Cidally again offered, gesturing to a spot directly across from her. "You're safe. Hamelton never comes in here."

Hamelton was the least of Eugene's concerns. Being alone with Cidally now topped the charts. Yes, this was what Eugene had dreamed about. No interruptions. Work temporarily on hold.

But even he, in his most outlandish reverie, never thought a one-on-one would come to pass. Could he meet the moment? Could he hold his own? Would the stage prove too big for him?

He had been given no time to prepare!

Eugene set his sugary drink back on the shelf and reached for a water. Wired as he was, additional caffeine would only put him over the top.

Closing the stainless-steel door, Eugene babystepped across the vinyl floor. Pizza in one hand, drink in the other, he made his way as if transporting nitroglycerin.

Cidally scrolled through her phone. She checked emails and texts. She opened an attachment, the color and movement of video reflecting in her eyes.

Eugene dabbed his pizza with a napkin. He pushed harder. Better to soak up the grease now than have it dribble down his face.

Why hadn't he packed carrot sticks or frozen grapes?

Eugene glanced about. For want of an opening line, conversation was lost.

Until, that is, a pat of butter broke loose from above. Like a skydiver without a chute, it descended from the ceiling until – plotch! It landed face down at the end of the table.

Down went Cidally's phone. Down went Eugene's pizza. Up went both heads in search of the next object to break free.

A sweep of the area revealed no further danger overhead.

"Rogue student," Cidally theorized.

"First name Darby," Eugene proposed. "Butter up! A home run!"

Surprised by his words – the ease and spontaneity with which they popped into his head – Eugene let out a "guh-huh." More hiccup than chuckle, the involuntary release amused as much as what prompted it.

The unforeseen dairy drop had done more than break the silence. It broke the ice.

"How did you end up here?" Eugene began, then clarified. "I mean not in this room, but how did you end up working for Darby—and Hamelton?"

Cidally dragged a fork through her vegetable garden. She scooped up a few morsels, holding them aloft as wisps of steam danced in the air.

"Do you have a game plan?" she asked, blowing gently on the pilaf.

A game plan? What game plan?

Did she mean a blueprint for growing their relationship? Did they have a relationship? Could they have a relationship?

Eugene didn't know how to respond. Thankfully, Cidally picked up the conversation before an awkward pause could develop.

"By the time I was in grade school," Cidally said, "I knew I was going to play basketball. That's pretty much all I wanted to do."

Major sigh. This game plan had nothing to do with their compatibility. He should know better. Eugene had to remind himself that his infatuation was more one-sided than a Möbius strip.

Her food having cooled, Cidally took a bite. Satisfied, she dug in for more.

"I had my dad put up a hoop. I played against girls older than me. I went to camps. I played against the neighborhood boys until I could beat most of them one on one. I had a game plan."

And just like that, the mounds of comic books and football cards Eugene had collected growing up seemed so juvenile.

"I played in high school and college," she continued. "When I didn't make the pros, I coached as a graduate assistant. And then ..."

Cidally hit pause. She needed a moment.

"Jayne Landsinger. They gave the job to The Landlubber!"

"What job?" Eugene asked.

"Hell, I scored thirty points on her in high school. We beat her Pirates ... every ... single ... time!"

"What job?" Eugene asked again, his hunger forgotten.

"Full-time assistant at St. Bee's. It came down to Landlubber and me. Flip of the coin, I was told. She got it and I didn't."

The passage of time had not alleviated the sting of disappointment. Coming up short was not in Cidally's DNA.

"Maybe she crushed the interview," Eugene suggested, a misguided stab at rationalization he immediately regretted.

Cidally's penetrating stare burned hot. Was that a red dot on Eugene's forehead?

"I could have applied elsewhere," Cidally insisted. "I would have landed on my feet. But something told me to leave the hardwood and pursue a different tack."

"Hamelton Skrean is different," Eugene agreed.

"Darby hired me," Cidally said, wiping the corners of her mouth. "He's been a booster of athletics longer than I've been alive. Hamelton had no say in the matter."

"So, you were never subjected to Hamelton's if-you-could-change-one-thing-from-the-past question?"

"Oh, he tried to drop it on me."

"And?"

"I declined to answer. I told him – politely – I am future forward. Eyes squarely ahead. He never asked again."

Telling Hamelton no to his face. How refreshing! How decisive! How powerful! He should hang out with Cidally more often!

"What's your game plan, Eugene?" Cidally quizzed again.

Still lacking a satisfactory answer, Eugene spit up: "Ah, I've written a novel."

Eyebrows raised, Cidally tilted her head. She was intrigued.

"What's it about?"

Eugene's admission invariably triggered that response. His comeback was just as predictable.

"I can't tell you," he said, adding a disclaimer. "I'd jinx it if I did."

"When can I expect it in stores?" Cidally inquired. "I'd like to read it."

Seriously? Even Eugene's closest acquaintances did not make that offer.

"Probably never," Eugene lamented. "I've been rejected so many times I've lost count. I can't get the ending right."

He braced for what was coming next. Why not self-publish?

"You keep working at it. Tweak it, change it. Get it right," Cidally ordered. "Mold that story so that you – your harshest critic – are satisfied."

Cidally's phone rang. She declined the call.

"When you're finished, I want a copy and I want it signed."

Yes, ma'am! Eugene's pen stood at the ready.

Even in Hasmire's classroom, two months removed from their lunch together, Eugene fed off Cidally's confidence and positivity. His self-esteem rose, his backbone stiffened.

Eugene stopped the video. He needed no help recalling the remainder of their time together that morning.

He had tried to be clever. Absent a game plan, his life had been a series of audibles and in-game adjustments. He had done the best with what he had been given.

What he didn't tell Cidally was that for as long as he could remember, he had searched for a calling. A reason for being. Now, halfway through life, with nothing on the horizon, this urgency to discover a passion chipped away at his soul. At eighteen and now at forty-five, he had no clue as to why he got out of bed every morning.

Seriously, what could he do that others hadn't already done and done better? What talent did he have that set him apart? What gift did he possess that might benefit the world?

Maybe he was trying too hard. Maybe he was putting too much pressure on himself.

Best to be honest. He was a blender, background noise, a harmless wallflower. He was vanilla aspiring to be tutti frutti. He was a grain of sand heading for the bottom of the hourglass.

Had he expressed this to Cidally, she would have torn into him. She would have ordered him to stop feeling sorry for himself. She would have told him to grow a pair. And she would have been right.

Eugene returned often to his lunch date with Cidally. He did so to confirm it actually happened. He did so to rekindle the emotions that had raced through his body during their hour together.

Most of all, he watched again and again because for a moment – however brief – Cidally's focus had rested solely on him.

Chapter Sixteen

"Eleven o'clock on the dot," boomed the larger-than-life Darby who filled the jumbotron at center court. Head down, the figure composed of millions of pixels studied his wristwatch.

"Eleven o'clock it is," agreed the same voice standing in front of the supercomputer. The Darby in the gym – the flesh and blood version – gazed not at his timepiece, but at Verne's console.

As Eugene strode across the hardwood floor, he noted the actual time to be closer to noon. Darby, he assumed, having finished his tinkering, had waited until eleven o'clock to herald the hour. By doing so, he could then send the drone back to the moment of his pronouncement. If Verne's readout displayed eleven o'clock in the past at the same time Darby's resonant voice announced the same, one could assume the recalibration had been successful.

"Good as Greenwich," Darby avowed, his knuckles rapping metal.

"I'll take the wheel, then," Eugene said, sliding into Darby's spot. The stool's new occupant wiggled about until the heat beneath his bottom was mostly of his own making.

"Listen," Darby said, turning serious, "I'm working late tonight. And so are you."

"Count on it," Eugene agreed without protest. He would have nodded in assent to just about anything to get Darby out of the gym. A certain cabin called out to Eugene from deep within the woods.

Darby moved closer. Close enough that Eugene quit the random reshuffling of papers that he had hoped would speed Darby's exodus.

"I know you like to freelance," Darby said, his eyes narrowing as Eugene feigned ignorance. "I've done plenty of it myself."

Eugene steeled himself. The bar stool had become a hot seat.

"It's not like I ...," Eugene stuttered, kicking himself for not having a plausible denial at the ready.

"Relax. I'm not here to play wet nurse to you," Darby said. "I get it. Cidally Short is once in a lifetime. Any guy in your shoes would do the same. But the Grim Reaper doesn't give a damn. He expects results. He's going to make a change."

"What if I told you...," Eugene started, only to be cut off.

"Don't talk." Darby ordered. "Listen. I've been around long enough to know when bending rules leads to a break. So tonight, you work until I tell you to go home. Come hell or high water, you will find the governor! Understood?"

Understood? What the hell, Darby! Stooping to Hameltonese? You're better than that, Eugene thought

Forming a solid base by centering his weight over his feet, Darby sprouted roots. He wasn't going anywhere.

Eugene would have laughed if the man weren't so resolute.

"Un-der-stood?" Darby repeated, drawing out each syllable.

Geez! Had someone dropped a deuce in his oatmeal?

"Yes, yes!" Eugene pledged again, flashing two thumbs up. "I'll stay until the sun rises in the east. I'll stay until it sets in the west. I'll stay until the end of time. I'm all yours!"

Having achieved his objective, Darby backpedaled, index and middle fingers forming a V which he aimed at his eyes, then at Eugene. He continued the "I'm-watching-you" schtick until colliding with a stray basketball, which he launched into the stands with an extra dollop of torque.

Screw Hamelton! Screw Darby! Screw Allerspan!

Eugene, until further notice, answered only to Clancy Wigwort. Even in death, the master tinkerer had more to say, and Eugene was all ears.

Punching in coordinates even before Darby vacated the premises, Eugene trekked back to Twigs Gathering. As the drone settled inside the cabin, Hamelton, not Clancy, was the first to speak. Eugene welcomed the voice as it confirmed he had landed in the right place at the right time. Darby had recalibrated correctly.

"I got it. I freakin' got it?" Hamelton whooped, then added: "Thank you, my friend. You did not die in vain."

Hamelton's jubilation boiled over exactly where it should have. And this time, when the uninvited opportunist set his prized possession on the arm of the sofa, Eugene could read every word on the cover page, including title and author.

Doubling Back on Time: Past Becomes Present by Clancy Aloysius Wigwort.

The words corroborated what Eugene had suspected: Wigwort, not Hamelton, had been the driving force behind time visitation. Clancy, not Skrean, had envisioned the possibility, formulated the theory, and applied the science.

And for what? To have his progeny stolen by some ne'er-do-well looking for redemption?

This is why Hamelton had ransacked the cabin. Why he had befriended the old man. Why he fetched groceries. Why he played chauffeur. Why the ugsome usurper with "me" embedded in his name chose to become subservient to another human being.

Even Hamelton, uninterested in the affairs of others, understood what awaited the fortunate soul who brought to bear this technology: power, fame, prestige—immortality. That he could be first to birth Verne keyed Hamelton's ignition, motivated his every move, and had him thinking long term for the first time in ages.

Perpetual motion had been Hamelton's downfall. Opening a window to the past would have him rising from the ashes like a phoenix.

And Wigwort? What would the purveyor of physics reap? Thanks to Hamelton, he had been stripped of his legacy. Thanks to Hamelton, he had been downgraded to just another Joe with no meaningful contribution to his name. Thanks to Hamelton, Clancy would be forgotten as soon as the last scoops of dirt covered his coffin.

Eugene kicked the bleachers.

"Life is so blatantly unfair," he screamed, only he didn't say "blatantly."

Eugene could not fathom being dispossessed of such an achievement. He could not fathom someone swooping in to claim that which belonged to another.

Sadly, he could relate to the anonymity to which Wigwort had been condemned.

Poor Clancy. He had persevered. He had done the heavy lifting. He had outfoxed nature itself. He, not Hamelton, should be reveling in what Darby referred to as the Repository of Re: Return, Replay, Relive.

If only Wigwort had rejected Hamelton's entreaties. If only he had rebuffed his advances. If only he had not been ... killed?

Murder. Was it possible? Had Hamelton Skrean, tired of waiting out a geriatric gentleman, taken matters into his own hands?

Eugene had to go back. He had to witness Wigwort's demise.

A backpack slapped the table. Though out of camera range, it startled all the same.

"Thanks, Clance," Hamelton squealed in delight. "Thanks for punching my ticket out of this mosquito-infested nature preserve."

Eugene muted Verne, cutting Hamelton off even as his lips continued to move. Why couldn't he silence the talking head in real time?

Eugene brought the drone back to the present. He scanned every inch of the gym. He did not want company as he and Verne were about to witness a second man make his earthly exit.

Death. The cessation of life. The final goodbye.

Eugene did not fear the physical act of dying. Sure, it might be unpleasant or painful or even messy. But he expected he would welcome the end, especially after quality stopped flowing through his IV.

For Eugene, his trepidation centered on what came after. What happened to those who were never heard from again?

The church said heaven awaited. Love triumphed. The many became one.

To Eugene, that sounded too simplistic, too contrived, too human to have originated with the divine. How, exactly, did one gain entrance through the Pearly Gates? Key fob? QR code? A special coupon from Sunday's worship bulletin?

The entire exercise did not ring true. It did not jibe with the vagaries of life.

Eugene knew precious little, but he did know this: he did not exist before he was born and he would not exist after he died. Nothing before and nothing after. Didn't the Bible say as much?

"For you are dust and to dust you shall return."

Think number line like the one in Hasmire's classroom. An individual is alive only for the small section that appears on the wall. The portions that stretch to infinity in either direction are the voids that come before and after. No living creature can avoid the voids.

This simple truth didn't come from a burning bush or a stone tablet. It came from within. And, it made sense. Enjoy the ride while it lasts. It's the only one we get.

Eugene rubbed his eyes. He sipped his soda.

Time to break out the acetaminophen. A dull heaviness had moved into his frontal sinuses.

With death so final, so irreversible, how could anyone contemplate taking another's life? The thought sickened him, especially when Hamelton Skrean might be the perpetrator.

Sure, Hamelton had his faults. Eugene and Darby had started a running tally. But neither thought to list the taking of a life among them.

Only one way to find out. Send the drone back and babysit Wigwort until he no longer required a nanny.

As Eugene returned to what had become his second home, Clancy hitched up his pants and deposited his posterior onto the sofa. Having touched down, he used both hands to ferry a cup of ice water to his lips. A small trickle ran down his chin. He dabbed at the runaway liquid, his drink swaying side to side.

A mound of unshelled peanuts overflowed a plastic bowl. Discarded husks sat atop the dirt and debris trapped within the carpet.

His thirst quenched, Clancy reached for the novel between the cushions and opened it. He raised and lowered it until the printed words became clear. Roughly twenty pages lined up behind his most recent dog-ear.

Was that a bodice ripper ol' Clance was reading? Good for him! Mr. Practical was more than logic and utilitarianism. He had a playful side!

Unhurried – think snail driving a Fiat with the left blinker on –

Clancy waded through the paperback. Ten minutes passed. His pupils glossed over. His eyelids drooped. His mouth fell open. Snoring took hold.

What commenced next was a discordant back and forth between soft palate, uvula and tongue to determine which fleshy mass could best obstruct Wigwort's airway. No clear-cut winner emerged; the loser, of course, the avid reader deprived of restful slumber.

The extemporaneous symphony – guttural bass, high-pitched wheezing, tin-pan percussion – rose and fell with Clancy's chest. Set to repeat, each refrain kicked in after a pause, a gasp and a snortle.

Until the music stopped.

The book slipped from Clancy's grasp. The melting ice in his tumbler shifted.

A minute passed. Then two. The wireless fidelity of the living had cut out.

Anyone entering the cabin would have assumed Wigwort had nodded off. His jaw had slackened and drool had pooled, but he otherwise appeared at peace.

"Hey, Old Fart, where you hiding?"

Hamelton approached from the right, Wigwort's back to him.

"Sleeping again?" Hamelton said in mock surprise. "You're never going to amount to anything!"

A backpack hit the floor.

"Got you some donut holes. Those glazed ones, you know, the kind you like. Had a couple myself."

Hamelton set the box down. He slowed his movements. Something was off. Sugary confections always rousted Clancy. He could sniff them out better than any bloodhound.

"The ladies at the library asked about you," Hamelton continued, circling Wigwort like a predator loath to approach further. "Another week and they'll have that microfiche."

Tiptoeing as if not to awaken a baby, Hamelton positioned himself directly in front of the motionless man. Chewing on his lip, the visitor looked left, then right. He put one foot forward, then back.

"Worried someone might see you, Hammy Boy?" Eugene taunted. "You should be, you brown-headed cowbird!"

Hamelton took a step to the right, his left leg then sliding to meet the other. He repeated the motion – the cowardly shuffle – until he reached a stack of periodicals.

Securing the top-most publication, he waved it about. He beat it against a nearby chair. He lobbed it at Wigwort, an errant shot that drifted high and wide.

Still unsure that death had come calling, Hamelton circled back behind the sofa, He grabbed Clancy's tumbler and held it directly over his friend's head. Looking the other way, Hamelton paused, stole a glance at the lumberjack in repose, then turned the glass over. Liquid and cubes fell to the earth as if discharged from a downspout. So, too, did the container as it clunked off the old man's noggin on the way to the floor.

Was the coast clear?

Hamelton counted backward from ten. He recited the numbers, each one arriving sooner than the last. Hitting zero, he pivoted ninety degrees, then turbo-charged to the bedroom.

Chapter Seventeen

Unimpeded laughter cascaded down the hallway as Eugene approached Hamelton's office for his three o'clock reckoning. The tomfoolery emanating from the most toxic workspace in the building was as foreign as another language.

Eugene loitered. He lingered. Dare he enter?

"Get in here," Hamelton ordered, anger despoiling any remaining levity. "You're late!"

And you're despicable, Eugene longed to counterpunch. You're a rat snake willing to devour your own tail to get what you crave. You're the CEO – make that EGO – of a sole proprietorship designed with one customer in mind.

That's what Eugene wanted to say. But, as he had done all his life, he backed down. He ceded control. He would let another dictate the terms and conditions regarding the next paragraph or two of his life.

And, in this case at least, maintaining a low profile might expedite his visit to the principal's office.

Crap! Hamelton had company. Big company.

"He thinks his time is more valuable than mine," Hamelton belly-ached to a hulk like-figure who – shoehorned into a desk intended for someone half his size – broke out the shame-shame finger motion. "Keeping me waiting! It's lucky he keeps his job!"

With arms as thick as footballs, the muscle-bound freak smirked as if eyeing his next meal.

"Brody Slattner, meet Eugene," Hamelton flatly offered with zero enthusiasm.

Brody wore a neatly pressed shirt, double-pleated cotton that struggled to contain his testosterone-infused torso. Knowing he had Eugene's attention, the Brawny Man leaned forward and popped his pecs.

Eugene choked back what he hoped was acid reflux.

Tanned, clean-shaven and visibly sweating, Brody dashed off an upward nod. Eugene extended a half wave.

"I knew a Gene once," Brody recalled as both wrists went limp. "Coke bottle-wearing desk jockey who played for the other team, if you know what I mean."

Hamelton tittered. Not a snicker, not a snort, not a guffaw, but a genuine titter. If this was what the dinosaur found funny, no wonder Eugene could never make him laugh.

"It's Eugene! Always has been. Always will be," Eugene countered.

King Kong puckered and blew a kiss.

"Brody's pursuing a career in criminal justice," Hamelton announced. "He's someone we can all look up to."

"Guilty, not guilty. I make the call," Brody stressed.

Eugene's acid reflux roiled again. Bilge water had that effect on him.

"Get this," Hamelton effused. "This big dog attended the same college as Cidally. What are the chances?"

"She's real easy on the eyes!" Brody winked. "If you know what I mean?"

This dude had to have Neanderthal tattooed across his boxers.

"She can take care of herself," Eugene asserted, his own cheeks tightening.

Cidally would have neutered this ape. Shredded his male ego. Reduced him to pablum. As a female athlete – make that as a female period – she had encountered jackanapes like this far too often.

"Get this," Hamelton clucked. "Brody starts Monday. You're going to show him how to time travel."

A tire iron to the head would have connected with less impact. Not only was Hamelton going to phase Eugene out, he was going to force him to train his replacement.

"I'm getting close," Eugene protested, gesturing with both arms. "Real close."

"Not according to what Darby pulled off Verne yesterday. The time stamps on those files tell me you have done virtually nothing this week and tomorrow is Friday!"

Hamelton smoldered. "You've been playing me for a fool, dragging your ass. Well, guess what? The joke's on you!"

Eugene simmered, sucking in as much air as his flared nostrils would allow.

"That's right, Hamelton glowed: "Once Brody can fly solo, you are history."

His back to Hamelton, Brody raised his middle finger.

"Tweet like a bird," he rasped. "Tweet like a bird."

Visions of Ned Beatty crawling on all fours in *Deliverance* popped as panic tapped Eugene on the shoulder.

Hamelton's whipping boy could live with getting canned. He had been let go before.

But Eugene was not prepared to say goodbye to Cidally or Verne. They defined him, motivated him, kept him grounded.

Yes, Eugene had understood this assignment to be temporary. But, in accepting it, he had believed he would leave on his own terms, not on the whim of some punitive powermonger.

Now, with a pink slip on the horizon, what recourse did he have? Had the time come to call Hamelton out? Expose him for the cheat he was? Have Mr. Criminal Justice take the transgressor into custody?

His mind in hyperdrive, Eugene sought to self-soothe. Dial down his emotions. Regulate his breathing. Clear his head.

What was his game plan? Cidally would have had one.

Assailed by thoughts – random, disconnected, impractical – one kept recurring, repeating, circling back. Like an alarm clock sans snooze button, the idea continued to buzz until not even Eugene could overlook it.

Verne. Verne held the answers. Eugene's binary buddy would come through as only he could. Verne would lead the way out of this mess.

"I need a drink," Eugene announced in an all-too-obvious bid to gain freedom.

"Don't we all," Hamelton agreed. "But you're going nowhere."

Going nowhere? That's false imprisonment! Totally illegal!

Perhaps Eugene should have objected. But with Brody serving as bailiff, he withdrew the motion. Better to get out in one piece later than to exit now – possibly on a stretcher – by challenging the ruling.

Still, Eugene considered bolting. Given his location near the door and the element of surprise, he might slip away before the desk-bound feces thrower could react. And once in the hallway, Eugene knew the lay of the land.

But *Toccata and Fugue in D minor* scuttled Eugene's flight to freedom. The opening notes to the sonic icon – a horror film staple – functioned as Hamelton's ring tone. Only the living dead would select something so ghoulish and macabre.

"I have to take this," the Phantom insisted, slithering away.

Swell. Chaperoning Baby Huey now fell to Eugene.

Or maybe not. Brody pawed at Hamelton's desk. He sifted through items, picking them up, turning them over, and putting them down with a vacant stare reminiscent of Michael Myers in *Halloween*.

Brody gave Hamelton's globe a spin. He twirled it faster and faster until it threatened to leave its base.

Then, with one well-placed hand, Brody brought the sphere to a halt. He reached for a stapled set of papers, the lone tenant on the top shelf of a grey storage cabinet. He brought the two-inch stack closer, exploring page after page with a gentleness that surprised.

Eugene considered volunteering to read anything contained within for Brody, but held off. Not because he feared the Cardiff Giant – he did – but because the document looked familiar. Where had he seen it before?

New toy in tow, head still bowed, Brody sidled up to the chalkboard. With each deliberate step, he clutched tighter the many sheets of twenty-pound bond.

"Time to say goodbye," he hushed to the insect rubbing its front legs in a sea of green.

Brody smacked the board. His deadly backhand scattered chalk and body parts to the four winds.

"Another one bites the dust," he leered, loosening his grip on his makeshift flyswatter.

Eugene blew his nose. He had to be dreaming.

"I used to pull the wings off these buzzards," Brody bragged. "They'd hop around until I flicked them across the floor with my finger."

"Everyone needs a hobby," Eugene shivered, terrified at what the loathsome beast might have done to small mammals.

"You're a funny dude," Brody grunted.

Up front, framed photographs of past principals lined up chronologically. Though never associated with higher learning, Hamelton had placed his image on the far left. His likeness, the only selfie, took up more space than the others.

"Know where I'm going after you show me how this time travel stuff works?" Brody asked, still thumbing pages. "Locker rooms."

Having tuned out, Eugene stayed with the headmasters of St. Anthony's. Only one had been photographed wearing glasses. Shouldn't there have been more? Roughly forty percent of males required vision correction.

"Chicks can come into a guy's locker room after a game," Brody reasoned. "Well, I'm getting into theirs."

Eugene couldn't shake the faded faces. He stared so intently that the wire rims of the bespectacled entrant went in and out of focus. Man, they were thick. Thicker than usual. Almost goggle-like.

That's it! Senseless goggles!

"Can we record all the stuff we're going to see?" Brody asked, looking at Eugene for the first time since Hamelton had cut out.

That's it! The manuscript in Brody's meaty paws was the one Hamelton had pilfered from Clancy Wigwort.

"That hottie. What was her name?" Brody asked. "Played basketball, didn't she?"

Eugene made a tent with his fingers.

"Mind if I have a look at what you found?" Eugene asked, feigning disinterest as best he could.

"I most certainly do," Hamelton thundered, breezing past Eugene to recover what he had neglected to safeguard. So effectively did he pickpocket Brody that the younger man was left clutching air.

Hamelton ripped open the lower drawer of his desk and slammed it closed in one continuous motion. That he had time to safely tuck the document inside between those nearly simultaneous actions was a sleight-of-hand worthy of a magician.

Such an exhibition should have ended conversation on the topic, but Brody plodded on.

"You're a game-changer," he marveled, surprising Hamelton with his sincerity. "You're playing like, like 5G chess, man!"

Hamelton glowed, albeit in a grotesque, Quasimodo sort of way.

"It's my life's work," the lying lout boasted.

If only Wigwort had dreamed bigger, Eugene mused. If only he had reached for the stars and cracked the code on how to resurrect the dead. If he had, Clancy could have dropped in and set the record straight.

Hamelton would have soiled his pants.

But Wigwort was gone, his ashes scattered among the pines and maples he so loved. If the innocuous innovator was to receive his due, he would have to rely on Eugene. He would have to entrust his good name to a blender who – short of being pumped full of helium – had no clue as to how to rise to the occasion.

"Get this," Hamelton said, still blushing from the bouquets Brody had bestowed. "The governor's grandson will be here in two weeks. He and his wife want to see Verne do his thing. Sooooo. Starting Monday, the two of you are on deadline. Find Allerspan! Understood?"

"We got this," Brody saluted.

"What about you, Gene?" Hamelton demanded.

Sure. Why not moonlight as a zookeeper? Feed the seals. Bathe the rhinos. Train the 300-pound gorilla.

"Absolutely," he concurred, bristling at his new nickname.

"You do or you – will – be – finished!" Hamelton promised. "Fini-to!"

Well, then, Eugene thought, let's have some fun. If Brody – empty between the ears – was Hamelton's idea of salvation, why not emulate the big guy.

Eugene would play dumb, a natural state for Brody. He'd use big words, confusing commands, pseudo-science. He'd spoon-feed Brody, enough to turn him into a liability that would fail spectacularly at crunch time.

Eugene would appeal to Brody's privilege. He'd cozy up to the Neanderthal's perceived infallibility. He'd encourage the Entitled Elephant to help himself to whatever he wanted.

Eugene would shovel bullsilt – thanks, Cidally – until he buried this unwelcome albatross.

This wasn't Eugene's first brodeo. But, by god, it was going to be his last.

Chapter Eighteen

What would he do, Eugene often wondered, if he found out he had one day to live?

Would he spend his final hours with family and friends? Would he check off items on his bucket list? Would he renounce decorum and engage in the forbidden?

This mind-bending hypothetical could hit Eugene at any time: when stuck in traffic, when sleepless in bed, or when tending to business atop the commode. Once in his head, the what-if wormed its way into his cerebral cortex, hunkering down like a squatter hellbent on gaining adverse possession.

Years spent wrestling with this brain buster had yielded but one answer: Eugene would never be given advance notice of his impending demise. But, if somehow he were, any plan he had formulated would get lost in the ensuing panic of being told he was about to die.

No alarms had gone off for William Allerspan. The former governor had no inkling his calendar was about to run out that Friday. Had he known, he might have delayed his trip or, at the very least, declined to take the road less traveled. Anything to avoid the fate that awaited him.

Eugene had witnessed Allerspan's denouement. He had solved the decades-old mystery more than a week earlier. He had ridden shotgun as the governor rode into the sunset.

Allerspan's last day and his inauguration could not have been more different. Alone in death, he was never more alive than when he addressed the throng of 5,000 that packed Capitol Square. Family, staff and former governors braved freezing temperatures to sit in chairs atop a platform adorned in red, white and blue bunting. A group of middle schoolers – essay winners – hooted and hollered and jostled each other as they waved flags.

Aglow in the winter sunlight, Allerspan beamed. He smiled. He applauded the day. This was the beginning of a new era.

Mindful that trouble never takes a holiday, state patrol helicopters hovered overhead. Snipers held down positions on surrounding rooftops.

Interspersed among the many supportive faces were those who believed Allerspan should never have left the ghetto. He was poking his nose where it didn't belong. His skin was too dark to represent the majority.

"Providence has delivered me here today," the great-grandson of slaves intoned. "And providence shall guide me for the next four years!

"I pledge to serve the citizens of this state – each and every one – regardless of creed, race or religion. Your needs are my needs. Your concerns are my concerns. Your fight is my fight.

"We. Shall. Prevail!"

Providence had not offered much wiggle room. Allerspan won by less than one thousand votes, and that advantage shrank after a mandated recount.

As a minority, Allerspan needed every vote. As a man of color with a woman on the ticket – a longtime colleague seeking the office of lieutenant governor – he could not afford a misstep.

"If we come in with a black and a woman, that ticket is a dead duck," bemoaned one party member. "We won't get the votes."

Allerspan tuned out the negativity. He canvassed white and black neighborhoods alike. He refused to sling mud.

"I'll walk a hundred miles in your shoes to earn your vote," he asserted.

Over time, the tide turned in his favor.

A month shy of fifty-five, the lifelong Democrat touted his experience. He had been tough on crime as a prosecutor. He had mastered the inner workings of government as a state senator.

Family first, he had been married to the same woman for more than thirty years. Country foremost, he had served in the military.

Allerspan prevailed with the help of Blacks, liberals, the poor, and those off-put by his opponent. That he squared off against a populist with a checkered past pushed independents and undecideds his way.

Allerspan navigated a budget crisis while in office. He held the line on taxes. He froze in-state tuition. He brought new business to the state.

Always, he kept himself in the news cycle.

After two years of what he trumpeted as a radiant rebirth, Allerspan announced he would make a run for the most prestigious office in the land. If Jesse Jackson could mix it up on the national stage, so could he. Allerspan became AllerCanDo.

"As an American and a champion of change, I can no longer tolerate what passes for governance in Washington. As your governor and a fellow citizen, I declare myself a candidate to become the next President of the United States."

Allerspan's decision likely cost him a second term as governor.

"It's nothing personal," said one citizen. "But he's not qualified."

"Traipsing to Washington," another scoffed, "He has a state to run. The nerve!"

"He never met a camera he didn't like," summed up a third. "Well, he'll get wall-to-wall coverage now."

Allerspan struggled to raise funds from the outset. He lacked name recognition. He failed to set himself apart from other contenders.

Advised to lean more left, he came off as less than genuine. Coached to be more forceful, he came off as angry – even uppity – in some quarters.

Polling last, Allerspan suspended his campaign. He returned home to a state-wide teachers strike and the resignation of his lieutenant governor.

He served out the remainder of his term while facing growing backlash. He was advised to forgo re-election.

Given little choice, Allerspan acquiesced. He stepped aside. He zipped his lip while affixing a chip squarely atop his shoulder.

The piqued progressive remained in politics and worked behind the scenes. No task was too small, no assignment too inconsequential. He crossed the aisle to broker deals. He served as mentor to those new to government. He warmed to the role of senior statesman.

However, he seethed as less-accomplished, less-talented actors jockeyed up the ranks.

Forced to confront his increasing irrelevance, Allerspan envisioned a comeback. He would again ascend to the highest office in the state. He would become more than an answer to a trivia question.

The human hand shaker dropped hints of a return to his friends, acquaintances and anyone willing to listen. He kept a running count of those who welcomed the news and those who didn't.

As his informal poll climbed into the hundreds and the ayes tipped in his favor, Allerspan requested a special meeting with party leaders. Rebuffed, he went public. He leaked his plans to the media. He sat for dozens of interviews. He stood ready to toss his hat back into the ring.

Allerspan finally got his meeting.

Had he showed up that Friday afternoon, Allerspan would have met with pushback. His name polarized. His time in office, despite an encouraging start, was viewed negatively, especially his bungled play for the White House.

His time, he would have been told, had come and gone. He was analog in the coming age of digital.

In a small way, Allerspan's failure to keep his appointment was a blessing. He was spared the humiliation of being told his place was at the back of the bus.

The Saturday after her husband was a no-show, Allerspan's wife contacted authorities. They insisted her MIA would turn up.

Days stretched into weeks, then months. No Allerspan. No clues, no leads, nothing to go on.

The former governor had ceased to exist. And life, as it always does, carried on.

Oh, there were those who said they had seen Allerspan. He was quaffing a beer at a local tavern. He had caught a cab uptown. He was placing leaflets on the windows of vehicles in a parking garage.

Such sightings were easily disproven. More difficult to discount were theories with a more sinister bent. Allerspan had been silenced by a political enemy. He had been the victim of a kidnapping gone wrong. He had been taken out by white supremacists.

Eugene ignored the speculation. Allerspan's wife had told the press she last saw her husband at roughly eight in the morning on the day in question. She was not expecting to hear from him until Saturday, as he expected a late night with friends after his meeting.

To get the truth, Eugene parked the drone near the city limits along the only interstate that fed into the capital from Allerspan's side of the state. Rather than tag along for the entire trip – an enormous undertaking as he would find out – Eugene would let the governor come to him. The politician, provided he limited his pit stops, should motor into the city sometime late Friday morning.

Except he didn't. Eugene monitored all three lanes leading into town. For hours. In real time. Without success.

Oh, Eugene saw plenty of dull gray sedans zip past, but not one was piloted by the state's first governor of color.

After days of reviewing footage, Eugene concluded that Allerspan had taken another route. But which one? This particular human locator had neither the fortitude nor the time to engage in a drawn-out guessing game.

So, Eugene started at the beginning. He would follow the governor – mile by painstaking mile – as the latter edged closer to his destination.

How to broker more than 100 miles of roadway? Going high – a bird's-eye view – led to fewer drone recalls, but Eugene risked losing the gray sedan among the many commuters. Going low eliminated that problem, but it entailed more back and forth between past and present as Allerspan – and everyone else – left the frame much faster.

Eugene employed both methods. He also fast-forwarded, jumping ahead five or ten miles until Allerspan appeared. That worked until Eugene again found himself hanging. No governor.

Allerspan must have ditched the expressway for country roads. Farmland. Cow pastures. Riding stables. Small towns with no stoplights.

On screen, Allerspan chewed up highway as efficiently as a combine harvesting corn. He paralleled a freight train until it dipped low and headed east. He waved at bicyclists who returned his greeting. He honked at teachers and children enjoying their first outdoor recess of the season.

These had been his constituents. And they might be again, if they pulled the correct lever come Election Day.

Ahead, Mossy Lake beckoned. In winter, the deep, murky body of water supported hundreds of shanties. Now, a week into spring, heavy rains and melting ice had increased liquidity to near record levels.

As clouds thickened, raindrops spattered the gray sedan's windshield. The only driver on the road scarcely noticed as he patted the passenger-side floor mat of his vehicle. Something — Eugene never found out what — had slipped from Allerspan's grasp.

Leaning further right — his face barely above the dashboard — Allerspan's fingers brushed against the AWOL object. Contact only drove it farther away.

He slumped further toward the open seat, his body draped across the center console as he raked the carpet. He extended his reach. He cursed. He took his eyes off the road.

In his determination to recover the wayward item, Allerspan scored a deadly trifecta. His car veered right, the mat under his feet shifted, and the accelerator stuck.

Two tires left the pavement, spitting up gravel as Allerspan's ride began the ascent to Kincaid Bridge. A tire blew. The steering wheel jerked. A second Goodyear radial imploded.

Allerspan's runaway car spun off the road and hit a ridge. Speed being a factor, it jumped the guardrail, clearing the metal barrier by inches. The governor braced for splashdown as the unconventional missile reached its apex.

Plastic, glass and metal crashed into the soupy drink as the vehicle bellyflopped. At impact, a geyser of spray arose as if a whale had cleared its blowhole. A second later, a surge of bubbling foam rushed in to fill the air cavity created by the intrusion of a foreign object.

Moments later, the upper half of the vehicle resurfaced as if rejected by the lake. The rear window bobbed into view as though it was coming up for oxygen.

The reprieve was short-lived. Water poured into every orifice, twisting and swirling and forcing its way into every empty space. Windows and trunk struggled to stay afloat even as gravity and foundering conspired against them. The rooftop, its dull gray sheen bumping up against algae green, was the last to succumb to submersion.

Allerspan, like Jonah before him, had been swallowed whole.

Eugene kept the camera rolling for more than an hour after the deadly plunge. A bus, a pickup and two vans passed by unaware of what had happened. Two inches of rain ensured everyone else would be kept in the dark as well.

Still shaking, Eugene went back for seconds and thirds. He captured the mishap from different locations. He recorded portions in slow motion. He even attempted to glean footage from inside the lake.

Hamelton would have wanted that. Hell, the sick twitch would be downright giddy. Not only did the accident make for must-see TV, but Allerspan's body might still be intact. His remains could be confirmed as those of the missing governor. Skrean Time could commence.

Allerspan's death had been a shame. Skrean's intention to profit from it was shameful.

More repugnant: Eugene had been a willing accomplice.

Chapter Nineteen

"You call it defense. I call it do-fense."

Do-fense? The term sounds comical, even laughable.

But don't tell that to the defender – or is it do-fender? – who coined the expression. Especially not on game day.

Brody Slattner, all six-feet-four and 250 pounds of him, is liable to deposit you on your backside, then dare you to get up. When this two-time all-conference linebacker speaks, people listen. Teammates and opponents dare not snicker, even when what he has to say is – how shall we put this – indo-fensible.

"Everyone talks about the offense moving the ball," the senior continued. "Well, we move it, too. We create turnovers, we sack the quarterback, we tackle for loss.

"We may not always know what play our opponent is going to run, but we make damned sure they don't try it a second time. We play do-fense."

Eugene reread the opening paragraphs. If only he could have traded places with the author.

"Hey, Brody! Do you practice do-fensive driving? If you were to have a heart attack, should we fire up the do-fibrillator? How many concussions must one sustain before do-mentia sets in?"

The inane questions exploded rapid fire in Eugene's head, piling high like so much doo-doo. Enough material flowed to fuel a sketch on *Saturday Night Live.*

Brody Slattner: All-American Doofus.

In poking fun, Eugene leveled the playing field. He cut Brody down to size, something many an offensive linemen had failed to do over the years.

Of course, had the Hulking Hothead stepped into the gymnasium, Eugene would have gone from smiley to frowney face faster than a tech-savvy tot could locate either emoji. But with Brody out of the building, the amateur comedian amused himself until he tired of devoting time to a buffoon unworthy of his attention.

The article that had triggered this jockularity was one of many retrieved using yorenewspaper.com. The other write-ups, many of which detailed Brody's exploits on the gridiron, didn't pack the same punch.

In scouring them, one fact became unassailable: Brody was a once-in-a-generation talent. He was the unquestioned leader of a record-setting defense. He tackled with the ferocity of a cheetah taking down its prey.

Such glowing praise roiled Eugene. He wanted scandal, chinks in the armor that could be used against the arrogant a-hole. Ammunition, an edge so to speak, should a confrontation materialize. He could not go into battle empty-handed against someone twice his muscle mass.

But Brody appeared unimpeachable – both on and off the field. If he had run-ins with the law, they had been kept out of the paper. The big lug was as clean as a bench warmer's jersey.

Perhaps Eugene should revisit the hilarity that had played out as he approached Hamelton's office just hours earlier. Perhaps something said then could yield a clue now.

Eugene swallowed the last of his soda, his face puckering as if biting into a lemon. The syrupy remains – featuring food particles floating amid room-temperature backwash – told him he had drunk from a day-old can. He shuddered as if that might drain the ickiness from his taste buds.

Eugene sat atop a stool and scooched over slightly to access more tush-friendly terrain. Clasping his hands behind his back, he thrust his chest forward and rolled his shoulders, rocking his head from side to side.

If anyone was a candidate for excessive screen time, it was Eugene.

Entering the data that would transport him to Hamelton's office, Eugene hit send. He waited. Then waited some more.

With no Shepard tone forthcoming, Eugene double checked his work. He looked for loose connections. He fine-tuned a dial or two knowing full well the adjustments had no bearing on whether or not Verne carried out his instructions.

Out of patience and out of ideas, Eugene banged the side of the console. The large screen crackled to life as flesh smacked metal.

Large screen? Eugene had requested the small monitor.

"If you could go back in time and change one thing about yourself," Hamelton intoned from above, "what would that be?"

What the hell? This wasn't Hamelton in his office. This was video of Hamelton conducting a job interview with Darby at his side. And the poor slob being raked over the coals was Eugene.

"I have to be honest," the Eugene of yesterday confessed. "I do have regrets. My life is not perfect."

Those words – inadequate then, cringe-worthy now – grew in volume.

"You can't change the past," insisted Hamelton. "What's done is done."

Eugene turned and faced the bleachers, scanning every seat and row. No Darby.

"That's Buster," came a young girl's voice. "He's taking a nap."

The cherubic face of Sabrina lit up the gym. Crayon in hand, sprawled on the floor, she colored. She was in the process of applying generous helpings of blue to a monstrous sketch pad that was nearly as wide as she was tall.

Had Verne slipped into autoplay? Was he dropping a greatest hits album?

"Line up for a free throw," Cidally ordered. "Everyone in the same place as before."

Verne had again changed channels. And as much as Eugene admired Cidally's skill and form, what would he do if the expert rebounder herself walked in? How could he explain her image holding sway above center court?

Not to worry. Verne again shifted location. Sasha Ankubar had Hamelton on the ropes.

"Tell me about perpetual motion," the journalist cooed.

Before he could reply, the Hamelton of the library vanished, replaced by the stall sitter in the bathroom. A pat of butter parachuted to earth. Wigwort settled in for his final read.

The snippets kept rolling, each shorter than the last: Hamelton poured water over Clancy's head ... Sabrina colored with crayons ... Cidally sipped wine.

The display intensified. The playback gathered speed. A carousal on amphetamines, clips flashed faster, stronger, louder. Blurring, overlapping, blending, discrete units became one, melding into a mosaic of pulsating light and sound. The sensory stimulating whirlwind bedazzled and hypnotized, enrapturing its audience of one.

One scene remained discernable. One scene cycled through on repeat: Allerspan into the lake ... Allerspan into the lake ... Allerspan into the lake.

Pancake. Belly flop. Cannon ball.

A dead man's float to the bottom.

The mind-numbing loop mesmerized, sucking Eugene in deeper. Swirling, twisting, coiling, the kaleidoscopic onslaught snaked past his cornea and into his brain. Each frame a tsunami. Each frame a fresh assault on his senses.

How to end this digital regurgitation?

Pull the plug? No one cord powered Verne.

Pull the flash drive? Yes, and pull it now!

Grasping the memory stick, Eugene tugged. He yanked so violently that the tiny object flew high into the air. Remaining calm, he snagged the precious cargo as it rocketed back to earth like an infielder under a pop fly.

Above, where video had unfurled, a shimmering circle radiated outward. Growing smaller, the grainy white noise aligned horizontally across the screen. Then, with one final twinkle, the light poofed into oblivion.

The hair on Eugene's arms stiffened. Every corpuscle taut and at the ready.

In the eerie stillness, no sound, no movement. Yet, Eugene sensed a presence.

A higher power? God? Hamelton?

He could swear he was being watched. But by whom?

Of course! How could he have overlooked the obvious? If he could visit the past, so too, could others. Eugene was being observed by an individual or individuals not yet born.

In that moment, Eugene realized he not given enough thought to time visitation. For being a so-called contemplationalist, he had dropped the ball. He had been treating TV as a harmless diversion, even though something buried deep within told him it wasn't.

For the first time, Eugene understood he would be a target. He should have known, but because he didn't point the camera at himself when looking back, he assumed no one else would want in on his business either. He couldn't have been more wrong.

Eugene and every other human – regardless of how unremarkable, how short lived, or how off the grid – would be put under the microscope. Each would be held up and examined. No one would be exempt.

People watching. Everybody did it. Since the dawn of time. Adam checked out Eve. Boaz took notice of Ruth when she was gleaning in his barley fields. King David spied on Bathsheba while the attractive Israelite was bathing.

Who could possibly be immune? Even the God of Eugene's previous employer kept tabs on every member of his flock. With Verne, everyone would become all-seeing, all-knowing.

Perhaps Eugene should have remained cloistered within the church. Never had he been more alone, yet never had he felt so closely watched.

What had Darby said about facial recognition and Abe Lincoln? One day, smart cameras would follow a person's every move, surrounding their target like mosquitoes at a bloodletting. Lenses and microphones would record every twitch, belch and bowel movement.

Anyone down for a little cyberstalking? See someone you like? Snap their photo. Take some video. Upload it to seeallofme.com.

Then download their entire life story whether it be the girl next door or the recluse who shelters behind a gate and high hedges.

Looking for more coverage? Sign up for the deluxe package. Instead of one, get four drones. Observe your homecoming queen from all angles. Move in closer. Pan from head to toe. Ogle the body part of your choosing.

Want more? Get alerts as to when the object of your desire disrobes. Set notifications for intimate moments. Replace your ring tone with the sounds of passion that are sure to follow!

Like what you see? Share it with friends. Cast it to your TV. Make that head-turner the centerpiece of your next party. Surveil 'til death do you part!

Good god! There had to be some injunction to counter this madness? Some authority to step in and prevent this sensory free-for-all from gaining a foothold?

If nothing else, the legal profession was sure to have a field day.

"Have you or your loved one been autopsied while still breathing? Don't roll over and die. Fight back. For less than you make in a lifetime, we'll expose the exposers. We'll record those recording you. We'll unearth enough dirt so you can bury your enemy before he buries you. Call 1-800-DIG-DEEP now!"

Jesus, Joseph and Mary! Were humans equipped to withstand such continuous scrutiny? How many would opt out – permanently – under the glare of an unrelenting spotlight?

That was an experiment, Eugene decided, that had to end before it began. He had to shatter the magnifying glass before it charred mankind to a crisp.

"Verne, buddy, I need your help," he pleaded. "What do I do? Give me a sign. I'll take anything!"

Unmoved, the Goliath of the Gym remained mum.

Eugene hopped back on the stool. Where to next? Would Verne even function after having unleashed his ill-tempered spasm of pyrotechnics?

Apparently, yes. Gone was the input from earlier. In its place, a number with many zeros blinked incessantly. Eugene recognized the integer for what it was: a lion in waiting.

Chapter Twenty

As a child, Eugene set out to find the world's largest number. His grandfather, an actuary, fueled his interest by extending the -lions for him: quadrillion, quintillion, sextillion, septillion, octillion, nonillion, decillion.

That last entry, a one followed by 33 zeros, reigned as king of the jungle for years. It was not until Eugene literally bumped into a dictionary so massive it rested on a stand of its own did that status change.

In paging through the expansive reservoir of the written word, Eugene discovered that the range of the big cats extended much farther. Their territory stretched from vigintillion (63) to duotrigintillion (99) to quinquagintillion (153) to centillion (303) and beyond. All one had to do to birth one of these monstrosities was to throw down a one and add extra zeros. Presto! The pride welcomed a new member.

But where did the vastness end? Did it end? At what point does the finite become the infinite?

Though Eugene loved to dabble in integers on a grand scale, he struggled to visualize such magnitude. How much was a million? How much was a billion?

A reference reader he purchased at a museum provided clarity. He learned that one million oranges would fill a swimming pool. One billion would pack a football stadium to the brim.

During an oral report on the book that so fascinated him, Eugene let slip his desire to become a billionaire. His goal – presented without a hint of irony – drew hee-haws in the classroom and ridicule on the playground.

"Hey, how's business Mr. Citrus Farmer?" his freckle-faced peers inquired. "Earn that first billion yet?"

Eugene, of course, never did. At best, his middle-aged self might fetch a few hundred thousand if he auctioned all he owned and sold his body to science.

No, to reach ten figures in net worth – an aspiration he should have kept to himself – would require thousands of lifetimes at this rate. And even at that, everything he squirrelled away would have to carry over from one go-round to the next, all while earning a sizeable return on investment.

Staring down the lion on Verne's console had Eugene again contemplating the far reaches of enormity. What would he find if he ventured that far back in time? Could he venture that far back in time?

The questions came easily. The answers not so much. Verne would require decades to send the drone back that far. Still . . .

The display on the console taunted. On, off – off, on, the lineup of digits and placeholders flickered like incandescent bulbs loose in their sockets. That the value was greater than the estimated age of the universe had Eugene curious as well.

Screw it! What did he have to lose? His days of gainful employment were numbered. Why not detour as Allerspan had done, albeit with both eyes on the road and both hands on the wheel?

Eugene initiated the launch sequence expecting a drawn-out energizing process. Not so. The light signaling all-go turned green almost instantly. The drone took flight.

A sneeze bounced off the walls of the gym. Then another. On the small screen, Cidally braced for a third ah-choo, but it dissipated before it precipitated.

"Bless you," Eugene said, knowing the sniffler could not hear him.

Cidally studied the computer monitor in her office. Lost in thought, she scarcely moved.

Had an army of onlookers suddenly materialized, each might have been struck by a different facet of her beauty. The sheen of her hair. The curve of her lips. The child-like dimples that deepened with every smile.

For Eugene, it was Cidally's eyes. Always her eyes. He searched those deep blue reflecting pools for a clue, a flicker, a sign that she reciprocated his feelings. That he came away disappointed every time did not deter him. He could have lingered a lifetime.

This time, Cidally's baby blues pierced his heart from behind designer frames. Eugene nearly puddled. No other item on a woman — not jewelry, not clothing, not piercings — quickened his pulse more. Eyewear transformed, enhanced. Glasses bespoke intellect, a mind crying out for exploration.

Cidally removed a notebook from a nearby shelf. Running her fingers down the page, she stopped mid-sheet, circled an entry with her pen, and then set the book aside. Pursing the writing instrument between her lips, she tapped out a message, her fingers gliding over the keys.

Eugene sat riveted, tagging along for every indent, tab and backspace. He adjusted to Cidally's moves like a cat to a laser pointer.

Cidally toiled in one of the best-maintained rooms at St. Anthony's. Spacious, with windows above the main entrance, the second-floor hollow kept her sufficiently removed from Hamelton and Darby, who conducted business at street level.

Eugene knew those portals of tempered transparency well. He glanced in their direction each morning, drawing comfort whenever the lights were on.

Cidally removed her glasses. She massaged her forehead, temples and neck. Eyes closed, she rolled her shoulders, straining to loosen the knots levied as a surcharge by stress and bad posture.

Oh, to be a masseur! Why hadn't Eugene given serious consideration to that profession all those years ago? Oils, lotions and creams! Oh, my!

Cidally tugged at her left sleeve. She lowered it enough so that her left arm no longer remained within its confines. She then did the same with her right arm and right sleeve.

Her limbs now inside her top, Cidally turned her bra around so the hooks faced forward. She unlatched each fastener, liberating herself from the finest Victoria's Secret had to offer. That done, she returned each arm to its respective sleeve, slipped free the supportive garment from within, and tossed it aside.

Eugene turned fifty shades of red. He hadn't knocked, he hadn't called, he hadn't texted. He had barged in without warning.

This felt wrong. Cidally had a right to privacy. She had the right to keep the nosy out of her affairs.

Yet, here Eugene was, taking it all in. What was he thinking?

Wasn't he supposed to be billions of years in the past? Wasn't Eugene supposed to be inhaling the hydrogen, helium and lithium present at the Big Bang? Wasn't he supposed to be watching the universe form, not the form of a woman?

Eugene checked the console. The mysterious number continued to wink.

Was it possible, Eugene thought, that the little hovercraft had gone back seconds instead of years? Maybe all those zeros had failed to register. Maybe Eugene was watching a live feed on a short delay.

One way to find out. He picked up the receiver of the phone near Verne and rotary-dialed as he had done when making outgoing calls at his grandparents.

"Hello," said a voice in Eugene's ear.

"Hello," said Cidally on screen.

The voices synced perfectly. The only holdup originated with Eugene. Now that he had Cidally on the line, what was he supposed to say?

"Ah, yeah, it's Eugene," he stammered, mouth numbed as if dipped in Novocain.

"Eugene who?" came the short reply.

The question touched a nerve. More than one girl in high school had blurted out the same after Eugene had worked up the courage to call. Cidally's ignorance, feigned though it was, laid bare old insecurities. Just who the hell was he?

The Eugene of old would have hung up. But the current version refused to bail. He would ride out this connection. He would collect on this call.

But he needed something clever. He needed Darby. The Improvisational Imp would not have missed a beat.

"Eugene, who?" he thought of saying. "Why, the man of your dreams! The lover who satisfies! The irresistible bad boy who will have you begging for more!"

Too strong! And way too in-your-face!

Eugene settled for: "You know, Eugene, the gym rat."

Not a home run, but a serviceable play on words. He did work in a gym. A lot. With Verne. For hours on end.

Maybe a small chuckle?!?

"What's up?" Cidally deadpanned.

No points for cleverness? Really? Not even a gold star for effort?

"What's up?" Cidally asked a second time.

Eugene floundered. "Uh, what time do you have?"

"Precious little and even less having talked to you!" Cidally said, bursting into a smile. She let go of her mouse, clapped her hands and swiveled in her chair.

"Sorry to have bothered you," Eugene apologized.

"No, no, no," Cidally jumped in. "My Aunt Edna used to say that. Not to us, not to her nieces, of course, but to the rude, the obnoxious and the unrepentant!"

Silence. Long silence.

Eugene was not one to experience deju vu. But something told him he had been here before.

"Which, by the way, you're not," Cidally appended when the lengthening pause threatened to become pregnant.

"I didn't think you would be working late," Eugene said.

"Mandatory overtime. Hamelton has a kink in his colon."

"True that," Eugene agreed. "Hey, did you lose power a few minutes ago?"

Cidally squared up a stack of papers.

"For about ten or fifteen seconds."

"Me, too," Eugene noted, relieved the interruption had not been directly solely at him.

Cidally placed the papers she had gathered into a folder and set in a bottom drawer. She pulled out a pack of Stim-U-Dent plaque removers from her purse. With the last one, she vigorously worked the area between two incisors.

"Do you ever wonder if we know what we are doing?" Eugene exclaimed, peering at the athlete-turned-dental hygienist through the outermost regions of his peripheral vision.

"What do you mean?" Cidally asked, smoothing over a particularly tender spot with her tongue.

"This technology we're working on. It's kind of scary, don't you think?"

"How so?"

"We're stirring up the past. Someday, someone will root out our past. Ever think about that?"

"You hiding something?" Cidally asked, swishing and swallowing with water from a bottle.

Was she going to answer his every question with a question?

"Private matters," Eugene clarified. "What goes on away from work – that kind of stuff."

Cidally retrieved her compact. "How is anyone going to know where to look?"

Whoo boy! Was Cidally truly unaware or did she prefer not to go there? How is anyone going to know where to look? How do hackers breach security? How do online scammers target the vulnerable? How do the underage obtain alcohol?

There is always a way.

"Ever hear of the infinite monkey theorem?" Eugene submitted.

"If you get enough monkeys pounding on enough keyboards you will eventually produce the entire works of Shakespeare," Cidally came back, mirror in hand, fingers tousling her hair.

"So, you see where I'm headed. Every day, apes go scrolling and swiping. Twenty-four/seven. We will be found. It is only a matter of time."

"Maybe," Cidally conceded. "But I counter your monkey business with the celebrity worship syndrome. Given a pipeline to the rich, royal and famous, who would want to dig into my life?"

Her life? Was this a set-up? Some sort of test?

Who would want to invade her personal space? Short of being served a restraining order, Eugene would have snooped high and stooped low to get to know her better.

But he could not let on. He had to remove himself from the discussion. Yes, he had been tempted to probe Cidally's past and so might others. She could easily become a celebrity in her own right. What, then?

"Once you've become a successful D-1 head coach, you might want to rethink that," Eugene said.

"I can handle it," Cidally countered. "Don't you worry."

There it was. The confidence Eugene so admired. Cidally, ready for any challenge. Short in name only.

But the opposition in this case consisted not of flesh and blood. Cidally versus Verne was more like chess grand master Garry Kasparov versus IBM's Deep Blue. Or the legendary power of John Henry versus the steam engine."

She stood no chance. No one did.

"I am sure you handled it well," Eugene glossed over. "But that was before Verne. This dude is a game changer."

Game changer? Really? Eugene came off sounding like Hamelton's misbegotten stepchild.

"With Verne, without Verne, I live my life the same," Cidally asserted. "He doesn't dictate how I operate."

Defiant. Unwilling to compromise. What was not to love?

Eugene should have stopped there.

"I get it," he said. "But this is not about you. This is about the obnoxious fan, the leering photographer, the depraved drunk. Verne will throw open the door and he'll turn on the lights. And he'll only leave – if he does at all – when he is good and ready."

How could Cidally argue with that? Deny it? Shrug it off? Bury her head in the sand?

She had to admit they were playing with a live wire. They were throwing down a welcome mat that would be overrun by the scum of the earth.

"It's getting late," Cidally begged off. "It's been a twelve-hour day. I need to recharge. I'll see you tomorrow, okay?"

Cidally's eyes – bright, eager – appeared to have dimmed. Was that doubt? Fear? Fatigue?

Backing her into a corner was not Eugene's intent. Instead, he had hoped Cidally would tell him he was wrong. That he need not worry. That he could rest easy. That Verne would do more good than harm.

Had he pushed her away?

Why? Why had he not kept his mouth shut? Why had he not played nice?

Lord knows he had lived his entire life excelling at both.

Chapter Twenty-One

"So I travelled, stopping ever and again, in great strides of a thousand years or more, drawn on by the mystery of the earth's fate, watching with a strange fascination the sun grow larger and duller in the westward sky, and the life of the old earth ebb away. At last, more than thirty million years hence, the huge red-hot dome of the sun had come to obscure nearly a tenth part of the darkling heavens. Then I stopped once more, for the crawling multitude of crabs had disappeared, and the red beach, save for its livid green liverworts and lichens, seemed lifeless."

The Time Traveller in H.G. Wells's story – sorry, Darby not Jules Verne's – *The Time Machine* traversed more than thirty million years in filing his somber report. He pushed limits, going to the extreme to determine what happened to humanity.

The traveller in Wells's narrative is never named. He's an eccentric, intelligent, highly driven British scientist.

In other words, he bears little resemblance to Eugene.

That said, Eugene couldn't help but feel a kinship of sorts with the one who navigated in the fourth dimension. In their respective work, both men had reached beyond what was thought possible.

Eugene had read Wells's foundational text as a freshman. The pages spoke to him as no novel before or since. It sparked a line of questions that might never be answered.

How old is the universe? How did it begin? How would it end? Would it end?

Most baffling: Why did something rather than nothing exist? Wouldn't nothing have been easier? More likely? No assembly required.

That brain-twisting bender could terrify, especially under cover of night.

The blinking number that had taken Eugene into Cidally's inner sanctum was far greater than the thirty million of Wells's protagonist. It numbered in the billions. The eleven-digit string was larger than the estimated age of the universe.

That random number – random to Eugene's way of thinking – had showed up after Verne's laser light show. Was it solely a result of that phenomenon or did it hold additional meaning?

Eugene hoped to find out. Emphasis on hope.

When first hired, Eugene had been told that the drone's energizing process required one second for every year of backtracking. So when he checked in on William Allerspan, at least forty seconds came off the clock before visuals began to populate the screen.

As such, this second-for-a-year rule should have precluded reaching back into prehistory. More than 500 years would have had to have elapsed before the drone could sufficiently charge for such an ambitious trip. Eugene would have been long dead before his flying friend left the building.

A check of Verne's console showed the number still in place. Why this whopper? And why now?

Could the late hour be affecting him? Eugene was coming up on a twelve-hour shift with no end in sight.

"Verne, my man," Eugene stated. "Help me understand."

In backpedaling billions of years, Eugene had landed in Cidally's office. He had spoken to her in real time.

Now, despite his aversion, he had to point the camera on himself. He had to go back, this time with the gym in his sights. If his hunch proved correct, he expected to come face to face with his ugly kisser!

He could not have been more right. Almost immediately, the small monitor began to function as a mirror. When Eugene furrowed his brow, so did his likeness on screen. When he waved, his digital counterpart did the same. When he jumped, so too did his other.

The camera, as he had intended, was positioned a few feet in front of him. Eugene couldn't see it, of course. But every readout indicated it had landed in the past at the same milepost as his visit with Cidally.

Eugene clapped his hands. His twin did also, the sound bouncing back in stereo. Eugene extended both middle fingers. His other uncorked a double bird as well.

As with Cidally, Verne appeared to be broadcasting in the present, as events unfolded. But that was impossible. Had it been live, the drone would have been visible. And since it wasn't, the drone had to have dredged up the past.

As improbable as it sounded, Eugene had to have been in this gym before. He had to have had performed these same actions eons ago. Gone through the same motions, with the same intensity, with the same befuddlement as he displayed at that moment.

What other conclusion could he reach?

Eugene recalled the drone. He tweaked the destination. He sent it back with the intent to record himself from behind.

Yes, sirree! When the feed appeared, Eugene saw the back of his head. And that head stared at a screen which displayed a slightly smaller back of his head which also stared at a screen which displayed an even smaller version of the back of his head. This lineup of the occiput, each tinier than the one before, telescoped backward into indistinguishability.

Call it a visual echo that continued indefinitely. Call it an infinity mirror.

Had he been an adherent of the Chinese philosopher Feng Shui, Eugene might have believed his life force had been thrown into a loop from which he could not escape. A never-ending tunnel that led nowhere. An illusion that added depth to an otherwise two-dimensional set-up.

Did existence – all that was and all that was to be – circle back 'round like the first day of spring? Was the arc of time simply a repeating background against which the same characters carried out the same actions with the same results?

For Eugene to have witnessed what he saw, each cycle would have to be an exact match. No deviations. For even one alteration – however minor – would have upset this stream of sameness. And if one alteration were permitted, there could have been a second and a third, potentially far more than even Eugene's lions could account for!

No, every one of Eugene's heads moved in unison. Every one a carbon copy of the one before.

This was synchronicity for the ages. Or, a terrible joke. What sane person would order reruns of a TV show with a single episode in the hopper? Creation had to be more than a one-hit wonder. Didn't it?

Eugene wrote down the massive number that had not stopped blinking. He doubled it, tripled it, quadrupled it, each time punching in a new multiple. And each time, the same never-ending, back-of-the-head display passed before his eyes. Either the cycle was real or Eugene had hit upon a malfunction that defied explanation.

The power outage. It had to be! Something had messed with Verne.

Eugene examined the drone. He subjected the console to a battery of tests.

No matter. Each time Eugene came face-to-face with multiples of himself. Even Socrates would have balked at so much self-reflection.

What do to next?

Eugene added one year to the number still lodged in Verne's console. No multiplication this time. Just simple addition. Theoretically, that would take him back an additional year. If so, he should get a front row seat to Verne being assembled in this very space.

As Eugene ordered Verne to dispatch the drone, the familiar Shepard tone commenced. Building and building, it headed nowhere. On and on, it confounded with its repetition.

While a newbie, Eugene had turned to YouTube to understand this type of Shepard. Some of the examples at that site came tagged with a warning that the audio could have psychological effects.

Eugene had never felt any sense of impairment. He tended to tune out when the Shepard sounded. His focus lay with the visuals.

But this tone persisted. Over and over. Snaking and winding, it soldiered on with no apparent end. The lengths to which it went would have tested anyone's patience.

Eugene aborted the mission. He ended the scheduled long-distance flight after just three minutes of energizing. He could no longer tolerate the incessant racket.

This getting nowhere was exactly what Eugene expected when he punched in the original number. Interminable waiting. Nothing but huffing and puffing as Verne spun his wheels trying to return to a time that predated civilization.

That number, the one that appeared after the great electrical fallout, must be a throughput, a passage between cycles where the tumblers of time align. Instead of churning backward, the drone just drops effortlessly through a wormhole, encountering no resistance as it chugs backward though as many cycles as requested.

Eugene was no scientist. But this conclusion – given what he knew – sounded reasonable.

The universe, apparently, was set to repeat, from big bang to big extinguish. The same show headlining the same theater under the same management.

Miss something the first time? Get it on the rebound.

Opening wide for a massive yawn, Eugene needed relief. This was a lot to process.

Cycle. Repeat. Cycle.

Faced with that reality, Eugene considered throwing himself down and gnashing his teeth. Maybe opening his lungs and screaming to the heavens.

As cleansing as that sounded, Eugene was too tired. Maybe tomorrow. Maybe his head would clear after a good night's sleep.

Tomorrow. The word stuck. The coming of a new dawn had always carried with it the possibility of something different, something new, something better. Celebrated in song and poetry alike, what was to come promised a new start.

Eugene wasn't so sure anymore. Having been let in on one of the greatest secrets in the universe, he understood the next twenty-four hours to be just as inflexible as the previous twenty-four. The concrete had cured. The future was set.

A depressing assessment, especially with the day running short. But Eugene was a realist. No troubadour, he preferred the straight scoop. Give him the facts, and he would take it from there.

Which, if he was thinking clearly this far past bedtime, meant he had a crystal ball at his disposal. One named Verne. An oracle so accurate, Nostradamus couldn't carry his jockstrap.

Eugene could peer into the future as he had done with the past if it was indeed predetermined. Well, technically not. What he could do is examine what transpired in the previous cycle after this night of revelation. He could know what was on tap as surely as the God of the Bible.

To get there, Eugene would enter the time component as a mathematical expression. He'd send the drone back via that billionoid number – a trip that should require no time at all – then have the little guy come forward a day, a week, or a month or two. Theoretically, the calendar yet published would be his.

Or maybe Verne would accept negative numbers. If so, that would simplify the process.

Whatever. Eugene had a game plan! That's all he needed. Cidally had told him as much.

New-found energy surged despite the late hour. Eugene had risen to meet the moment. He, a contemplationalist, had brain-powered his way to a solution.

Then, just as quickly, his euphoria faded. His sense of accomplishment fell by the wayside.

Eugene had done nothing new. He had come up with nothing innovative. Nothing other than what he always did during his time here on this planet.

That billionoid number. Why had it been there? Why did it blink so unmistakably bright?

Because it always had. In the never-ending story, this was the place – and time – where it showed its face.

Similarly, why had Eugene decided to look forward? Because he always did. His looking was the next bout on the main card.

Eugene pulled open the drawer just south of the console. He tore loose the child-resistant cap on a bottle of aspirin and placed two caplets on his tongue. He washed them down with the last of his soda.

Weary from abiding by cogent reasoning, Eugene let his mind go. He let it wander unburdened from the discoveries of the past few days. His grey matter deserved as much.

Unrestrained, free to roam, Eugene's brain cells hit upon one additional conclusion. One that had him seeing red.

Hamelton had been right. Perpetual motion was real. Set to auto pilot, the merry-go-round in the sky never stopped revolving. It had to. Cycling on repeat was the law of the land.

Anyone for the Bobby Fuller Four? As much as Eugene wanted to fight back against this notion of perpetual motion, he was inclined to lay odds that the law would win.

Didn't it always?

Chapter Twenty-Two

The mustachioed, heavyset barkeep parked two pints in front of Darby and Eugene. He scooped up a twenty and headed for the cash register.

Part watering hole, part sports bar, Gastmeyer's had become popular with the college crowd as a fixture on one of the area's busiest street corners. The establishment had occasionally doubled as lodging for Darby who, years earlier, had awakened in the basement storeroom after a night of revelry.

In a stand against time, the saloon utilized printed menus, rotary desk phones and word-of-mouth advertising. Its reluctance to modernize, however, did not extend to amenities such as ultra-high definition, lightning-quick broadband and tap-to-pay credit card readers.

"So, what do you think of the new guy?" Darby asked, savoring a swallow of suds.

"Brody? He's okay, I guess," Eugene answered, adjusting his palate to the bitterness of the IPA Darby had suggested.

"Okay? My God, his body is a temple," Darby protested, faux annoyance rising. "It's sacred space. Prostrate yourself at the altar of Brody!"

The barkeep, his forearms thick with bristled hair, slapped change upon the bar. Puffing out his chest, he chipped in two cents of his own.

"My body used to be a temple," he boasted. Then, his thumbs pointing back at himself, he added. "But for too long I have worshipped at the altar of food and drink!"

Darby raised his drink. Eugene held his aloft as well.

An hour earlier, Eugene had been ready to explore the future as it played out in the previous cycle. He never got the chance as Darby swung by to inform him that a pair of Saint Pauli Girls had requested their presence at Gastmeyer's.

Eugene's efforts to beg off went nowhere. Darby craved liquid refreshment and he refused to drink alone. Besides, he was buying.

Reluctantly and under protest, Eugene agreed to go. Who knew what Darby might say when sufficiently sozzled?

As the two men sluiced their gullets with additional citrus, other narratives played out, many reflected in the large mirror behind the bar. In a corner cubby, roommates fumbled through a game of Fuzzy Duck. Up against the jukebox, a hands-on couple shared their first kiss. Near the fireplace, grad students debated politics, their convictions as loud as their voices.

"Let's assume you're right," Darby said, holding a quarter upright with one forefinger while giving it a spin with the other. "Let's say there is a cycle. So what?"

Eugene squeegeed the condensation on the outside of his glass. His finger damp, he traced circles around his coaster.

"You've asked me that question billions of times," Eugene replied. "Doesn't it get old?"

"You tell me," Darby fired back, glancing at the wall calendar. "In my book, this is the first time we've been to Gastmeyer's together."

Eugene's penetrating look had Darby reconsidering his response.

"Okay. The first time I can *remember* going out after work together. So what if we've been here before? What's the big deal?"

"We're stuck," Eugene stated flatly. "Plain and simple, we don't advance any farther than we did last time."

"And how far is that?" Darby asked, eyeing a strawberry blond stirring her martini.

Honestly, Eugene didn't know. A satisfactory comeback eluded him.

"Truth is, you don't know," Darby said, giving voice to what Eugene had been loath to express. "You don't know what tomorrow brings any more than the next guy."

Eugene balled his right hand into a fist and rapped wood.

"I'm limited," Eugene declared. "I can never improve on who I was in the previous cycle."

"Improve? You want to be a doctor? Go back to school. Want to stop smoking? Try hypnosis. Want more friends? Buy a round of drinks!" Darby lectured. "The self-help industry generates billions of dollars every year. They would welcome your money."

Eugene rubbed his forehead. He wiped his chin with his left hand.

"Remember when you could set your VCR to record a game while you were out?" he began. "Later, not knowing who won, you'd watch it back the next day.

"Well, let's say that as you sit there, eyes glued to the screen, you notice that the opposition cannot stop the toss sweep. Keep running that play and your hometown boys win.

"You get the coach on the phone. You tell him to keep running that play. It could mean the difference between winning and losing.

"Problem: The game ended hours ago. All you did was awaken an ornery cuss who finally got to sleep after a heart-wrenching loss to an old rival. The final score had been posted hours ago. You were a loser before you hit play, and there is absolutely nothing you can do to change that."

"And you feel like a loser?" Darby guessed.

"No," Eugene protested. "I'm the guy who can't change the outcome!"

"How is that any different than if you're cheering live in the stands?" Darby questioned.

"The end result has yet to be determined," Eugene clapped back, his frustration mounting.

"Clearly, you're not a professional wrestling fan," Darby joked.

A wrestling reference? That was the best Darby had to offer?

Eugene had been hoping for a sympathetic ear. A sounding board that would appreciate this new reality. Confirm its magnitude and implications.

Apparently, he was asking for too much. Time to abandon the toss sweep.

"Hey, Casanova," Eugene addressed Darby. "Bad news. You're going to die by the hand of a jealous husband. In this life and all that follow, you wind up dead because of your philandering. What are you going to do?"

"When, exactly, do I meet my maker?" Darby asked, admiring the speed with which three sorority sisters downed shots of Fireball.

"Sooner than you think," Eugene warned.

"All the more reason to introduce myself to some of the fine clientele here tonight." Darby concluded as he surveyed the premises for the exciting, unusual or absurd.

Eugene mouthed an "OMG." Darby's head no longer manned his tiller. Control had been usurped by a nerve center a little lower on his body.

Nearby, a man and woman held hands, each scrolling through a phone. The bartender shook dice with a couple celebrating their anniversary. A pair of twins – on tiptoe – waved in an attempt to flag down a group that had just entered.

Eugene risked slipping into a discomfiting solitude even as a steady stream of incoming youth added to the social setting. Never to be confused with a Greek god, he nevertheless found himself shouldering the burden borne by Atlas.

Whap! The smack of flesh on timber turned heads.

Eugene, his hand stinging from having slammed wood, whispered into Darby's ear. He leaned in close, far enough that those who took note probably thought he had kissed the older man.

"What?" Darby asked, unable to decode what Eugene had said.

Eugene leaned in again, making no attempt at clarity.

"Speak up," Darby ordered. "I can't hear you!"

Eugene murmured a third time. Then a fourth. Each time he made sure Darby could not decipher what he was saying.

"You think I'm stupid?" Darby boomed, catching on to Eugene's ploy. "You think I don't know what you're doing?!"

"What!" Eugene retorted, raising his arms as if innocent of any charges that might get leveled. "You tired of this game? Already? And I wanted to play for all eternity."

Eugene steered a bowl of pretzels his way. Perhaps a snack might offset his rising blood alcohol content.

"Listen, I'd be okay with returning as long as the script got tweaked, even just a little," Eugene admitted. "But it doesn't."

Cheers erupted to Eugene's right. High fives gave way to orders for more libations.

"Grand slam homer in the bottom of the ninth. Don't see that every day," marveled a voice over the din.

"It's control you're after, isn't it?" Darby speculated. "That's what this is all about."

"I want to drive the bus," Eugene agreed.

Noting Eugene's somber mood, Darby broke into song.

"And the wheels on the bus go round and round, round and round, round and round. All through the town."

"You're a diphthong," Eugene unloaded. "I expected more from you."

Darby slugged the last of his beer and requested a refill. Eugene, too, ordered another.

Maybe Darby's refusal to engage had more to do with the messenger than the message. Eugene had become accustomed to being ignored, so much so that he often followed the gaze of those to whom he was talking to see what they found more compelling.

What really stung was when these same folks – bored and distracted with his presentation – later floated the very same ideas that had originated with him. These sneaky plagiarists got others to buy in because they could play to an audience better than he could. Eugene's insights – DOA in his possession – flourished when promoted by loudmouths with far less imagination.

Eugene had coined a nickname for them: air controlling traffickers, or ACTs. In blowing hot air, they could give flight to just about any inane notion.

"Ever notice how many people stare into their phones?" Darby remarked to no one in particular. "Even amid wall-to-wall humanity, they choose bells and whistles over physical interaction."

"That a problem, old-timer?" a miffed Eugene asked.

"Problem, no," Darby corrected. "Opportunity, yes."

A truncated burp slipped past Eugene. The eructation bolstered the rich flavor of pretzel headlining his taste buds.

"How 'bout a game?" Darby suggested. "When someone comes in, let's see how long it takes before they check their phone?"

Eugene slammed a handful of popcorn, losing a few kernels as he repositioned to face the entrance.

"Well-built hottie at the door," Darby announced. "What do you think?

"She looks around. Cranes her neck. Where can her party be? Ah, over there. She waves. Smiles.

"And down she goes, checking her phone before joining the others. How long was that?"

"Fast!" Eugene replied, getting the word out between bites.

"Damn right," Darby concurred.

"And look at those bozos," Darby redirected. "Faces in their phones as they walk in. I suppose I should give them credit for multitasking."

"What's your point?" Eugene queried, his fingers dipped in butter and salt.

"Everyone suckles at the teet of 5G," Darby observed, back resting against the bar. "We have a rapt audience. Verne's gonna be the next social media sensation."

Darby elongated the *meee* in media.

"That brunette who just came in," Darby pointed out. "She suffers from vasovagal syncope. She faints at the sight of her own blood."

"And those two lug nuts?" he prattled on. "They removed a stop sign when they were kids. Thanks to their stupid prank, two elderly women died."

"What are you talking about," Eugene asked. "How do you know?"

"With Verne in business, people will be known by their afflictions, their mistakes, their most intimate moments, not by their real names. That brunette? She becomes Vago the Vixen. Lug nut One and Two? They are the Sign Swipers."

Darby forged ahead, plowing into realms Eugene had yet to contemplate.

"We – you, me, the world – will know a person's every tattoo, whether they pick their nose and what sexual positions they prefer. We will know their net worth, their criminal past and their medical history. We'll know them better than they know themselves."

Eugene looked around. Were others listening to this air controlling trafficker?

"A person will be judged – acceptably or unacceptably – before we meet them."

"Scarlet letter," Darby rambled on. "Today's Hester Prynne would merit a time stamp. A big red flag to mark where she sank to her lowest so we all can go back and watch her fall."

"And that is something to celebrate?" Eugene pushed back.

"They say history is boring. Not when it involves your neighbor," Darby rolled on. "Forget googling. People will be Verning – digital Dumpster diving – the good, the bad and the ugly. Every life fair game. Every second ready for review.

"That includes you," Eugene pointed out. "People are going to be looking at you!"

"They had better," Darby agreed with gusto. "Especially as I laugh my ass off on the way to the bank!"

Darby spewed with a glee and ease that startled. Where were his scruples?

"You're suggesting the end of privacy," Eugene declared.

"Suggesting?" Darby repeated. "I'm guaranteeing it!"

Darby rocked and swayed atop his synthetic swivel seat. "We cannot be lied to anymore. We cannot be kept in the dark. The playing field will be leveled," Darby prophesized. "The never-blinking camera will usher in an age of truthfulness, understanding and accountability. We will never look back by always looking back."

As Darby sucked in oxygen to fuel his rant, Eugene teed up a frightening scenario.

"You okay with your never-blinking camera recording a serial killer dismembering his victims?" Eugene proposed, hoping to sober Darby.

"Get the time and coordinates right ...," came the cheerful reply.

"That's sick!" Eugene protested.

"And profitable!"

Had the Devil himself slipped in unnoticed?

"You really haven't thought this through, have you?" Darby chided, aware for the first time how little thought Eugene had given the subject. "Anonymity is dead. No one can hide from his past."

Eugene squeezed his liquid refreshment tighter. How easy it would be to pour it over Darby's head and run. With surprise on his side, he might even reach the exit before his drenched companion did.

But Darby, he of depraved and addled mind, was only part of the problem. He and Hamelton were but symptoms of the same infectious disease: fame and fortune. They were merely building upon – albeit without his permission – the work of Clancy Wigwort.

Clancy had to have known the ramifications of the secret he had unlocked. He had to have known the extent to which it could devastate. What wounds it would lay bare. What lives it would destroy.

Perhaps that's why he had never put his theory into practice. He had a conscience, something Darby was ready to write off for a few pieces of gold.

"Oh, come on," Darby said, shifting gears. "Nearly everything known to man can be used for good or bad. Medicines can have dangerous side effects. Cars can mow down crowds of spectators. The life-saving syringe can kill with an air bubble to a blood vessel."

"Is that going to be your advertising campaign?" Eugene spewed. "We are not to blame. Some material may not be suitable for children? You've been sitting here touting the dark side of Verne with crazy-assed enthusiasm. How you are going to exploit vulnerabilities. How misery will fill your coffers.

"Well, count me out!" Eugene declared with a certitude that would not be shaken.

"Whoa, big fellah," Darby said, grabbing the younger man's arm. "Let me finish."

With a violent tug, Eugene shook free. No way he would allow contact with one who embraced evil.

"Look," Darby reset. "Everything I just said – forget it. It's not going to happen."

"You seemed pretty damned sure while running your mouth," Eugene stressed.

"Listen," Darby ordered, palms facing outward as he dialed down. "Governments, law enforcement, the courts – they are going to shut down Verne and his offspring or regulate the hell out of them. No way we get a free pass. No way they allow cameras behind closed doors."

"And that's okay," he continued, "because we will be long gone. We will have sold out to the highest bidders."

So, that was the plan. Score big, get out, and leave the cleanup to others.

"How many lives are you going to ruin? How much pain will you inflict? How many pounds of flesh?" Eugene flared.

"That's the cost of doing business," Darby intoned.

"You mean the price of peddling poison," Eugene corrected. "What kind of monster are you?"

With logic and reason getting him nowhere, Eugene went personal. He broached the unthinkable. He delved into territory best left uncharted.

He also prepared to duck and cover.

"I'll be posting video of your daughter, Sabrina, getting molested at day care. Janitor takes down her pants and has his way. She's crying; he's defiling. I'm betting it goes viral!"

Darby's little girl had never been molested. A hand had never been raised against her.

And Eugene had never said something so audacious and inflammatory. Not even close. Especially not to one who controlled his livelihood, one who could end his career, such as it was.

Eugene's words – so despicable, so raw, so close to the heart – shredded the smugness under which Darby had been operating. It obliterated his holier-than-thou attitude, forcing him to choke on a small sample of the damage to come.

It was an air bubble that could kill.

"You son of a bitch," Darby roared. "Get the hell out of here."

"Has the cost of business gotten too high?" Eugene taunted.

In a flash, Darby was up, his bar stool clattering to the floor. He took a swing, a looping roundhouse so wide of the mark it nearly dropped its originator to the floor.

"You go to hell," Darby shouted, as a bouncer closed in. "You crossed a line, you piece of crap!"

Yes, sir! Eugene had crossed a line and he'd do it again. And again. He'd cross it as often as he pleased; as often as the cycle persisted.

Eugene had finally gotten through. He had knocked Darby off his high horse. He – not some plagariast – had gotten his message across.

Entering Gastmeyer's, Eugene had been consumed by a universe on repeat. Leaving the establishment, he fixated on a technology that would destroy.

Hamelton had to be stopped. Permanently.

Even without a show of hands, Eugene understood he was the only man for the job. A daunting task, yes, but an assignment he could complete by cheating. Eugene – the teacher's pet – would sneak a peek at the paper turned in by the Eugene of the previous cycle. He would once again become history's greatest copycat!

Friday

Chapter Twenty-Three

Bar hoppers, a half dozen or so, slipped inside Gastmeyer's as Eugene held open the door. The last to file through, a dead ringer for Cidally, winked as she passed by.

Eugene had to look twice to confirm the playful patron was not the woman for whom he pined. Her resemblance was such that he had to fight the urge to head back inside.

This was not the first time Eugene thought he had seen Cidally outside work. He had spied her in an aisle at a home improvement outlet. He had glimpsed her behind the wheel of a Corvette. He had caught sight of her playing fetch with an Alaskan Malamute.

Each time he had been mistaken. Each time he had been disheartened.

How Eugene would have loved to have discussed the cycle with Cidally rather than Darby. Unlike the fulminating fool he had just shut down, she would have listened, empathized and offered insight.

But Cidally hadn't asked him out. Darby had extended the mandatory invitation. So until Eugene could harness sufficient courage, a date with Cidally would remain a pipe dream.

Eugene closed his eyes as he stepped into the night air. He savored the warm breeze tinged with garlic and oregano from nearby Spiganelli's.

In the street, passersby negotiated light traffic skipping from one side of the roadway to the other. Cars slowed for the less nimble. Horns blared at the intentionally obstructive.

On the sidewalk, scores of night owls strolled about seemingly with no destination in mind. Friends posed for photos. Frat boys did push-ups, one for every chime that emanated from the two-dial street clock as it struck midnight.

Most did not have to work on this Friday before the Fourth of July. Most did not include Eugene.

Beginning the considerable walk to St. Anthony's, Eugene noted the pan-tilt zoom security cameras affixed to Millar's Drug Store. He waved to the dome cameras attached to Stubner's Jewelers. He stuck out his tongue at the bullet cameras that dotted the exterior of Hixnar's. And he came within a belt buckle of mooning the fisheye setup that clung to the covered walkway leading into the courthouse.

Could he have wondered into Taiyuan, China, the most surveilled city on earth?

While navigating the gauntlet of lenses – an invasion of privacy in Eugene's book – he had to credit their honesty. Clearly visible, the cameras made no attempt to mask their intentions.

"Yes," they announced, "we are here." "Yes," they admitted, "we are recording your every move." "Yes," they promised, "There will be more of us – many more – in the years to come."

Bordering on the ubiquitous, the cameras nevertheless had their limits. Eugene could and did move out of their range. He could have avoided them altogether had he taken another route.

Verne, on the other hand, faced no such restraints. He could move through space and time with the ease of smoke filling a room.

More terrifying, the Big Guy operated on the down low, out of sight. His accomplice, the drone, was the definition of discreet, the ultimate uninvited guest.

Like Big Brother, Verne would be everywhere: listening, watching, recording. Every hair of every head numbered. Every action of every individual documented. Cyberstalking on speed.

Eugene bit his lip hoping to stanch the negative. Maybe he was wrong. Maybe society would function better under the glare of a spotlight. The intense scrutiny might serve as a disinfectant, destroying thoughts of wrongdoing before they could germinate.

Eugene had heard that people behaved more altruistically in the presence of an observer. Dishonest behavior dipped. Property theft decreased. Burglaries diminished.

Hamelton could market Verne as the ultimate cop: McGruff, the seeing-crime dog. Spayed, neutered and house broken, this canine sniffs out corruption in real time. As a member of the paw patrol, he can't be bribed or influenced. His bite is more formidable than his bark.

The idea held promise. Until it went to the dogs.

Cameras had no significant effect on violent crime. The possibility of being recorded did not neutralize out-of-control emotions or prevent spur-of-the-moment mayhem. Those set on wreaking havoc would carry on regardless. No supercomputer could dissuade the stupid or the reckless.

Verne, of course, would be utilized for more than law enforcement. He would poke his nose into bedrooms, back rooms and bathrooms. He'd roll in the lurid, the obscene and the gross. He'd drop turds of deep, dark depravity.

The demand for the base and twisted never wanes. Video games promise intentional harm and graphic violence. Torture movies traffic in killing, maiming and dismemberment. Literature had offered up morally reprehensible themes as far back as ancient times.

Even the day's headlines touted the terrible. If someone wasn't shooting up a school with semiautomatic weapons, they were mowing down pedestrians with a vehicle. If someone wasn't poisoning a relative, they were strangling a stranger.

And Mother Nature? That old broad dished out earthquakes, cyclones, wildfires, floods and famines. Pick a number, make a wager and lose it all on her roulette wheel of destruction.

His mind awhirl, Eugene leaned against a Do Not Enter sign. He welcomed in the moist summer air with big, drawn-out gulps. Not through his nose, but through his mouth. If he continued down this path, his head might explode.

His wouldn't, of course. But others had not been so fortunate. Like the teen he had read about years ago, the one whose death unleashed a strain of inhumanity so repulsive it sickened.

In dredging up a story he would rather have forgotten, Eugene's eyes moistened. Replaying this tragedy would again break his heart.

This young lady, a college freshman living with her parents, got into an argument with her father. After he left for work, she went into the garage and took off with his Porsche 911 Carrera. She had never been behind the wheel of this high-powered sports car and had been forbidden from driving it.

Didn't matter. Hitting the accelerator, she raced down the highway at speeds topping 100 miles per hour. Weaving through the congested thoroughfare, she clipped a slower-moving Honda Civic, which sent her careening into an unmanned, concrete toll booth. She was killed instantly.

Her family was devastated. But their nightmare had only begun.

Photos taken by law enforcement were leaked and found their way onto the internet. Anyone with a computer could gawk at pictures of the nearly decapitated teen.

Despicable trolls did more than look. Some said the out-of-control driver was a spoiled little rich girl who deserved to die. Others lamented the accident, saying a good car had gone to waste.

Human scum mailed the photos to the parents with a note saying their daughter was still alive. They mocked the family, making their life a living hell.

The images had yet to be taken down from online sites two decades after that horrific accident. In death, the aspiring photographer had become known as the "Porsche Girl."

How many more Porsche Girls were out there? How many lives would be ruined if Verne was hidden in every phone, tablet and electronic device?

Darby, damn him, had been right. Everyone would get labeled by a past episode. Everyone would be distilled down to a moment they longed to take back.

Kicking a soda can, then smacking it again, Eugene recommitted to his prime objective: torpedo Hamelton. Kick the legs out from under the mother searsucker. Thank you, Cidally!

But how?

Warn the public? He'd get no further than he did with Darby at Gastmeyer's. Poison Hamelton? Out of the question, but the thought did afford some perverse pleasure. Set fire to St. Anthony's? His knowledge of arson did not extend beyond striking a match.

A fourth avenue, one Eugene repeatedly disregarded even as it overspread his thoughts, gnawed at him. Why not sabotage? Disconnect a cable, remove a semiconductor, disable a CPU or lay siege to a motherboard? He might even rig a debilitating sequence that could be actuated by Darby or Hamelton without either being the wiser.

It sounded simple. And within reach. But such acts would harm his binary buddy. And that was verboten.

Verne shouldered no blame for this mess. He had done nothing but what was asked of him. It was those pulling his strings who needed to be held accountable.

Ahead, the weed-ridden cemetery of St. Anthony came into focus. Leaves skittered across pine straw. Branches swayed in the breeze. Eugene's arms turned to gooseflesh.

Cold and stoic, the rows of headstones testified to the finality of death.

Eugene usually quickened his pace when passing by those who had passed on. In a routine culled from childhood, he hurried to keep the dead from becoming jealous of his living, respiring ways.

But not this time. Eugene surveyed names – Lund, Walsh, Rheintgen, Budde, Leptich. He imagined how each would have appeared in his or her prime. He studied the years engraved, using that information to calculate lifespans. He lingered, unable to countenance why some reached old age while others were snatched in childhood.

A weather-beaten cross in the back row – an outlier in distance – had fallen into neglect. Based upon the surrounding mud, crabgrass and dandelions, not even the caretaker came near. A good place, perhaps, to bury something that might otherwise land one in trouble should it go missing.

The name on the marker: Edward Broscott. The accompanying message: "Given too little; given not a lot!"

How true! Not just for Broscott, but for every soul resting within! Given a choice, how many would have returned for more? How many would have opted to continue living: one more sunrise, one more triumph, one more heartache?

Living – even on a hamster wheel – was always more enticing than the alternative.

And what of those who would never be called? Those individuals never born because this lone reel of reality never got replaced? Might they, given a chance, outperform those who continuously came and went? Might they not avoid the mistakes made by the familiar ensemble that marched on stage with every turn of the wheel?

Who advocated for them?

Eugene was no John Lennon, but the same chords moved him. He could imagine. It wasn't hard to do.

Of course, in a new cycle, humans might fail to evolve. A new breed – manipulative, egotistical, vengeful, exploitative – might come to power. Hamelton and his ilk would become the norm, not the exception. Law abiders might go the way of the golden toad.

Or, maybe no earth would be forthcoming at all. No planets. No solar system. No Milky Way. No intelligent life.

Would that be so bad?

In bailing on Gastmeyer's, Eugene had hoped to clear his head. Instead, he had more food for thought than he could stomach.

Back peddling from the matrix of the deceased, Eugene entered the asphalt expanse in front of St. Anthony's. The pockmarked lot, its many stalls empty, provided ample space for six middle-schoolers to dribble by, each searching for the pretty lady who could rebound.

Eugene, like those figments of his imagination, also yearned for that lady. Cidally could sneak into his thoughts as easily as she could glide to the rim for a layup.

Ahead, the blinds to her office remained open.

"Cidally, Cidally, let down your hair," Eugene play-acted, dropping to one knee. "Fair maiden, I wish to gain entrance by climbing your flaxen tresses."

Eugene cupped one hand to his ear. His eyes widened in anticipation, then squeezed shut. He hung his head, disappointed again.

"I see," he said, continuing the charade. "You'll let me into the building, but not into your heart. 'Tis not what I want, but I shan't get greedy."

Getting to his feet, Eugene climbed the cobblestone that led to the school. How to gain admission to the brick fortress?

From Day One, he had been told to stay away from campus unless Darby or Hamelton was present. The two had given him no means by which to gain entrance.

No problem. Verne had long ago validated his ticket.

Every morning, Cidally and Darby blocked the pin pad when they punched in. Not so Hamelton. Cocky and defiant, he refused to act as a human shield. Discovering his code was as easy as having the drone spy on him as he entered the sequence of numbers that granted him access.

What a fool!

For months, Eugene had no reason to utilize Hamelton's PIN. Now, the old fart's failure to safeguard beckoned as an open-ended invitation.

How fitting that Hamelton's arrogance might precipitate his downfall. And if the cocksure codger needed a little push, Eugene was ready to apply one just as he did to the now-unlocked front door.

Chapter Twenty-Four

"Shuffle, ball, change," exhorted the elderly woman at the front of the studio.

Sashaying with the energy of an individual half her age, the instructor modeled every dance step as two rows of second graders sought to mimic her movements. The octogenarian doled out encouragement at every turn, keeping her charges on their heels until one too many fell out of line. Then, with a wave of her flappy arms, the discordant motion ceased.

Mrs. Dee had been choreographing dance routines set to music for children of all ages for fifty years. Generation after generation had returned to her so that she now worked with the children, grandchildren and even great-grandchildren of former students. Her waiting room overflowed with notes, cards and photos from those who had celebrated life with her.

Called to order, the bevy of ballerinas awaited further instruction. Eugene, too, came to attention as best he could.

Droopy-eyed, cotton-mouthed and unshaven from having spent the early morning rooting through time, Eugene had again taken leave in Hasmire's classroom. He had put Verne through the paces in the hours after midnight as if a prize fighter. The two hopscotched into the future, bouncing from one coming attraction to another. They pushed on, maintaining their feverish pitch until fatigue trumped fact finding and Eugene called timeout.

Dead on his feet and aching in his joints, Eugene had grabbed his laptop. He mounted the stairs as if in a trance and shuffled to his familiar third-floor getaway. There, as always, he bummed a ride to the past, this time rolling footage of the spinster in her element.

Mrs. Dee's troupe of aspiring Rockettes gathered once a week. Eugene looked forward to their tap-tap-tapping not because of his love for children, but because a certain former student volunteered her time and talents.

Off to the side, Cidally fiddled with the shoe of a girl raring to join her friends. She reminded the bundle of energy to wait until the music stopped before zooming headlong into the fray.

"What's the word of the day?" Mrs. Dee asked, encamping atop a three-legged stool.

A chorus of, "I know, I know!" surged, each respondent inching closer.

"Discipline, yes, discipline," Mrs. Dee agreed as shouted answers pinged off the walls.

Since Eugene had discovered Cidally's side gig, he had come to understand that Mrs. Dee taught life lessons as well as footwork. Instilling character and integrity ranked higher than preaching straight lines and rhythm. Good people made good dancers.

Cidally had taken Mrs. Dee's words to heart. Not a week went by that she did not reference her ballet and tap days, expressing a fondness for the woman who handed out pennies for bubblegum after a workout.

"Discipline," Mrs. Dee continued. "You know, like when there's a big bowl of candy on the table and Mother is gone. You could eat the whole thing, right? But you have to discipline yourself. And how many pieces do you take?"

"Three," piped up a swinging pair of pigtails from the back row.

As the noise level dipped, the little girl knew she had overstepped. Three for one child? How selfish! She couldn't get away with that. Or could she?

"One for me and two for my brothers," she improvised, citing a generosity she rarely practiced.

The littles in leotards broke into giggles. Everyone knew Jenny Lou had no siblings.

Eugene, too, always got a kick out of Jenny Lou's comebacks. Her timing and delivery matched that of a seasoned comic.

So full of life, these youngsters couldn't tell a Hamelton from a Darby. They had no clue their childhoods would soon be stolen, their innocence a quaint relic of yesteryear.

As rays of sun poked through the blinds in Hasmire's Hangout, yesterday, today and tomorrow melded, a singularity of time that had Eugene knocking on the door of enlightenment. Or sleep, whichever came first.

Sounds faded, taking on a faraway tinniness. Objects appeared to liquify, melting as if brush strokes in a Dali painting. Rest, so lacking, finally gained a foothold.

Eugene's snoring, mild at first, hardened into the stridor that comes with an obstructed windpipe. Exhausted, the globetrotting timekeeper renounced control, his subconscious taking the wheel.

Even in slumber, Eugene could not escape the gymnasium. Within its confines yet again, he recoiled as his two former bosses stoked a throng that overflowed the bleachers.

"Welcome to the Amphitheater of the Always!" Hamelton intoned, costumed in top hat and tailcoat.

"Yes, we know you have seen this show before," Pastor Paul noted, vested in cassock, alb, stole and chasuble from St. Anthony's. "But you waited for hours to get inside anyway."

The two preachers – only one ordained by the church – spread wide their arms in welcome. They spoke – each atop their own pulpit – from where the scorer's table had been.

Eugene sat mid-court in a folding chair that wobbled. He could not get the fourth leg to make contact as did the other three.

"Eugene, my friend – may I call you my friend?" Hamelton ridiculed. "We have noticed that for all the time you spend in the past, you don't turn the camera on yourself. Why?"

The wobbliness under Eugene worsened.

"My guess," ventured Pastor Paul, "is he can't bear to look. No one aspires to be Eugene. Not even Eugene."

"How insightful!" Hamelton praised. "Can I get an alleluia?"

The jaws of those present clicked open and shut.

"Hey, you," Hamelton called out. "Yeah, you! Mr. Nobody. We need that canister over here. Yes, the one that encompasses forty-five years but weighs less than a pound."

A wizened man, clad in a sleeveless shirt and shorts, threaded a movie projector. The stooped figure advanced the celluloid frame by frame. He stopped short of the disclaimer: "This film has not yet been rated."

Pop Top!

"Afraid of your shadow, are you boy?" Hamelton toyed with Eugene. "Well, prepare to be scared out of your skin. Light up the Big Boy!"

Screen ablaze, the raucous venue came alive as never before. Eugene rocked back and forth as his life story commenced. He couldn't cover his eyes because his arms were zip tied in back.

"What's the problem, my son?" Pastor Paul probed. "Not yet a disciple? You'll come 'round!"

The camera, unrestrained by convention, pushed its way into a neonatal intensive care unit.

"Those who are squeamish might want to look away," Hamelton advised. "The blender is about to be born."

Eugene's mother, younger than he remembered her, writhed in pain. She sought to jettison the source of her torment.

Eugene squeezed his eyes shut. He kept them closed even as the announcement, "It's a boy!" rang from the rafters.

"You really should watch this." a friendly voice encouraged. "I'll hold your hand."

Cidally, her tight body throwing off heat, had sidled up to Eugene. She placed her arms on his shoulders.

"Don't you want me to get to know you better?" she purred. "The real you. The you when no one is looking?"

God, no! Eugene did not want to look at the Eugene when no one was looking.

"Everyone wants to be on camera," Cidally asserted. "Instagram. TikTok. Snapchat. Haven't you been classically trained? Wag your tongue, flap your arms, go goofy when in the frame? All the world is a screen!"

"No," Eugene countered. "I don't own a cell phone."

Pastor Paul stopped sprinkling holy water. Hamelton passed out his last cigar.

"Blasphemy!" they rebuked in unison.

The men dismounted their towering perches and circled Eugene, the man of the cloth going with the clock, the carnival barker going against.

"He doesn't want to recall what he's done or what he's failed to do," the pastor explained. "He'd rather remove his eye than see a past littered with failure."

"This, then, is an intervention," Hamilton concluded. "A forced reckoning. A long overdue reminder of who he was and who he is."

Eugene strained to find an ally – where had Cidally gone? – someone who might release him from the center square. But craning his neck only brought Hamelton and Paul closer.

"A blender among blenders?" Hamelton declared.

"Chaff among the wheat," Paul agreed.

"Zero stars," Hamelton said, his thumb pointing down.

"His father said as much," Paul added. "Don't you remember?"

Eugene did. He remembered as if it had happened yesterday. And then, as now, he wrapped himself in an overcoat of unworthiness tailor-made for him.

Not yet ten and supposed to be in bed, Eugene instead listened at the top of the stairs as his parents hosted a rare get-together. The voices. The jokes. The fun.

If this was adulthood, Eugene couldn't wait to grow up!

The merrymaking rolled on for hours until an unfunny bit hit the fan. Eugene's father – BAC up, inhibitions down – delivered the coup de grace: a punch line so offensive it left everyone speechless. As guests rushed in to limit the damage, Eugene's father repeated himself, thinking no one understood the joke.

"My son was a Eug mistake! A Eug mistake! Get it? E-U-G. Huge."

The gathering broke up almost immediately. As noisy as the party had been, its volume couldn't match the yelling that followed. Eugene's mother lit into her husband, ordering him to spend the night in the garage.

Eugene, who cried throughout the night, never mentioned the incident to anyone.

"How's that for an oldie but a goodie?" Hamelton crackled, his pupils fixed and dilated.

"Do you know why we hired you?" the gleeful goon pressed on.

"I'll give you a hint," Pastor Paul offered. "It wasn't because of any skill or talent."

"You follow orders," Hamelton summed up. "You always have. You always will."

"Tell him how we know," Pastor Paul squealed. "Tell him what we did!"

Hamelton put a finger to his lips. With one digit, he stilled every voice.

"Verne vetted you," he revealed with relish. "We screened countless hours of your life before we brought you into the fold. We saw everything. We saw you sleeping. We saw you awake. We saw you when you were naughty and we saw you when you were nice."

Of course they had. Logic dictated as much. Going forward, background checks would include a heavy dose of Verne. Embellished resumes would be flagged and shredded. Nobody's business would become everybody's business.

"Nowhere to hide, my friend," Hamelton promised. "These drones will only get smaller. They will enter every crack and orifice. They will monitor blood flow, enzyme levels, lipid panels, heart rate – the whole package. Sneeze, and someone in Singapore will shout, 'Bless you!' Pass gas, and the EPA will label you a contamination site."

"Those buggers will chew their way into your brain," Pastor Paul continued, taking the baton. "Cerebrum, thalamus, temporal lobe, cerebellum ... these tiny flyers will infest faster than locusts. They will seize total control.

"They will do a better job of being Eugene than you ever did!"

Hamelton broke into a Cheshire cat grin. He squeezed Eugene's cheeks until the buccal regions turned white.

"If you could go back and change one thing in your life, what would that be?" Hamelton queried, trotting out his old tried and true. "Would you: a) decline to interview for this job; b) rat out Pastor Paul; or c) make a move on that little vixen of yours?"

"I can't change the past!" Eugene spit up with the force of a toddler expelling unwanted vegetables. "You told me so yourself!"

"Oh, but you can!" Hamelton insisted. "You'll get another chance. And another after that. This blessed cycle will lead you here again and again. The same nightmare over and over.

"Terrifying, isn't it? But you have the power to make a difference, to start fresh. Not in your past, but in your future. You could point this Amphitheater of the Always in a totally new direction."

Hamelton added this rejoinder to his motivational speech:

"But you won't. You don't have the guts. You don't have the balls!"

The gymnasium erupted. The crowd sprang to its feet. A standing, whooping, no-holds barred ovation ensued.

Hamelton and Paul strutted, waving to the multitudes. They bowed as additional applause threatened to raise the roof.

"You know," a tiny voice advised, "you don't have to fight fair."

Cidally once more placed her hands on Eugene's shoulders.

"Are you telling me it's okay to lie?" Eugene asked, his hearing thrown off by rhythmic cries of "Skrean Time! Skrean Time!"

"How do you think we women deal with the male ego?" Cidally purred, her aura never brighter.

Still shackled, Eugene scooted his chair forward in increments, hoping to break free. The on-again, off-again of metal scraping wood caught Hamelton's attention.

"Guards," Hamelton thundered. "Grab that woman!"

Four men, biceps the size of Eugene's thighs, surrounded Cidally. They grabbed her, sausage fingers covering her mouth.

"No!" Eugene shouted. "Let her go!"

Cidally attempted to use the men's leverage against them, but to no avail. Four against one, especially when the detainee was smaller in stature, amounted to no contest.

"Off with her head!" the crowd chanted. "Off with her head!"

Chest tightening, heart in overdrive, Eugene slammed the metal below him against the floor. Blow after blow, ka-thunk after ka-thunk, yet the chair remained intact.

"Off with her head!" the cries went up again. "Off with her head!"

The repetitiveness disoriented. The chanting overwhelmed.

"Off with her head," Hamelton hissed to Eugene. "Care to do the honors?"

As Eugene swatted away the knife presented by Hamelton, the ground beneath him fell away. Like a rocket shedding a core stage, the hardwood floor grew smaller and smaller until it faded from view. The chair in which he sat began to rotate, gaining speed with every turn. His seat, as if at the end of a long arm, spun like a gondola. As blood translocated into his lower regions, Eugene became a human centrifuge.

This disruption played out on a smaller scale in Hazz's Hideout. Eugene's limp body functioned as a carousel in the plastic-backed chair in which he had fallen asleep. An off-kilter gyroscope, angular momentum held him in place until he awakened. Then he – all of him – went off the rails.

Jaw smacked floor. Tongue kissed tile. Eugene's body, dead weight all, crashed to earth.

Eugene stayed down. In the throes of a diaphragmatic spasm, he twitched as if tasered. Struggling to breathe, he flirted with hyperventilation, the wind knocked from his sails.

Mentally, Eugene checked body parts. Head? Throbbing. Knees? Dinged, but functional. Everything else? Shaken, but none the worse for wear.

"Eugene? Eugene!"

Cidally's call carried throughout the hallway.

"Eugene! Eugene!"

Normally, Eugene would have welcomed a visit from the Good Samaritan. But not while lying face down as if the local drunk. Not when having to explain his klutziness to a world-class athlete.

Crap! Cidally had spotted him through the glass in Hasmire's door.

"Eugene, what is going on?" she demanded, pressing her weight against the unyielding mahogany.

"I took a digger. I'm fine."

"You're on the floor? Let me in!"

Oh, the irony. The man who ached to have Cidally in his life now wanted her as far away as possible.

"There's no blood," Eugene insisted. "Nothing's broken."

"Did you hit your head?" Cidally asked. "You might be concussed."

"Negatory," Eugene replied, following that lie with another. "Never felt better."

"What's your name and date of birth?" Cidally demanded.

"Cidally Adira Short," he recited with a twinkle. "Born in the summer of not very long ago."

"Open this door, wise ass!" Cidally fired back. "I am not leaving until you do."

Not fond of ultimatums, Eugene embraced this one. Cidally could have threatened to call Darby or Hamelton. She could have thrown up her hands and walked away. She could have taken him at his word and let him lick his wounds.

Instead, she stayed. She saw through his bogus claims. She cared enough to remain.

Hell, she might even kiss his boo-boos and make him feel better!

Cidally's compassion buoyed Eugene. It salved his pain. It refocused his mind.

As he struggled to his feet, Eugene placed one more item on his injury list. His heart! It hurt more than his head. How could he possibly carry on without Cidally?

Chapter Twenty-Five

"I have seen the future," Eugene stated as if announcing the next port of call.

"You must have really taken it on the bean," Darby said, legs atop his desk, hands interlaced behind his neck.

With thumb and forefinger, Eugene worked the corners of his mouth. Elbows resting on his knees, he sat in Darby's office only because Cidally had ordered him there. She brushed aside his every protestation and guided him through the hallways as if she were the school nurse, even insisting he down two Advil before she returned to work.

"Tell me about the future," Darby offered, his disinterest unmistakable. "Powerball is up to half a billion dollars."

"Let me rephrase," Eugene clarified. "I have seen what constitutes the future in previous cycles."

"You have three minutes," Darby offered, tapping his watch.

The good news was the financier appeared to harbor no grudges despite brandishing fisticuffs at Gastmeyer's the night before.

"Last night you told me I hadn't thought this all the way through, right?" Eugene reviewed.

"I did," Darby agreed.

"Well, I say you're the one who is shortsighted. With Verne, we should be touting the future. That's where the real excitement is."

"Do tell," Darby mumbled, picking up his phone.

"Where do you see yourself in five years?" Eugene asked.

The HR bromide, long having exceeded its shelf life, had Darby looking up from his face magnet. The old chestnut seemed especially out of place coming from one who was interview-averse.

"God, I hate that question," Eugene continued, "But with Verne, no problem. No guesswork. I can tell you where you and I and Hamelton will be."

"Wanna know?" Eugene teased.

"What's your point?" Darby sighed, again scrolling on his hand-held like an infant suckling a teat.

Funny. Even without Verne, Eugene could envision what the future would have looked like if he had not stayed overnight at St. Anthony's. Yest Fest would have been a huge success, though it would have occurred later than planned. The ever-resourceful Darby would have secured buyers for the technology. Hamelton would have been immortalized, his sneer chiseled into the Mount Rushmore of Science.

But that reality wasn't going to happen if Eugene played his cards right.

"Remember that number I told you about, that billion-dollar baby? I call it the constant of repetition, or CR for short. With it, the tumblers of time align. Use it to move from cycle to cycle."

"I have a better tale to tell," Darby informed. "Lone wolf gets his ass fired after breaking and entering in the middle of the night."

The threat meant nothing. Darby was bluffing, something someone with a window to tomorrow could plainly see.

"After Gastmeyer's, I used a simple mathematical expression to dispatch Verne," Eugene explained. "CR minus however far into the future I wanted to go."

"Two minutes," Darby cautioned, unimpressed.

"Want to know what happens Monday?" Eugene ventured. "Since today is Friday, punch in CR minus three days. That gets us to the upcoming Monday in the previous cycle.

"You see, we don't want to go back the full CR as that would land us where we are right now. So, we pull up short which lands us in the future. Get it?"

"I gotta admit," Darby groaned, his perturbation rising. "I never pegged you for a BSer!"

Eugene stretched, his body still sore from his face plant. Sucking in air like a windsock, he helped himself to a butterscotch from Darby's personalized bowl.

"Just one?" Darby scoffed. "Why not take them all?"

"I would," Eugene said, "But I don't have any siblings."

Somewhere, Jenny Lou was giggling.

Eugene removed the plastic from the confectionary. He rolled the sticky candy between his fingers and launched it toward the ceiling.

Reaching its apex, the yellow disc plummeted. Eugene dodged right, then shimmied a tad left. Tongue out, he welcomed the sugary sensation into his mouth. He completed his high-wire act with a wrapper drop onto Darby's desk.

Amazing! From the gravity-defying aerobatics he had just performed, to his give and take with Darby, everything was unfolding as it had on Verne's big screen in the hours after midnight. Eugene had watched more than once, enough so there would be no surprises.

"Darby the Skeptic," Eugene mused. "Going to have that printed on your tombstone?"

"One minute," Darby scowled.

For Eugene, reality had become dream-like, he the only lucid performer. Words crystallized in his head. Internal cues told him when and how to speak. If he stuck to the script, everyone else fell into line. Nothing could have been simpler.

Of course, Eugene assumed he could make a change if he wanted. He could say or do something different from the previous cycle. He could deviate from that which had always been.

Want a fresh start? Call Eugene. Want to maintain the status quo? Call Eugene. Yes, that lowly computer operator was driving the bus!

The responsibility was almost too much to bear.

And Hamelton fancied himself a god. Who was he kidding? The old sourpuss didn't return for another go-round without Eugene's say so.

"You need convincing. I get that," Eugene allowed, reaching for paper and pen.

Scribbling a few words, he folded over what he had written and handed it to Darby.

A knock sent both men's gaze to the door. Darby waved in Cidally.

"Hamelton wants to see you both in the gym in an hour," she stated. "No excuses."

"Hold up," Eugene ordered Cidally. "You'll want to see this."

Eugene's boldness surprised. But the mild-mannered medium had more up his sleeve.

"Darby, check out what I just handed you."

"Forget it," Darby came back. "Time to move on."

"Grow up," Eugene returned fire. "Take a look. I wrote down exactly what Cidally said before she said it."

Darby stared at the paper he had balled up. Should he indulge Eugene or toss it aside unseen? Curiosity had him wavering.

Eugene counted ten. Darby relented. He placed the wadded-up

words on his desk and smoothed them out.

"Read it out loud," Eugene ordered. "I know you won't."

Darby passed the note to Cidally.

"This man doesn't believe," Eugene proclaimed. "That's to be expected, I suppose. Who am I but a prophet without honor among his peeps?!"

"How's your head?" Cidally inquired. "Any pain?"

Eugene submitted to a visual checkup as Cidally searched for signs of distress. That the potential for injury – not physical attraction – drew her to him mattered not. Getting her undivided attention – especially at close range – had him savoring the snap inspection.

"You, me, Darby – all that we know and don't know is trapped in a cycle," Eugene explained. "Over and over, we show up, take our places, spin our stories, take our lumps, curse our fate, and disappear until summoned again."

"Eternal recurrence. Nietzsche had a name for it," Cidally informed, monitoring Eugene's speech and movement. Aside from the rubbish exiting his mouth, he displayed no ill effects.

"Answer me this," he continued. "Would you live your life again and again knowing nothing would change?"

"Count me in," Cidally volunteered. "Immortality with a twist."

Still hovering, she redirected: "Do you feel dizzy or groggy?"

Shaking his head no – stupid, as the motion touched off a low-grade lightheadedness – Eugene pressed on.

"Think about it," he marveled. "All the highs – leading the conference in scoring, winning a state championship – will come to pass again and again."

"And the lows?" Cidally questioned. "Beaten out by Landsinger? Busted for speeding? Having to tend to a patient spouting nonsense? Come on, Eugene. You are not yourself right now."

"You are absolutely right," Eugene agreed. "How could I be knowing what I know?"

Cidally approached Darby. The two whispered as if deciding the fate of the mentally incapacitated.

"I am not concussed," Eugene protested. "And I'm not taking the afternoon off."

Darby, now vested in events as they happened, flattened the paper with a ruler.

"Show me how you did this," he commanded, engaging with an earnestness previously lacking. "How did you know what Cidally would say?"

"That's nothing," Eugene bragged. "I can change the future."

Synchronized eye rolling. Had it been an Olympic event, Cidally and Darby would have taken home gold.

"So can I," Darby harrumphed. "I can throw you out of here."

Unmoved, Eugene plowed ahead: "What would you do if you found out you had a short time to live?"

"I'd get a second opinion," Darby sniffed.

"Short, time, to live?" Cidally repeated, inserting a pause between each syllable. "What do you mean?"

Eugene held up his arms as if silencing a crowd.

"Given a choice, would you get off the merry-go-round? Would you jump even if it meant the end of your existence?"

"Yes," Darby bellowed emphatically. "If it meant putting a stop to this lunacy, I would jump, hop, leapfrog, and catapult myself clear. I'd get up and get out."

Eugene had hoped for more. But Darby remained bound by powerful, time-honored constraints.

"Yes, we could jump. We could start from scratch. Wipe the slate clean," Eugene agreed. "We could welcome a whole new cast of characters to the set."

"I'm going to drive you home," Cidally decided. "Truth be told, you're scaring me a little."

Whoa! Had Eugene heard correctly? Was Cidally going to drive him home? What a proposition! One that, if acted upon, would change the course of history. But one that, if he were being honest, would lead nowhere.

So he lumbered on.

"Tell me, by staying the course, am I not denying the gift of life to countless future generations?" Eugene pondered. "Am I not slamming the door on those who would get a chance should I end this redundancy?

"What do you say? Should I make a change? Should I eliminate us all? I could use a little help here. It's not like I'm ordering takeout!"

"Keep him here. I'll text you when I'm ready," Cidally told Darby as she hurried from the room.

"I don't want to be forgotten," Eugene murmured.

"How about another butterscotch?" Darby asked. "See if you can stick another landing."

Eugene ignored the offer, instead burrowing deeper into his psyche. How does one demonstrate that time visitation is possible? That it is not a hoax? That Verne and his drone can function as advertised?

In the same vein, how does one convince others that he has seen the future? That a cycle exists? That he is not bat-guano crazy?

The answer had eluded him as he began his early-morning exploration of what was to come. But after consulting Verne, his makeshift crystal ball, Eugene knew how to proceed. He'd do what he'd always done. Why reinvent the wheel?

Suddenly, Cidally's scream ripped through the hallway. Short in duration, it did not lack for decibels.

Darby sideswiped a chair and upended a trash can in his haste to reach the startled woman. Turning the final corner, he pulled up short. Cidally, gesturing with both hands, pointed to the wall.

Eugene had painted a message hours earlier that he knew would not go unnoticed. That he had chosen speed over skill – dribs of black had tracked to the floor – only enhanced the creepiness of his first rendering on a nontraditional canvas.

"Truth be told," he had slathered on with broad strokes, "you're scaring me a little."

Cidally's words splashed upon a wall like graffiti on a train car. Call Eugene a tagger. Call him bummed.

As always, Eugene regretted this decision. Why spook Cidally? Why make her question his judgment? She had no dog in this fight.

No, this cycle and all it entailed was his cross to bear. Skrean Time – the final act – was but an hour away. Eugene had a demon to exorcise.

Chapter Twenty-Six

Eugene could lose himself in a library. The odd man out nearly everywhere else, he came alive among the vast collections arranged by subject and call number.

As a child, Eugene wandered from shelf to shelf, seeking out the largest, the smallest, the heaviest, and the lightest books. He'd open each, his interest rising or falling depending upon what he found within.

What, he wondered, did grownups write about? What drove them to fill hundreds of pages with words and ideas beyond his understanding? How did they know what to include? What to exclude?

How did they know when to stop?

Not yet a teen, Eugene eventually lost interest in the affairs of adulthood. What his elders deemed important could wait. He had a bevy of two-dimensional friends idling in the children's section. And off he went.

It troubled him that no single word existed to describe his affection for these storehouses of the printed word. Bibliophile? No, that was someone who had a great passion for books. Bookworm? No again, as that was just an avid reader regardless of setting. Library enthusiast?

Well, that was two words, not one.

So, with nothing satisfactory out there, Eugene turned inward. He would coin a term so catchy it would gain immediate entry into the lexicon.

That was thirty years ago. Eugene had yet to deliver on his promise.

Fresh from having irritated Darby and spooked Cidally, Eugene had time to kill before his meeting with Hamelton. But his decision to visit the library at St. Anthony's was driven by mission, not by the hands of a clock.

Eugene's goal? To retrieve a document he had stowed away in the wee hours of the morning. One for which he now had a final disposition.

"Ashes to ashes. Dust to dust."

Once inside the temple of tomes, Eugene soaked up his surroundings. He welcomed the vanilla/almond bouquet of aging paper and binding materials. He turned 360, allowing the objects in the room to come to him rather than the other way around.

Sasha Ankubar's chair, the one from which she had conducted her interview, remained unmoved. So, too, the seat that had supported Hamelton's backside.

St. Anthony hung from his usual place on the wall behind the circulation desk. Forever ensnared, he appeared as devoid of answers as Eugene.

"Humility can get you only so far," Eugene asserted as he passed by.

Blink and one might miss the science section for which Eugene was bound. The items there numbered less than half of what comprised the religious studies section. Most were older, too – rudimentary texts – nothing so cosmological as to stir up controversy.

Sure enough! There, atop *A Short History of Nearly Everything*, rested the stapled pages Eugene had dropped off earlier that morning. He chuckled as he recalled Operation Extraction.

Having breached the building in the wee hours, Eugene headed first to Hamelton's office. As expected, the door was unlocked, and the room as dark and foreboding as its tenant.

Eugene flipped on the overheads and sized up the desk. As with the door, nothing prevented him from gaining access. He slid open the lower left drawer, the one Hamelton had slammed shut the day before. The compartment was empty save for Wigwort's masterpiece.

Eugene picked it up. He brought it close. He ran his fingers over the title page.

Doubling Back on Time: Past Becomes Present, by Clancy Aloysius Wigwort.

Intent on the treasure he now possessed, Eugene switched muscle control to automatic. As his eyes scanned left to right, his torso shed altitude as if his legs were hydraulics. Continuing to sink lower – balance iffy, calf muscles shaky – he dropped bottom into Hamelton's chair.

Eugene placed his reading material on Hamelton's desk. He moved from page to page as if wearing white gloves. Diagrams, tables, mathematical expressions, and the occasional photograph scrolled past.

The engrossed trespasser imagined Wigwort at his back, pointing and leaning in as the master tutored an inferior mind. The author of the work might have even squealed in delight as a concept or two clicked with a student who had twice failed chemistry.

Nuts and bolts aside, Eugene wanted to know what made Clancy tick. What inspired him? What kept him going?

Did he regret the science he had so expertly articulated?

The circumstances and forces that drove people to do what they did always fascinated Eugene. Why time visitation? Why perpetual motion?

Why the irretractable Skrean, first name Hamelton? What powered his engine?

Years ago, likely in a library somewhere, Eugene had read that much could be learned about an individual based on the content of their drawers. Such a search could provide insight into their personality, their habits and priorities.

What luck! Eugene just happened to be parked smack dab in front of Hamelton's away-from-home storage unit. And, if everyone's life was to be an open book because of Verne and his offspring, then surely Ham Sandwich could not complain about an underling rifling through his privates.

Eugene slid open the top compartment. Shallow, yet expansive, it housed paper clips, rubber bands, twist ties and dust bunnies. Rolaids, Tums and prescription medications hugged the side rail. A shoehorn, letter opener and magnifying glass congregated in the middle.

Amid the clutter, one item stood out: a box of staples that contained no staples, but instead a yellowed scrap of paper. Torn from a wide-ruled notebook, the portion that survived had Eugene furrowing his brow.

Believe, don't believe, it matters not. Your skepticism will not alter the truth.

Life IS cyclical. The carousel goes round and round. You and I and everyone with us shall return. And in this next life, I will again pen this note to you – same words, same paper, same message. And you will again hedge your bet as I will again fail to sway you.

Eugene bobbed his head in agreement.

Clancy knew. Clancy knew the cycle was real. His intellect had uncovered the truth and he would not be convinced otherwise. Certainly not by a nosy neighbor with a stubborn streak.

Eugene tucked the note into his pocket. This chicken scratching was coming with him. The message it conveyed resonated with him more than it did Hamelton. Of that he was sure.

Clancy's words confirmed that Eugene was not bound for the looney bin. In tagging along with Verne, he had stumbled into a new reality, yes, but his eyes, ears and mind still worked. As did reason and logic.

Humor maintained a place, too, something Eugene was eager to put into practice. He would leave a calling card. He would replace his divot – the missing Wigwort manuscript – with something sure to have Hamelton fuming.

Eugene craned his neck toward the rogue's gallery overhead. Somber portraits, each one. Unsmiling. Tight-lipped. No nonsense. Mugshots of every principal employed by the school.

Except for one. One didn't belong. One was coming down.

A chair under his feet, Eugene removed Hamelton's puss from the wall. He resisted the urge to bounce it off the floor, instead placing it in the drawer he had emptied. Then, peeling off a sticky square, he scribbled: "What comes around goes around!" and pinned the note to the donkey's face.

As much as that pre-dawn stop-off had provided a laugh, it did nothing to ease Eugene's burden. He had a cycle to deal with regardless of whether he was invading Hamelton's office or lingering in the library as he did now.

Before the Great Reveal, Eugene had navigated his day with relative ease. Nothing so out of the ordinary crossed his desk that he couldn't handle. Nothing was so challenging that he had to think outside the good book.

That seemed a lifetime ago. Exploring the past had yielded surprises at every turn, with one – the cycle – impossible to reconcile. Should Eugene stay the course, opt for change, or bury his head in the mud?

That he had stared straight into an infinity mirror led him to believe that he, and he alone, bore responsibility for this interminable autoplay. The looping continued because he failed to act or failed to act appropriately.

Eugene was history's biggest loser. Or was he?

Eugene hadn't asked for this. He had not auditioned for this longest running show on Broadway. He had not agreed to have this dilemma thrown at him midway through every performance.

So why was he, and not some other sap, afforded a peek behind the curtain?

Pure and simple, this was his fate. But could it be more? Could the cycle be his eternal punishment for having asked too many questions? For wasting too much time trying to know the unknowable? Was he a modern-day Sisyphus, condemned to forever pushing a metaphorical boulder up a hill only to have it roll back upon each attempt? Had Eugene, and not the fallen Greek god, become the poster child for futility?

Unlikely. For as often as he played the victim, Eugene balked at this possibility. For as often as he felt put upon, not even Eugene could fathom an entire universe created solely to play mind games with him. He was only joking – mostly – on those occasions when he cried out that all of heaven and earth was conspiring against him.

As he reflected on this, Eugene realized his incessant questioning was getting him nowhere. Sisyphus had a boulder. He had a rerun.

Case closed.

Perhaps he should embrace the cycle rather than bellyache about it. The fact that he served as gatekeeper meant he mattered. He had a say in what was to come. Not only did he have a home in the Amphitheater of the Always, he was its lynchpin.

Eugene, and no one else, decided if the perennial cast returned for another season. He alone would determine if his childhood pals – Ben, Rich and Tom – again overran the neighborhood. And Eugene – not Hamelton, not Darby, not Cidally – would make the call as to whether his beloved grandfather received another lifetime in which to dispense his brand of homespun advice.

These individuals all had a future in Eugene. Yes, their time would play out as before, but not one of them would care. Their lives would be as new and exciting as that which awaited Eugene in the coming decades.

Eugene, of course, had no knowledge of his future, at least nothing beyond the next twenty-four hours. He declined to peek ahead because he wanted the sights, sounds, emotions – everything he had remaining – to arrive full force. He wanted to sift through every experience – sand beneath his feet, the smell of rain, a view from a mountaintop – as if for the first time.

Celebrating life, even one already lived, trumped the alternative.

Eugene had two choices. He could deviate from the script, live out the remainder of his life, and then head straight into the abyss to the right of the number line. Or, he could stay the course, essentially wrapping the number line onto itself, and eliminate the voids at both ends.

Eugene would not be forgotten. No siree! As long as the lions roamed – from million to centillion – he would be back.

But in that, Eugene was getting ahead of himself. At just forty-five years old, he still had a second act to enjoy. One that promised more fulfillment than the first. One in which he drove the bus. One in which he no longer operated as a blender.

Eugene had held his own with Hamelton. He had flirted with Cidally. He had faced down a cycle.

This longtime church secretary had been promoted. Of his own volition.

Cue the new challenges. Roll out the new experiences. Eugene stood primed and ready. He would take the rut out of routine and place the act in impactful.

Cycle be damned! Never had he felt more in control.

His spur-of-the-moment pep talk finished, Eugene had business to attend to. He had a manuscript to burn. Clancy Wigwort's blueprint was about to be introduced to a fully functional Bunsen burner down the hall.

Chapter Twenty-Seven

The scuffing of heel on floor told Eugene he had company in the first-floor restroom. But the prelude to a cough – one laced with mucous and phlegm – came too late to be of any benefit.

Tethered for the moment to the urinal, Eugene glanced over his shoulder. Sure enough, someone – most likely Hamelton – had camped out in the middle stall.

Eugene needed a minute to finish. Less, if he skipped washing his hands.

Why he had opted to make a pit stop with another perched upon the porcelain eluded him. He could have visited the second-floor facility. Although a housekeeping disaster, at least it afforded some semblance of privacy.

Now, with Hamelton set to emerge post-haste, urgency directed Eugene to void his bladder. Unlike the time he had just spent in Darby's office, Eugene had not previewed what was on the docket between now and his upcoming rendezvous with Hamelton. The next sixty minutes would be as new to him as it would be to his co-workers.

Urgency morphed into panic. The boogeyman had shifted his weight one too many times. Eugene had to complete his transaction. Instead, he tensed up, a once promising stream reduced to a trickle.

Hamstrung, Eugene prayed Hamelton might develop an upset stomach, a blocked bowel – anything to keep the human specimen cup on lockdown. Hell, even explosive diarrhea sounded reasonable if it prevented the enlarged prostate from getting to his feet.

A concussive whooshing of water flushed away those possibilities. Pants got raised, shirt tails got tucked, and the latch – the last line of defense – slid right.

With a final shake, the "prize" behind door number two stepped out.

Pressing in almost to the wall and with nothing forthcoming, Eugene resorted to humming. He would not leave until the coast cleared.

"What's all this crap about a cycle?" Hamelton asked, computer printouts in hand.

"I think you'll find it interesting," Eugene submitted, eyes taking in the ceiling.

"No one is paying you to think," Hamelton snapped, slapping the sink with his rolled-up reading materials. "This is just another one of your delaying tactics. Go ahead. Drag your feet. I'll have Brody drag your ass out the front door!"

Eugene buried his head in his chest. His cheeks swelled, puffing up as he fought back laughter. So this was how a balloon felt before it burst.

"I certainly wouldn't want that," Eugene conceded, choking back the bubbles of hilarity brewing within his nostrils.

"It's not about what you want! It's about what I want!" Hamelton hollered, pounding the metal towel dispenser. "Put Willie to bed and get your carcass in the gym."

Willie? Carcass?

Eugene lost it. Comedic release sprayed the lavatory like steam from a burst pipe. The outflow – emotional, seismic, giggle-ridden

– splashed wall, ceiling and floor alike. Echoing, reverberating, the catharsis relieved Eugene in a way he had not intended when he diverted to the loo.

Willie! Carcass!

The words had Eugene convulsing again, every thought – serious or not – an accelerant that fueled the frenzy. Tear ducts opened. Snot bubbled. The tickle in his snoot – muted at first – overpowered, manifesting itself in a series of blasting-cap sneezes that had Eugene backing away and zipping his fly almost before he could holster his manhood.

Willie Carcass! Big game hunter, Willie Carcass! Male gigolo. Willie Carcass! That's my stage name!

The two words, repeated over and over, lost meaning. Gibberish. Jabberwocky. Semantic satiation.

Hamelton, unnerved by the rapid-fire succession of bodily functions, bolted. So in a hurry was he that he clipped the right side of his forehead on the door as it failed to open sufficiently.

"Bye bye, Willie!" Eugene slurred. "I mean Dick."

Bent at the waist, Eugene eased into a corner. He slowly slid downward as the absurdity within mercifully abated.

Touching bottom, he wiped his eyes, brow and nose with a handkerchief. He stared straight ahead without blinking, head against cold ceramic, legs fully extended. A minute to decompress. Sixty seconds to marvel at how his life had taken a sharp turn into the different.

Three months earlier, Eugene had taken a flyer on a new line of work. Tired of a revolving liturgical year, he had hopped on board the bandwagon of innovation. He wanted new, exciting, different.

Now, slumped amid the acrid scent of urinal cakes and degreasers, Eugene wondered if he had made the right decision. Should he have stayed put? Should he have remained a church mouse?

In swapping a house of worship for a house of mirrors, Eugene had traded certitude for uncertainty. He had traded routine for spur of the moment. He had exchanged comfort for soul searching.

How to proceed?

"Know your opponent," Cidally had whispered to Eugene on his early-morning walk to St. Anthony's. "Stay a step ahead of Hamelton."

Good advice. Especially coming from someone who – Eugene assumed – was fast asleep in bed as he trekked from downtown to graveyard to gym.

Good advice he would follow. After punching in Hamelton's passcode, Eugene concentrated on the future. He studied the next twenty-four hours – with the exception of the sixty-minute interlude that so far had landed him on the bathroom floor. He memorized what was to come. He ensured he would not be caught off guard by anything that transpired in the next few hours.

At peace with the soon-to-be, Eugene jumped farther ahead. Where would Cidally and Hamelton be in five years?

Eugene tracked his hoop hottie to Spain. There, in Valencia, she was named head coach of one of the sixteen teams in Europe's pre-eminent women's basketball league.

Operating as if it were take-your-secret-crush-to-work day, Eugene tuned in during a game. He ignored the competition on court, instead zeroing in on Cidally. Passionate, energetic – her soles never stationary – she motivated with gestures, hand signals, penetrating stares and the occasional shortcuss. She drew up plays, huddled with her charges, and launched bouquets or zingers depending on how the officials ruled.

With each basket, a fist pump. With each turnover, a foot stomp. For every on-court action, Cidally had an equal and appropriate reaction.

Fixated though he was, Eugene didn't stay until the final buzzer. He did not set foot in the winning locker room.

But he did loiter as Cidally accepted kisses from a gentleman outfitted in tailored chinos and a button-down shirt. The tan, physically fit Adonis popped off a series of besitos as if a human nail gun. He concluded his public display of affection with an extended smooch and a declaration: "Greatest coach and wife, ever!"

Instant applause. Then, a pause.

"And after a loss, Gino?" Cidally asked, as those gathered awaiting the appropriate comeback.

"Greatest wife ever," her husband replied, concluding what Eugene assumed to be a ritual that followed every victory.

Whoa! Back up the minivan. Eugene needed another look. Instead of going back live, he played the recorded version, freezing the hands-on hunk in mid peck.

So, this was who Cidally had chosen? A foreign-born Brody? Machismo mucho!

Eugene did not approve. Not in this world or any other. He would have made that clear in the form of an objection had he been a guest at the wedding. Or, at the very least, he would have demanded an explanation.

How could she? How could Cidally, the unconventional free-spirit, settle for a stereotype? For a dime-a-dozen jock? For the prettiest face in the room?

How could she when others – he in particular – offered so much more?

Eugene recalled the drone. He couldn't compete. Not with the sexiest man alive.

But maybe not all was lost. Upon further review, Eugene came away with a silver lining. Cidally could not possibly forget him. Not entirely, anyway. He would remain with her until death did she part. He would resurface – time and again – with her every embrace of Gino, short for Eugenio, the Spanish equivalent of Eugene.

The ugly American could live with that.

Locating Hamelton proved easier. Eugene figured the bathroom sitter would never leave the acre of land on which he resided, and so he sent the drone there.

On first try, Eugene landed inside Hamelton's workshop, an outbuilding as large as the house. Power and hand tools lined shelves or hung from pegboards. Miscellanea – bird feeders, flowerpots, watering cans, table lamps – overspread much of the counterspace. Big ticket items – a snowblower, riding lawnmower, refrigerator, gas grill, ATVs – made straight-line travel within the structure darn near impossible.

Overshadowing all was a DYI machine so ugly as to require further inspection. The monstrosity resembled an octagonal hot tub minus the water. A pair of railroad ties had been fastened to the rim at the vertices. Running parallel to each other, the timbers divided the eight-sided shape into a rectangle and two trapezoids. A paddlewheel, roughly six feet in diameter, was affixed to the massive beams.

The set-up reeked of perpetual motion: a spinning wheel that, once actuated, never stopped turning.

Eugene returned a day later. Gone were the big ticket items. In their place were a key light, fill light, backlight and more.

A small group had gathered around the makeshift construction. Hamelton assured those assembled that he could get his contraption rolling if they could do the same with their cameras.

Yes, Hamelton had resurrected his hoax. The fraud had reached back, tilling his past and sowing seeds among a new generation of gullible.

Apparently, his nonsense had taken root. From what Eugene could see, Hamelton had spread enough manure to warrant the making of a documentary.

Jesus, Mary and Joseph! Why did this P.T. barnyard animal deserve 100 minutes of fame? Why did this clown prince merit a fawning biopic, working title *Perpetual Devotion*?

As much as Eugene didn't want to, he watched. He gawped. He rubbernecked.

Where was Sasha Ankubar? She would have cut this scam artist off at the ankles!

Instead, those involved with the project handled Hamelton with kid gloves. Their questions framed him as a misunderstood genius. They treated his answers as gospel.

If Hamelton was unhappy with a take, they'd reshoot. If he was unhappy with a questioner, someone else slid into the interviewer's chair.

But even as they bent over backward to please him, Hamelton simmered. Anger boiled beneath the surface, a geyser set to spout.

Why should he have to explain himself again? Why should he have to promote his energy machine a second time? He had done all this before. Didn't anyone remember? Had no one listened?

Growing more agitated, the combative geezer anointed himself victim. He had not been taken seriously. He had not been given his due. He had been ridiculed, marginalized and rejected.

People were slow learners. Uneducated. Ignorant. Plain and simple, people were stupid. And Hamelton was tired of playing to an audience that could not possibly understand the magnitude of his accomplishment!

Asked to expand on that claim, Hamelton turned on the film crew. He attacked the one group that could provide the publicity he so craved.

"Don't tell me what I can do and can't do," the martyr detonated. "You don't know me from crap. I know what I've already done and it's a hell of a lot more than you'll ever do in your damn life. All your life you'll never be remembered. I will be remembered."

The outburst was the last captured by the drone. With Hamelton having reached his nadir, Eugene recalled the little guy. He decommissioned the frequent flyer – dismantling it and burying it in the cemetery. Hamelton, from what Eugene could see, would die a lonely, disgraced death.

As he covered the remains, Eugene questioned his decision not to check in on himself five years hence. He told himself he didn't want to know, that tomorrow was fluid and not set in stone like the weather-beaten markers delineating the dead.

Wouldn't knowing where he ended up limit possibility and potential? Wouldn't knowing diminish intrigue and excitement?

Or would the journey be just as rewarding despite being privy to all that lay ahead?

Maybe more than anything, Eugene did not explore his future because he did not want to witness his own death. He always assumed it would come too fast. Attaching a date and time to his earthly exit would start a countdown upon which he would obsess. It would activate an alarm clock that had no snooze button. Death Con One: Eugene's body in the chalk outline.

The good news: Eugene's future was not yet locked and loaded. He could make a change, one that would put him on a different path, one that, theoretically, would break the cycle.

The bad news: Would deviating be fair to others? If Eugene zigged right instead of left, would Cidally find Gino? Would Hamelton get his documentary?

Eugene had been given a gift. He had seen the future. But he had been given no instruction manual.

So, what was his next move?

Perhaps he did not have to do anything. Odds were another Wigwort would come along fifty or a hundred years from now and unlock the secrets to time visitation. That poor sap could then wrestle with all that had rattled through Eugene's head the past few days. He or she could decide how to move forward.

Grabbing hold of the sink, Eugene pulled himself up. A blind date awaited. Blind because he had kept the camera away. Blind because he wanted to believe anything was still possible.

Chapter
Twenty-Eight

For as often as he ventured into the past, Eugene did not need Verne for this trip down memory lane. Sucking in a deep breath outside Cidally's office, the forty-five-year-old teleported back three decades on his own.

Eugene's surroundings fell away as a movie might transition from one scene to another. The door frame to Cidally's place of work dissolved, replaced by a two-story Colonial Revival from his old neighborhood. The hallway disintegrated, giving way to elm trees and Titan boxwood shrubs. The tiled floor dropped out, with lush, green lawns and well-trimmed hedges taking its place.

Eugene knew the home well. Elizabeth Fitzenbaugh resided within. He had directed his binoculars to her bedroom window so often he feared nearby paint might fade. His unobstructed view lasted seven months each year when the elm trees were bare of leaves. Though he checked in almost daily, only once did he glimpse Beth in full frontal. Caught off guard and afraid she'd see him, he dropped his hand-held visual aids. His foot ached for days.

Eugene so wanted to be a part of her life. He so wanted to be on the other end of the lens.

Then, as now, his nerve endings skewed into the red. Then, as now, he wrestled with a simple question: ring the bell or flee like hell?

Beth, beauty oozing from every pore, sat in the desk directly in front of Eugene. Though just fifteen, she packed as much maturity into her body as a college freshman.

Most mornings a simple "hi" was the only word shared between the two. For Eugene to have offered more would have required a confidence and command of the English language he did not possess. Not in her presence, anyway.

To Eugene's way of thinking, he would have said more if only Beth had appeared receptive. If she had given him a sign. If she had thrown up a flare. So inept was he at reading others that he never graduated to complete sentences with Beth, someone equally as shy as he.

Nervous, intimidated, Eugene clammed up. He kept to himself. Better she think he was disinterested than a selective mute.

Day after day, week after week, the sameness led nowhere. Eugene in awe. Eugene missing out. Eugene in a bubble of his own making.

On test days, Beth would reach over her shoulder and hand Eugene his copy. Only occasionally would she turn and face him before making the exchange, likely a wellness check to ensure he still numbered among the living.

Eugene was very much alive the day he approached Beth's front porch to deliver a letter addressed to her that had been mistakenly delivered to his house. The mixup, his mother said, was his ticket to visit the young lady and turn over what belonged to her.

"Man up," Eugene pep-talked from the front walk. "Don't be a wuss."

Knees knocking, Eugene climbed four stairs. Sweat beading, he located the doorbell.

His right arm, functional seconds earlier, calcified. His stomach, queasy on the way over, roiled like the surf ahead of a massive storm.

"Just ring the damn bell," a voice from within cried. "You're such a loser!"

No argument there. What was he going to do if Beth or – God forbid – her dad answered the door? Aside from mumbling "This is yours," he had nothing else to offer. Nothing to keep a conversation from imploding. Nothing to save himself from himself.

Such a scenario terrified him. So, too, did the fact that the longer he hung around, the more likely someone would approach and confront him. And that possibility had him racing the squirrels into the street.

Fully grown now, Eugene vowed he would not beat a hasty retreat from Cidally's door. A fast getaway was not possible at his age anyway. What's more, Cidally was waving him in.

With a gentle turn of the knob, Eugene entered on quiet feet. Cedar and vanilla hung in the air – warm, earthy, comforting. An oscillating fan, set to low, ensured the scent carried throughout the room.

Cidally was on the phone, air pods protruding from her ears. She pointed to a mesh-backed computer chair. Eugene sat, eyes roaming.

On an adjacent table, save-the-date notices awaited stamps and mailing labels. The decorative cards – a shout-out for Yest Fest – bumped up against unopened boxes of vellum envelopes.

"That's not what I was promised," Cidally asserted to whomever she was speaking. "Check your records."

Cutouts of the governor leaned against the wall. Dozens crouched there, each offset enough so that they could be easily counted.

"I'd like to speak to your manager," Cidally demanded in a voice Eugene had last heard courtside in Spain. "Maybe she can clear this up."

There was a thought. Cidally as his manager. If Eugene reported to her, he would never call in sick. He would arrive early and leave late. He would encourage daily check-ins. His productivity would skyrocket.

Oh, my! Cidally's pet. While some might have balked at the label, Eugene would have worn it as a badge of honor.

Eugene had read that there were four types of women: the maiden, the nurturer, the enlightened, and the untamed. Cidally transcended all, a force of nature. She was the total package.

Never had Eugene aimed so high. Never had he operated without a safety net.

That he had no chance with the woman he idolized made the moments he could steal from her more gratifying. Having no chance meant he did not have to aspire to be Gino, only an improved version of himself.

And make no mistake, Eugene had changed. Not only had he come calling for Cidally, he had Hamelton stewing in the gym while he did so. Eugene was driving the bus.

"Unless you can come up with a solution, we're done," Cidally closed out. "Thank you for your time."

She secured the blue pen she had been twirling impatiently and put a line through an entry on a scratch pad.

"They couldn't make a simple change," she announced. "I can. I'm getting another caterer."

The off-put blonde had twisted her hair into a pencil bun, a yellow Dixon Ticonderoga placed horizontally across her ponytail. The bun, Eugene had learned, was the power hairstyle of multi-taskers.

Power. Eugene had always been content to let others lead. Many – namely Hamelton and Pastor Perv – did not deserve the considerable influence they wielded. Others, like Cidally, led with an even keel that fostered stability, reliability and trust.

"I told you," Cidally addressed Eugene, sternness baked into her every word, "I wasn't talking to you until you saw a doctor."

"I have an appointment at three-fifteen," Eugene reassured. "I'll go once I've dealt with Hamelton."

"If I find out you're lying," she warned.

She wouldn't. She couldn't. Eugene would be unemployed by that time.

Cidally reached for a stapler. She drove a chisel point through the upper left corner of a stack of papers.

"What's up?" she asked, leveling a gaze that had him weighing his options.

Should he put on his stovepipe and play Abe Lincoln? Should he tell her this was the last they would see each other? That he was breaking it off before she could? That this was goodbye?

Or should he play it cool? Pretend this was just another visit? That nothing unusual was in the works?

Eugene chose the latter, croaking out this gem.

"What are you going to do after Yest Fest?"

"Funny you should ask," Cidally said. "I'm going to be coaching basketball overseas."

So, this really was goodbye. For keeps.

"Congratulations," Eugene managed, hoping to sound genuine.

"I miss the game. And who can say no to the Valencia Basket Club of EuroLeague Women and getting to live in Spain?"

Eugene could. He became homesick when crossing state lines.

"Going back to something you love," he replied with manufactured enthusiasm. "That's great."

Already, Eugene missed her. How could he not?

And so, he allowed himself one last look. One last chance to cat-alogue every detail: the burgundy, sleeveless A-line dress. The slim heels. The wire-framed glasses.

Simply stunning! And yet Eugene could find countless others just as breathtaking on television, in fashion magazines, and across social media. Everywhere, a slew of genetically gifted – or surgically altered – creatures who, on the surface at least, benefitted from the halo effect, the tendency to assign positive qualities to the physically attractive simply because of their outward appearance.

While Cidally certainly possessed that type of beauty, she offered far more. Much of her elegance manifested itself in the way she treated others, especially Eugene. She could have minimized him, communicating only when necessary. She could have patronized him, whispering behind his back. She could have toyed with him, flaunting her superiority at every turn.

But she hadn't. She had welcomed Eugene, accepted him, even looked forward to seeing him. She had injected a spark into his humdrum existence. She had instilled hope.

Above all, she believed Eugene to be a better person than even he, himself, would allow.

"Eugene," Cidally asked, rousing him from his zombie-like trance, "is there another reason you're here?"

Absolutely! He wanted more time with her. Wasn't that obvious? He wanted their futures to intersect. He wanted to trade places with Gino. He wanted to test drive those lips!

But he couldn't say that. Even the new and improved Eugene understood that to be a bridge too far.

"Did you know a Clancy Wigwort?" he rambled on, the words escaping as if on their own.

Wigwort? Really? Good Lord! How could Cidally possibly have a connection with a cabin-bound recluse? She was going to think he was still concussed!

"He was my great-great uncle. Did you know him?"

The revelation surprised him. It made the looming faceoff with Hamelton more personal.

"I came across an old article," Eugene stammered. "Something about senseless goggles."

"My grandfather had a pair. Strangest thing I ever saw."

"What can you tell me about him?" Eugene stalled.

"I never met him, but heard he was quite eccentric."

"What did he do for a living?" Eugene inquired, procrastinating.

"I don't mean to be rude," Cidally halted. "But I have a busy afternoon. And you were supposed to be in the gym fifteen minutes ago."

Hamelton, again! Inserting himself where he didn't belong like an oversized catheter. A cockroach in the salad of life.

"I'll get going," Eugene said reluctantly, pulling up stakes. Sticking around would only detract from this final farewell.

As he stepped toward the door, the debate raging within spiked. Should he? Shouldn't he? He had to decide now or forever wonder how she might have reacted.

Would he turn tail? Or would he stand and deliver?

Voiceless for so long, Eugene rose to the occasion. Cidally meant too much to him to remain silent.

"I've never met anyone like you, Cidally Short," Eugene confessed, not holding back. "I'm better for having met you."

There. He hadn't wimped out. The selective mute had spoken.

No, he hadn't said he loved her – he did – but the pronouncement carried the same risk. He had put himself out there, placing his fragile ego in her hands. If so inclined, she could snap him in half like the pencil tucked into her hair.

As the clock ticked, blatherer's remorse set in. Why had he not stayed quiet? Why had he not maintained his honorary standing among the Trappist Monks?

And then a response. A reply better than he dared dream. A comeback to remember until he could remember no more.

"And you're a different kind of cool, Eugene S.," Cidally declared firmly, her eyes finding his. "Now, get out of here, and give Hamelton hell."

Chapter Twenty-Nine

"**Y**ou're late!" Hamelton bellowed.

Eugene raised his right hand as if a game official had whistled him for a foul. He took slow, measured steps toward Verne, his only ally in the gym.

Directly ahead, Hamelton twisted and stretched the wristband of his watch. He scowled, testiness darkening his face.

Darby sat atop the scorer's table. Legs resting over the edge, he fiddled with his phone as he attempted to install *Deathloop*. Two would-be investors with bundles of bitcoin had recommended he download the action-adventure game.

"Sit down," Hamelton ordered, pointing to a plastic ottoman that sagged in the middle.

"And sink to your level?" Eugene said, ignoring the footstool that would have put him at a height disadvantage. "I'll stand."

"You'll sit or I'll ..."

"You'll do what," Eugene challenged. "Sic the big goon on me?"

Arms folded like a circus strongman, Brody emerged from behind the bleachers. A dark, tight-fitting rib knit top accentuated every peak and valley of his musculature. A larger-than-usual opening gave way to a neck and trapezii so over-developed as to render his head small by comparison.

"You want I should ..."

"Leave him," Hamelton said, commanding Pea Brain to stand down. "I can fire him just as he is."

"Wrong," Eugene corrected. "You'll find my letter of resignation on your desk. Here's the short version: You suck! I quit!"

The four-word summation, each syllable offloaded rat-a-tat style, strafed its intended target like machine gun fire. So unequivocal, so abrupt, the staccato blast had Darby setting aside his face magnet.

"Don't do it, Eugene," he objected. "I can get Hamelton off your back."

"The hell you can," Hamelton contradicted. "I'm running this show. If the blender wants to quit, let him."

"Running the show?" Eugene repeated. "Not in this cycle."

"Your cycle doesn't exist," Hamelton lashed out. "A discovery of such import would not have been made by a diddly squat like you."

Diddly squat. This was Ham at his flustered best.

In the past, such character assassination would have cut deeply. Now, it motivated.

"You are correct," Eugene conceded. "Someone who mattered did learn the truth: Clancy Wigwort. And unlike you, I'm giving credit where credit is due."

"Stop with this loopity-loop hooey," Hamelton ordered.

"And stop with your damned denials," Eugene hit back. "You know the cycle is real because Wigwort knew it was real. His invention – that's right folks, Wigwort's invention – works because we go round and round like hamsters in a wheel."

"You piece of crap!" Hamelton snarled.

"Poor Clancy," Eugene lamented. "He deserved so much better."

"Wigwort was going to put a match to an accomplishment without equal," Hamelton defended. "Incinerate it as if it were hazardous waste. In essence, abandoned property, free for the taking."

"What's a Wigwort?" Brody asked, clueless as a newborn.

"Clancy understood," Eugene affirmed. "Loss of privacy. Lives destroyed. He wanted out."

"What about the upside?" Darby interjected.

"Behavior modification," Hamelton said, taking the lead. "People will think twice before doing something stupid."

"Really? You're going there?" Eugene uttered in disbelief. "Verne, the computer canine, is going to take a bite out of crime!"

"I have a lot of money tied up in this," Darby cautioned.

At long last, honesty! Darby and Hamelton were in too deep to let this go.

"But at what cost?" Eugene challenged. "Every life an open book. Every shortcoming, misstep, and regret catalogued, cross-referenced and accessible."

"I am not liable for how my invention is used," Hamelton retorted.

"What the hell!" Eugene blazed. "Do you have no conscience? Are you for real? You're going to strip naked every soul who ever lived, all of us a child at one time or another. You're going to line us up and put us on display. A 24/7 peep show steeped in venereal voyeurism. Absolutely, this is on you!"

"Really," Hamelton said, drawing the word out as if patronizing a saint. "Don't tell me you haven't spied on that little wet dream of yours, Mr. High and Mighty. Dropped in on her in various stages of undress. Pleasure yourself, did you?"

At high and mighty, Eugene balled his hand. At pleasure yourself, he had drawn a bead on Hamelton's craggy chin.

Oh, to take a swing. To release pent-up energy. To bring Smugness Supreme to his knees.

Eugene could have taken out Hamelton with one blow. Bloodied him with one well-placed strike.

And why not? Why not join forces with those who relished violence? Why not impose his will simply because he was younger and stronger? Didn't might make right?

"Don't do it!" Cidally implored.

Eugene cocked his head.

"Don't do it!" the call came again, a cry for civility from a conscience that had been working nonstop.

Don't do it! The admonishment interrupted the primeval rage that gripped Eugene. Well-timed, well-placed, the plea for mercy put a stop to what could have been a full-scale beatdown.

Eugene would not resort to violence. He would gain satisfaction in a more calculated way.

The fly in the ointment? In preparing to wage war with Hamelton, Eugene had forgotten about Brody. Brody had no such memory lapse.

Certain of Eugene's intentions, the linebacker charged. In a tale of the tape, he had a leg up in every department: speed, youth, strength, size and ferocity.

Eugene's singular advantage: hours earlier he had watched and rewatched Brody's attack. David had seen Goliath's every move.

As the beast came at him, Eugene dodged right, leaving Brody grasping air. When his athletic adversary mounted a second offensive, the less nimble darted left. As the flummoxed gargantuan lobbed profanities, the less powerful legged it to safety.

The actions belonged to Eugene. The impetus and timing originated elsewhere.

In essence, Eugene operated on autopilot. He need to do nothing except lean into the pull exerted on him. His strings were being manipulated elsewhere, he a marionette practicing self-preservation.

Scrambling, Eugene reached his next mark. He would use Brody's momentum to end this skirmish.

As the wild boar lunged anew, Eugene stood tall, collapsing to the floor as Brody left his feet. Airborne and with no guidance system, the mastodon flew headfirst into the metal fencing surrounding Verne. Steel prevailed over skull, the aggressor returning to earth devoid of consciousness.

Darby ran to the fallen bully.

"He's out cold."

"He'll be fine," Eugene diagnosed. "Back to his rabid self before you know it."

"I'm calling 911," Darby informed.

"Don't," Hamelton ordered. "He's okay. You heard Eugene."

Since when did Hamelton put any stock in what Eugene said? Simply put, he didn't. Boss Man didn't want any outside interference.

"I have something to say to this sniveling snot," Hamelton barked. "You think you can stop progress. You think you can rain on my parade. Think again. You're nothing but a fungus I tracked in here one day! You're a bottom feeder!"

Having fended off the bull named Brody, Eugene pivoted to face the bull that required shoveling.

"You still don't get it, do you?" Eugene said with confidence. "Wigwort's invention. Yest Fest. They don't happen without me."

"See this flash drive?" Eugene said, tossing and catching the precious memory stick he was never without. "I wiped Verne clean. A blank slate. I have everything here in two inches of plastic."

Hamelton sprinted to Verne as if a starter's gun had gone off. Face contorted, eyebrows distorted, he stabbed at the controls, flipping what should have been pressed, and sliding what should have been turned.

Despite the frenzied manipulations, the binary big boy, like Brody, remained unresponsive.

"Darby, get this thing up and running!" Hamelton screeched.

Leaving Brody in a heap, Darby clicked through the sequence of steps he had demonstrated when training Eugene months earlier.

"Check the hard drive!" Hamelton shrieked, pounding the scorer's table.

"Wiped clean," Darby confirmed, examining the many folders Eugene had emptied before sunrise. "Nothing here."

"Suddenly, I've become veeeery important." Eugene taunted.

"Screw you," Hamelton blasted.

Eugene eased past the two men glued to the console. He opened the drone silo.

"Oh, my!" he gasped, pretending to be taken aback. "What happened to Fly Boy?"

Hamelton jumped in front of Darby. Turning his phone into a flashlight, he directed the beam into the darkened chamber.

"Where's my drone?!? Where's my drone?!?" he caterwauled, accosting Eugene by the shirt.

"If you'd kindly take a seat, I'll tell you," Eugene promised, twisting free.

"I don't have to ..." Hamelton corrected, blood pressure on the rise.

Darby squatted near the hangar where the drone should have been. He ran one hand through his hair.

"I'm starting to believe the kid," he mused, recounting recent events. "I think he knows what he's talking about."

"Bully for you," Hamelton jeered. "I want my drone!"

"Then sit ... your ... ass ... down," Eugene hissed.

The verbal IED exploded in Hamelton's face. So brazen, so unexpected, the fusillade landed with such force as to startle recipient and author alike.

His dominion challenged, Hamelton had to regroup. He had to save face. No way would he kowtow to an underling bent on mutiny.

For a full minute, absolute zero encircled the gymnasium at St. Anthony's. Molecular motion ceased. Nothing moved. Not Brody prostrate on the floor. Not Darby on the lowest rung of bleachers. Not Eugene nor Hamelton who, in sizing each other up, defied the other to act first.

As the visual game of chicken entered extra innings, time favored Eugene. Having given his notice, he had nothing on his calendar. Nothing but a lifetime to revisit the decisions he would make this day.

Perhaps sensing Eugene could wait him out, Hamelton caved. He cursed as he dropped his posterior a few feet from Darby.

The tone, Eugene thought. Tone was key to getting his way. If only he had known. All these years he could have been winning friends and influencing people.

"This cycle," Eugene began. "The one Clancy predicted and the one you, Darby, are coming to understand is real – can be changed. I have that power.

"And we want change, why?" Darby inquired.

"To get this asshole out of our lives," Hamelton grunted.

"You want change," Eugene corrected, "because Yest Fest doesn't happen in this cycle. Never has. Never will. No fame. No glory. No return on your investment. You're finished."

"What you want is a new cycle. A different cycle. A cycle that gives you a chance to introduce time visitation to the world. One where Skrean Time earns a 100 percent share across all platforms."

"Sound promising, Hammy boy?" Eugene goaded.

"Go to hell!"

"It's so simple," Eugene enthused. "I hand over this flash drive, something I've never done in any previous life, and the cycle changes. We enter uncharted territory. Yest Fest can go on as planned.

"Want more? How 'bout this? I found Allerspan. Yes, I solved the mystery. I have video. Lots of video. All right here. With it, you can prove time visitation is possible."

Darby, now the voice of reason in an afternoon that had sailed beyond the pale, turned lawyer pro bono. "Legally, everything on that stick already belongs to us. You'll surrender it regardless."

"Sorry. Not going to happen." Eugene objected. "I am two steps ahead of you."

Even at that – even knowing everyone's lines – Eugene stayed on script. He would bring nothing new to the table. Nothing so clever as to break the impending impasse.

Truth be told, he looked forward to locking horns. As one who usually backed down in an argument, Eugene had migrated to the edge of his seat in anticipation of the self-produced morphine that would result when exchanging stubborn for stubborn in a stalemate that would put Hamelton in his place.

And so Eugene again extended the offer he always did. He placed the conundrum he had been grappling with – to change or not to change – squarely in Hamelton's court.

No one said he had to be nice about it.

"Ham Bone, the power I possess is yours. You want me gone? You want me out of your life? "Give Clancy Wigwort his due. Tell us you stole his life's work. State for the record that you are nothing without him.

"You do that, and I bequeath all my files to you. I wash my hands of you forever. You win. I lose."

You win. I lose. Couched that way, how could Hamelton not accept Eugene's terms? Acknowledge Wigwort and the circle is broken. A flash drive is surrendered. TV – time visitation for the ages – goes on the air.

For Hamelton, that should have been low-hanging fruit: a new beginning with a favorable ending. So why, time and again, did the old bird stay silent? Too stubborn to honor Eugene's request? Too conceited to admit Wigwort's superiority?

Or could the source of his reluctance lie elsewhere? Could his hesitation be traced to time visitation itself?

Should Hamelton get his way, should Yest Fest take place as planned, Skrean's entire life would – as all others – enter the public domain. Fodder for the curious. Fuel for the masses. Food for the thoughtful. Could the lying cheat live with what others would uncover? Could he go to his grave knowing he would be outed for the sham he was?

Had the cost of doing business climbed too high?

"Need more incentive?" Eugene taunted. "Get this. The cycle ends sooner than you think. Darby and I don't make it to old age. We never do.

"That's right. The checkered flag is out. This race is ending. We're running on fumes."

"You're bluffing," Hamelton stated, unease coloring his response.

"Take my offer," Eugene challenged. "Do it to be remembered. Do it for the adulation. Do it because Skrean fits so neatly between Roentgen and Tesla!"

Eugene set his jaw: "Give Wigwort his due."

Hamelton spat on the floor.

"Believe, don't believe, I don't care," Eugene came back. "All I can tell you is the last time I sent the drone out, he didn't return. He got caught up in the black hole that swallows all before the next big bang does its thing. Nothing survives."

Darby's phone beeped. Then a third time.

Overhead, the lights hummed. In the far corner, the drib-drib-drib of the drinking fountain.

Outside, traffic crawled. Horns blared. A pedestrian toe-tapped his way from one side of the street to the other.

Then, from the cheap seats, a declaration of independence.

"I don't need you," Hamelton growled. "By God, I don't need you. Chicken Little crowing that the world is going to end. I'll end you!"

"Like you killed Wigwort?" Eugene announced, floating a theory that was long on guesswork and short on evidence. "Yes, Darby, your business partner is a bona fide, unrepentant killer. He couldn't wait for nature to run its course. Poison, wasn't it?

"Gee, if only someone had the evidence to back that up. Something – anything – to put Perpetual Motion Man behind bars. Oh, silly me! I do!"

Hamelton brushed aside the threat. Drawing on new-found energy, he turned to depart.

"You going to kill me, Ham Sandwich?" Eugene taunted. "Snuff me out like a candle?"

"Too easy!" Hamelton dismissed as Eugene moved to intercept. "Better a debilitating accident, one that puts you in a chair!"

Then, with added zeal, he appended: "One that gives you a permanent seat from which to watch me get every ... last ... thing ... I ... desire."

The threat, as chilling as dried ice, left Eugene numb, despite his having heard it multiple times earlier that morning.

"You won't see it coming," Hamelton vowed. "You're already dead from the neck up. I'll turn you into a vegetable, paralyzed from the neck down."

Having gotten the angle on Hamelton, Eugene inserted himself between his former boss and the exit.

"Just one question, Ham Job?" Eugene baited. "How you going to rebuild the drone?"

"Get out of my way!" the detainee snapped.

"Going to use Wigwort's instruction manual?" Eugene guessed, continuing to bar the door. "You know, maybe I shouldn't have torched that booklet on the Bunsen burner. My bad.

"But, hey! No problem! You can tape the cross-cut confetti back together because rumor has it you're not smart enough to build a flyer on your own."

Eugene had only read about spontaneous combustion. Hamelton's fit of apoplexy served as his first encounter with auto-ignition in the flesh.

As if buffeted by high winds, the big con shook uncontrollably. His veins surfaced, pockmarking his neck, face and head. Forced air, as if someone were breaking wind, escaped his lips, a teapot in tempest.

With Hamelton self-immolating, Eugene addressed Verne for the last time. He bent at the waist, bowing before the co-worker he considered more humane than most.

"We made quite a team, big fellah! Wouldn't you say?"

"He's going to press charges," Darby said of Hamelton. "You're going to prison!"

"Darby, Darby, Darby," Eugene triplicated. "What's more fun than stopping Hamelton from getting his way? How about doing it .... for all eternity?"

And while that scenario again appeared likely, alteration was still possible. Eugene had options. Should he wish to change the cycle, he could attend a basketball game in Spain. Should he wish to halt the endless repetition, he could mess with a documentary that had no business being made.

Atop Eugene's head, a chauffeur's hat. He steered the bus.

"Get the hell out of my way!" Hamelton howled. "Brody, remove this piece of trash. He's garbage."

The appeal to the torso with half a brain was a ruse. Brody would be out for another ten minutes. The coast remained clear.

In his forty-five years, Eugene rarely got in the last word. His father had threatened: "My way or the highway." His girlfriend had informed: "I need my space." His friends had insisted: "You don't know what you're talking about."

All his life, Eugene had been put in his place. All his life, he had gritted his teeth.

Now, the last word belonged to him. He held the upper hand. He could speak his truth.

Eugene wasn't about to blow it.

He cleared his throat. He swallowed hard. He took a deep breath.

Then, he made sure to bite down hard on the tenth word of his parting shot.

"And you – you son of a bitch – you will *never* find your governor."

This story's original title and book cover concept

The Trillion Cycle

(Written circa 1980)

The ringing finally came to a stop. Hamilton stretched his weary legs and stood up.

"It was a mis-connected wire," he announced flatly. "It should work fine now."

Eugene, Hamilton's assistant, certainly hoped so. He had been observing and assisting Hamilton all day as they struggled to find and correct the problem. They had thought everything was under control yesterday, but when they had hooked up the scanner to check the machine, it showed something was amiss. Too tired to track it down, they had retired to their private quarters hoping to get a good start the next day.

Well, here it was nearly dusk of the next day and they had finally found and corrected the problem. The scanner was silent now so the only thing that could possibly keep them from success was their theory. It might be incorrect or inaccurate or filled with faulty reasoning and errors, but if everything went as planned, they would be famous. The two men were constructing a time machine which could take them into the distant past or the far future. They could watch as molten mass transformed itself into the very earth they were anchored upon. They could view the solar system or galaxy forming, even watch the universe begin to take form. All the mysteries and secrets of the long-forgotten past or of the unseen and yet-to-be-encountered future could be unlocked with this key. The future . . .

"Eugene," Hamilton called, bringing Eugene back to the present, "wouldn't you like to test the machine and see if it really works?"

"Of course," he answered, almost fully awake now. "Oh, yes, very much. For where and when should I set it?"

"That's your choice." Hamilton replied calmly. "However, we must go into the past and not the future for a trial run. Personally, I'd like to see the signing of the Declaration of Independence."

Eugene's hand trembled as he set the clock to minus 223. Now was the moment they had been struggling to achieve. Eugene's mind raced back to a warm, clear summer day three years ago. Eugene was graduating from the university. He had spent 10 long years there studying and slaving and he was glad he was leaving. Diploma in hand, he left the main building only to be approached by another professor. Like Eugene he was graduating . . . graduating from teaching. Eugene immediately recognized the man as Professor Fineshin, the astronomy expert. Fineshin wanted to set up a partnership with Eugene and Eugene readily accepted the chance to work with the genius.

Almost immediately they devised a complicated theory about time travel and had begun extensive research. Two years of paper work and then the building began. They had made so many mistakes along the way. Many times they had become discouraged but the discouragement soon passed. Now, after climbing and sometimes crawling the long staircase of success, they had reached the moment of truth.

Eugene pushed a few more buttons and set a few more controls before everything was set. Then Eugene, heart pounding, pushed the "on" knob. Eugene and Hamilton froze. Their hearts stopped. They held their breath. The screen flickered and there appeared to their eyes, right out of the history pages, many men gathered around a table. Eugene watched in fascination as he saw someone that appeared to be Thomas Jefferson entering the hall. Hamilton and Eugene studied a man who appeared to be Franklin. He looked just as they expected, round, scholarly, aged, and bespectacled. Eugene heard voices, too, the voices of the long dead but once again alive. Soon the signing started and John Hancock scrawled his name large at the top. Then the others offered their names to the paper.

It took a while for it to sink in. They had succeeded. The three years of Herculean toil and sweat had paid off.

Eugene also realized he was involved in a turning point in history. He and Hamilton would be the foundations for time exploration. Maybe someday people could go back and not just see the past but actually be in the past. Eugene felt joy, happiness, success, satisfaction, wonderment, and fear, fear of what could happen if the past was changed. But that was silly he thought. Hamilton always claimed the past was past and could never be changed. He always compared time to the reading of a book. You'd start reading and the pages you read were the past. You knew what had happened on those pages and they couldn't be changed. The pages you were reading at the moment were the present and the pages not yet read represented the future all written out in plain English. The future, like the past, was not changeable according to Hamilton but Eugene didn't know if this was so. Once time ended it was as if the book had been shelved.

Eugene woke as the screen flickered off. His eyes had been watching the pictures but his mind was elsewhere. Now fully awake he wanted to try some more dates.

"It looks like it works," Hamilton stated softly.

Eugene noticed again how calmly Hamilton took in the whole situation. How could he stand there virtually immobile and speak as if he were on the phone while Eugene's whole body was alive. Eugene perceived that Hamilton had always been this way and really was feeling something inside. How could he control it so well? Eugene was like a puppy with a new bone. He wanted to wear either the machine or himself to exhaustion. He spoke with control as he said, "Can we try another date?"

"Well, of course," Hamilton answered.

The caged lion in Eugene was set loose as he fumbled with the dials. He watched as the cavemen fought, as the dinosaurs ate, as the Magna Carta was signed, and as the earth was formed. His hunger for knowledge was insatiable. The universe at its inception was something Eugene desperately wanted to see.

"I'm going to set the machine back one trillion years," Eugene stated.

"Yes, I'd like to see just how old the universe really is," Hamilton agreed.

The two didn't realize it but they had been at it for four frantic hours. Questions had popped into their heads as fast as popcorn popped in a popper. By the time they had found an answer to one question, they had four more just waiting to be answered. Innumerable questions still raced through their minds but Hamilton was feeling hungry. He wanted to quit after one more setting and he said so.

"Okay, Hamilton, we'll close up after this one final time journey."

As the screen glimmered and flashed on, both men let out a gasp. The first thought that landed in their minds was "Has the machine malfunctioned?" If not, then something truly amazing had happened, something no one knew about. For on the screen was a view showing the same room they were standing in. In the room on the screen were themselves watching another screen which showed themselves watching still another screen with themselves on it. It seemed to go on into infinity. It was just as if someone had placed a mirror in front of himself and one in back and was seeing himself getting smaller and smaller. Another strange thing was that everytime Eugene or Hamilton moved so would the Eugene or Hamilton on the screen and so on down the line. If either Eugene or Hamilton spoke, the Eugene and Hamilton on the screen spoke also. Eugene was confused so he asked Hamilton.

"Is it a malfunction?"

"The scanner is quiet, so it must not be."

"What does this mean?" he questioned hoping that Hamilton would have a different idea than the dreadful one he had thought of.

"I think it means we were doing the same thing one trillion years ago as we are doing today. And, judging from the fact that we saw not just two of us but uncountable pairs, I'd say we not only did the same thing one trillion years ago, but two, three, four, and even more trillion years ago."

"Then what I'm saying right now is something I've said once every trillions years."

"It would appear to be the case."

"Well, if we have repeated everything so many times in the past, then we are probably going to do the same things in the future."

"Seems logical," responded Hamilton. "Let's check it out."

Hamilton's hunger was put aside for the moment as they set up the dials. Again the same scene flashed before their astounded eyes. It seems they were bound to appear in another trillion years.

"Well, it looks like we have a contract to perform for another few trillions years," Hamilton said.

"I hate to repeat myself then," Eugene said, trying feebly at a joke. "But what is the purpose of it?"

"I don't know. I really don't know. God only knows, if there is a God."

"After we live out our lives, we must then forget about it and not remember anything when we start to live again. We won't know about it until we make this awful discovery again."

I think so. I suppose when something thinks he has done something before, he probably has, a thousand times."

"That's another thing. I wonder if our thoughts can change."

"I doubt it. If our thoughts could change, then we would do things differently. No. I think people's thoughts stay the same also."

Eugene realized for the first time he felt uneasy. This discovery seemed too much. Eugene thought about himself coming back in a trillion years. He wouldn't be wise to the fact that he had lived before. He would go through his whole life not realizing he had done everything before and would do everything again. And then Eugene would make the discovery again. Maybe Eugene could try to remember this life now so that next time he'd remember he had lived before and that would change the future. But Eugene realized he had thought of all of this before and he had not remembered. Then Eugene thought of all the people who would never know. They would keep journeying the road of infinite time forever without ever knowing they had lived before. Just how long had this cycle gone on? Did it have a beginning or an end? Eugene wanted to change it but he didn't know how. Then Eugene got a thought that he had thought of trillions of years ago.

"Hey, it might be possible for us to change the cycle," Eugene proposed.

"If we could change it, yes. But surely we thought of that a trillion years ago and you can see everything is still the same so don't get your hopes up."

We could set the machine to see what we will do tomorrow and then when tomorrow comes we could do something totally different."

"Yes, I like that idea," praised Hamilton. "Let's get to it."

Once again they set the machine. Could they escape this cycle, or were they for some reason doomed to continue to repeat their lives? What if somehow they could break the cycle? What would happen? Would breaking the old cycle mean they would have to repeat this new cycle into infinity instead of the old? Would this never end? When did it start? What was the purpose? All these questions gnawed at their minds.

Suddenly the screen lit up. It showed the universe being formed. It didn't take but a moment for both to realize that the cycle was to start all over tomorrow. They couldn't change tomorrow after all because tomorrow they'd be dead.

Hamilton spoke first. "I'm going to eat." And he left. The door closed and it seemed to Eugene that his life was closed. He'd be back again to discover the horror of the discovery. He'd live through this all again. Or was he dreaming? Maybe he actually was in bed dreaming. But no, he didn't seem to be dreaming. Maybe he was in hell. Maybe this was his punishment. Maybe he was already dead. With Hamilton gone, Eugene, for the first time, felt the loneliness. It crept up on him like a caterpillar, slowly and slowly. He felt like a leaf being blown wherever the wind decided to take him. He thought back to Hamilton's telling him that time was a book. Hamilton had told Eugene that the past, present, and future were like a book being read. When the book was shelved time ended. What Hamilton hadn't realized is that a book can be read by another who has never read it before, just as Eugene was going to live his life over as if he had never lived before. Eugene was thoroughly alone and terrified.

Maybe, Eugene thought, he could set the machine ahead five minutes and see what was going to happen. Then in five minutes he could do something different and change the cycle. Yes, it seemed like a good idea . . . a great idea.

The door swung open. Hamilton entered. A gun pointed as his temple spoke in place of him.

"No!" cried Eugene. His legs like springs rocketed him at Hamilton. In the next instant flesh met flesh and hammer met cartridge. The bullet went wild. It grazed Hamilton and then plunged into the machine. As the two fell to the cold cement floor the machine burst into flames and exploded. It was as if the universe had split. The flames leaped and danced taunting the men. It was as if the flames knew they would consume the men but they wanted to make it more dramatic. But it was all wasted. Hamilton and Eugene were unconscious.

Eugene found himself on a merry-go-round. He went around and saw the scenery. As he went around again, he saw on a large throne the operator. After many times around and after seeing the same surroundings Eugene cried," Let me off!"

The operator bellowed, "I forbid it!"

Eugene then found himself shrinking. He was in a dark corner all alone. He was getting smaller and smaller until he was gone.

Suddenly he was at a card table. He picked a card. It was the two of hearts. He put it back and shuffled. He picked again, and again he found himself staring at the two of hearts. Eugene took the two and threw it away. He shuffled and drew again. Another two of hearts. He spread the deck. They were all two of hearts.

Eugene felt a hand on his shoulder. He woke realizing he had been dreaming.

"Are you okay?" asked a blurred image.

Eugene's mind began to clear. Focusing in Eugene saw it was another scientist. Eugene saw two more. They were all bend over him.

"Got to set the machine," babbled Eugene. "Five minutes . . . must set it . . . got to change . . . got to break free . . . let me go!"

"Don't go in there," restrained one. "The room is a mess."

Eugene's mind finally did clear. He remembered the discovery, Hamilton's entry, the explosion, and how he and Hamilton had been knocked unconscious. He and Hamilton. Hamilton. How was Hamilton?

"How's Hamilton?" Eugene inquired.

The men bit their lips.

"He's dead," answered one slowly.

Oh my God, thought Eugene. "Dead," he asked aloud.

Yes, but how are you?"

"I feel okay physically," Eugene announced.

"Let's take you home."

"Wait," cried Eugene. "How is the machine?"

"Is that what blew?" asked one. "It's totally destroyed now."

"Oh," Eugene replied slowly thinking of Hamilton and himself now. "How did Hamilton die?"

"He was burned before the sprinkler system came on."

"Let's go home," ordered a second.

"I think we have come as far as we will ever come," Eugene said staring at a clock as it began to chime twelve. "See you all again in a trillion years."

Before the three scientists could ask any questions the earth began to shake. Then as it had done so many times in the past and as it was doomed to do so in the future, the universe split open and everything began all over again.

THE END AND THE BEGINNING!!!

My teacher's comments

A+

Please bring me a manuscript copy to submit for you in a writing contest next fall. Your story is excellently told as a narrative. Your writing mechanisms are admirable. Only major suggestion – avoid the "lazy it." (See ?it.) Nouns, phrases, re-wording of sentences are ways to avoid ?it and make your meaning even more vivid.